MARTIN LOST AND FOUND

a novel

Katie Gates

Cover photograph by Gerald F. Condit. © Gerald F. Condit. All rights reserved worldwide.

Book design by Integrative Ink.

Cover design by Debbi Andrews.

Martin Lost and Found

First edition: August 2012.

ISBN: 978-0-9853591-0-2

Channel Press
PO Box 27272
Los Angeles, CA 90027-0272

ACKNOWLEDGMENTS

When I began the acknowledgments for my first novel, *The Somebody Who,* I stated that it was a book about family. Fact of the matter is, *Martin Lost and Found* also is about family. Sometimes, though, the family you need at a particular time is a family that shares no blood connection.

Like Martin, I was blessed to find a family in Los Feliz. And I will always be grateful for the surrogate siblinghood I enjoy with Debbi, Julie, and Tim. For so many years, the four of us slept under the same roof. For so many years, we grew together, and we grew to love each other. I thank you three from the bottom of my heart.

Like Martin, I know that family is not always of the human species. And I have been blessed since childhood to appreciate the companionship of cats. Vesta, who circles about me as I type, has seen me through a great deal. Lotto, who is elsewhere at the moment, showed up at my door just five or six weeks after Dude appeared to Martin. Do I write these cats into my life? Well, if I do, more power to me, because I can't imagine a home without them.

And out from under my immediate roof, the support continues. As I was developing *Martin,* I shared early versions of this manuscript with several friends and colleagues, and their feedback was greatly appreciated and altogether encouraging. Thank you so much to Alyssa Bonilla, Michael Frishberg, Sue Frishberg, Monique Raphel High, Kathy Kappes, Diana Kyle, Linda Polk, Maria Simpson, and Alex Torres.

Readers along the way also included those formidable blood relatives. Martha, I appreciated your feedback. Mom, I know you also enjoyed the manuscript, and I'm really, really sorry for all the "f-bombs." (That's just the way people talk in the 'hood, Ma. What can I say?)

I also want to extend my gratitude to the family of bloggers with whom I've exchanged comments and emails and love. I didn't believe, when I began my own blogging venture, that I would come to enjoy a virtual community, but there are some very special souls out there who write beautifully and who are completely unselfish when it comes to support and encouragement. I don't dare list names here, because I know there would be omissions if I tried.

Finally, I thank the communities of Los Feliz, East Hollywood, and Silver Lake. This area of sprawling Los Angeles is a remarkable muse and a source of great energy. If it didn't exist, I would undoubtedly have an East Coast address.

Katie Gates
Los Angeles 2012

This is for my wonderful NYC friend

Tanya Kamens

Our virtual book-club-of-two
has spanned nearly 30 years
and has yet to have a formal meeting.

(Bless you, my fellow reader.)

ALSO BY KATIE GATES

The Somebody Who

MARTIN LOST AND FOUND

a novel

CHAPTER ONE

I

The elevator's stained, pock-marked mirror has a crack in it, and during the slow ride from the first floor to the fifth, Martin plays with his reflection. He moves his head so as to put the crack in different locations. The resulting distortions reflect his mood.

Once the elevator arrives on the top floor and the doors have worked their way open, Martin leaves the cage and begins his walk down the long hallway. It strikes him as odd that he never sees any of the other tenants. With so many units on each floor, he'd expect to run into someone from time to time. But he doesn't. There's something vaguely ghost-like in the atmosphere. And that sensation is in direct contrast to the busy Los Feliz block on which the building is located.

Arriving at his door, Martin starts to insert the key into the deadbolt lock, but just as he does that, he realizes that he doesn't have to. The door is not completely closed, and he immediately gets a sinking feeling in his stomach.

He pushes the door open, and his sense of anxiety makes his throat feel tight.

"*Hello?*" he calls in, his voice as forceful as he can make it.

For some reason, he decides to stomp his feet on the floor a few times. Maybe he thinks this will sound like he's more than one person. Maybe he thinks that, if the intruder is still within, the stomping will send the guilty party out the window.

"*Hello?*" he calls again, as he passes the door to the kitchen and enters the living room.

He immediately notices the blank space that was once occupied by his large flat-screen television.

"Fuck!" he says.

He tosses his briefcase on the couch and proceeds to the other rooms. He first checks the "bonus room," which is slightly smaller than the walk-in closet he shared with Lisa. He's glad to see that his computer—and all its components—are still there. He's glad the intruder didn't have time or room for them.

He returns to the hall and opens the large storage closet between the living room and the bedroom. He scans the shelves that were built for linens (as if he needed the extra storage; as if he had more than one set of anything). He sees a gap. A gap where his DV-cam had been stored.

"Damnit!" he says this time, as he slams shut the closet door.

Then, he goes into the bedroom. The bed is a mess. Dresser drawers are opened. Clothes are thrown all over the place. Mismatched shoes seem to be walking in circles.

"I'm such a fucking loser," Martin states, angrily. (The room looks exactly as it had when he left it that morning.)

He wonders if he should call the police, but he also knows that he's got a lot of competition for their time. A television and a DV-cam? Sure, there's probably more. Things that will "turn up missing" in the days ahead, but he wonders if it's worth the call. What can the cops do, anyway? Still, he heads for the phone.

But when he notices there's a message to play, the blinking light back-burners any other intentions. He pushes the *Play* button.

"Hi Martin," comes Lisa's voice, sounding oddly sweet and conciliatory, "it's me. I'm calling on Wednesday. The twenty-fourth. I hope you're having a good week. Um, Martin, I know we're not supposed to be talking to each other directly until everything is settled, but, I don't know, I just felt like I should share this with you. Um, Glen and I have decided to get married. We're going to wait, of course, until the divorce is absolutely final, but anyway, it's all good. And I just wanted you to know. Um... hope you're well!"

"Fuck you, Lisa!" Martin yells to the illuminated and no-longer-blinking numeral 1 on the answering machine. "And, no, I'm *not* well. I don't have a goddamn television. I got fucking *robbed* today."

"Fuck!" he says again, as he walks to the kitchen. He's starving, and he's not in the mood to deal with the cops. He's not in the mood for cops, for Lisa, or for this apartment. Things just really suck right now.

II

For several minutes after placing the Weight Watchers Thai Chicken in the oven, he just stands there. His soon-to-be-ex-wife is already planning her second set of vows, and he isn't even ready to date again. He can't imagine going through the process. It's been too long...

He returns to his front hallway and looks at the door. He opens it and studies the jamb. There's no sign of someone having forced an entry.

Reaching into his pants pocket to confirm the presence of his keys, he steps into the building's hallway and pulls the door shut. There's a soft clicking sound, but it isn't enough. He pushes on the door, and it opens easily. No key required.

He realizes it's his own fault. He must have neglected to lock the deadbolt when he was heading out that morning. That also doesn't surprise him. There's been a certain fog around him lately. A fog that seems to bring on whatever he deserves.

III

Since there is no longer a television in the living room, Martin takes his dinner to the bonus room, and after placing his plate and his Diet Coke on the tray table, he settles into his squeaky chair. He hits the *Enter* key on his computer. Now, the monitor will know that he is there.

He logs onto his email and clicks on "Check." The system indicates that it is receiving four messages. He's not surprised that three are from Aunt Betty. And they are all "Forwards." To Aunt Betty, these emails are probably funny. (Otherwise, why would she feel compelled to pass them along?) But Martin has never felt an affinity with this particular aunt (even *off*-line), and this lack of connection was confirmed more than a year ago, when Aunt Betty discovered cyberspace. He used to open her emails and peruse them. Now, he doesn't even bother with those keystrokes. If he sees **FW:** at the beginning of the subject line, he just goes right for the delete key.

"Sorry, Auntie," Martin says, as he trashes all three messages in a practiced move. "Just don't have the time."

Even as Martin says this, he knows it is bullshit, and it fills him with shame somehow. He does have time. Plenty of it. And how could he not make time for his mother's favorite sister? What's his problem? Couldn't he at least acknowledge all her Forward's with a reply of some sort?

He thinks about sending her a genuine, person-to-person message, but he's more interested in opening the one email in the bunch that is not a Forward. An email from his nephew, Zac.

Martin has always enjoyed Zac. Their connection seemed to have kicked in really early. Martin remembers playing air-guitar with his nephew back when the kid was four. They both were clearly in sync. It's as if they didn't just have a band, they had a *bond*.

Zac has been particularly communicative with Martin since he started at Penn last year. And although the messages have become less frequent—or at least, less detailed—as Zac cruises into the end of his sophomore year, Martin is always happy to receive them. He's also very good about replying—better, in fact, than he is with his other email communications. He always feels comfortable when he writes to his nephew. He feels that he can be frank.

Martin opens the message and reads:

`uncle marty, hows it goin in la? hows your new`
`place? things are cool here. classes continue`

```
and the homestretch is in front of me. cant
believe finals are only about 2 months away.
should be cool tho. history and psych are my
strongest, i guess. the english lit require-
ment is for shit. i dont mind reading books,
i just dont want to analyze them. i'm think-
ing about this summer and wondering what i
should plan to do. and i'm going to be really
bold here - any chance i could spend some time
with you? the womens ranch doesnt interest me…
write soon, Z
```

"Z," Martin thinks. *At least he still capitalizes that!*

Martin re-reads the message. There's a lot to take in. Zac, apparently, thinks that he might enjoy witnessing his uncle's life in L.A. At the moment, this concept is unfathomable to Martin. *He* doesn't even enjoy witnessing his life in L.A. At fifty-two years of age, he is not exactly where he thought he might be. But, Martin also realizes that he has always been dubbed the "cool uncle," and given his status as the only brother between two rather intense sisters, he knows that this moniker was unavoidable. His older sister, Reggie (Zac's mother), was five when Martin was born. Another five years passed before Rachel came along. During that half-decade, Reggie honed her doting skills, and by the time Rachel was walking and talking, she had learned to mimic her older sister's mannerisms. In some families, Martin realizes, the middle child gets "short shrift." In his family, he just got "shrift"—and too much of it.

Martin understands Zac's situation. His nephew has double the estrogen on either side. Like Martin, Zac is a middle child, but Zac is one among five. And the other four are all female. Martin can't blame him for referring to their home outside of Lancaster as the "women's ranch." Martin can't blame him for not wanting to sprint back there for the three months of summer vacation.

Viewing his place through someone else's eyes (for the second time in the last hour), Martin wonders what Zac might think of these post-marriage L.A. digs. He doubts if Zac is envisioning this place—a one-bedroom where break-ins might occur. Granted, the building is in Los Feliz (which is—or once was, at least—the coolest neighborhood on the planet), but it isn't standard California fare. It's a building that might exist in New York. It's old. It's relatively tall. It even has *fire escapes*, for God's sake. And Martin knows, from the trips he's made to the laundry room downstairs, that it is primarily filled with pink-haired, multiple-tattooed, overly-pierced thirtynothings. Their lives, they believe, are ahead of them. Martin believes that his is not.

"I'm such a fucking loser," Martin says, as the phrase threatens to become a mantra.

He can't send Zac a reply just now, not in his current mood. But, he's curious. His mood is so distinct. His attitude toward self is so relentless...

He goes to Google, gets the main menu, and when he has the search window in front of him, he types the words he just uttered. He puts them in quotes: "I'm such a fucking loser."

He clicks on the Search button. There are more than one million hits.

Martin bookmarks the page and decides to take his dinner into the living room. He's starving, and he needs to focus on that.

IV

That night, in Martin's dream, Prince Charles has finally been handed the throne. He is the new King of England. At the age of sixty-plus, Charles is finally assuming the position for which he's been groomed since he was a fetus in the womb.

Martin doesn't question the content of his dream. But the noise—the noise on the fire escape that takes him out of that dream—gets his attention almost immediately. When he wakes from the coronation, he remembers that he had returned home that night to a burglarized apartment. He looks toward the window and wishes he were more prepared to defend himself.

The venetian blinds continue to shuffle as the intruder makes its way in, and when the intruder proves to be a tabby cat, Martin relaxes. (He even smiles.)

It's not often that two strangers, when they first meet, say hello to each other at exactly the same time. It is even less often that the synchronicity occurs between two beings of different species. But for all those who witness this event (and only Martin and the cat do), it can be safe to say that the greeting is absolutely simultaneous. Just as Martin says, "Who are you?" the cat says, "Mao."

Shortly thereafter, the cat is lying on Martin's chest, and Martin is petting the cat.

The hunger for love is palpable, and it seems to come from both of them. Within minutes of their meeting, Martin realizes how much he sacrificed when he accepted Lisa's allergy. And the cat realizes that, of all the windows it had to choose from, it just might have walked through the right one...

CHAPTER TWO

I

In the morning—before he leaves for work—Martin is glad to notice that he had stored up so many small cans of "people tuna." His new friend is more than happy to scarf down the contents of one. And when Martin leaves for work, he doesn't close the bedroom window and thereby prevent this stranger from returning to some preferred other life. Martin just pets it on the back and says, "Good luck, buddy."

II

Martin's attitude at work has been changing, somewhat quietly, over the past several months. He is able to hold his own in the most important meetings, and he still dresses the part, but he knows that he isn't giving a hundred percent. He knows, because his patience is really short. The forced smile he returns to his assistant, Brenda, has begun to tell her not to ask any questions about his weekend or his life. And Brenda, being attuned, has quickly learned not to try to make small talk about anything outside the office routine.

Martin has noticed how she is becoming much more like the efficient secretary of some sort of high-powered executive. When there are documents for him to sign, she no longer enters his office and walks him through the process, chatting as he approves of this and that. Rather, she has created a "For Signature" folder, and she has even incorporated into the routine some of

9

those *Sign Here* post-its (complete with an arrow, in case the high-powered, six-figure-wielding executive doesn't happen to notice the blank space above his name). She leaves the folder in his in-box; retrieves it later from his out-box. And, if he is present, during either event, they both smile courteously. But: there is no small talk.

Martin no longer frequents the office's kitchen space, opting instead to bring with him the largest Latte he can purchase from the deli in the building's lobby. And when he wants more, he goes to the Starbucks around the corner. He just can't go into that kitchen anymore. The conversation makes him angry for some reason. He doesn't even watch *American Idol,* and yet, the last time he was in that kitchen, listening to the conversation, there was a part of him that just wanted to yell out: *"Danny's* going to win! Don't you people *get* it? It's a <u>done</u> deal."

When he passes Brenda's desk on the way to his own this morning, Martin is almost tempted to tell her about the break-in, about how vulnerable he feels. But, he realizes that their relationship has changed. She barely looks up when he walks by. Rather, she ends her phone conversation quickly, saying, "Oh, no, I think Adam's got it *sealed!*"

And the rest of Martin's day is as impersonal as its beginning. He adds numbers, figures percentages, reads the latest indicators, gets updated on regulations, and tries not to look at his watch.

III

On the way home, Martin stops at Ralphs, where Aisle 6 awaits him. It's the frozen dinner aisle, and it has become his go-to corridor on the western edge of his newfound neighborhood. He peruses the offerings from Lean Cuisine, Smart Ones, and Healthy Choice, and he remembers when such products were collectively called "TV dinners." Since he doesn't—as of yesterday—own a TV (and *The Ed Sullivan Show* is ancient history), Martin is particularly glad that this category of food has been promoted to a type of meal that is not only tasty and nutritional, but also can be enjoyed without the distraction of some prime-time routine.

Although he doesn't feel compelled to budget, and he's not one to scout out a deal, Martin cannot help but be floored by the offer: if he buys 20 Lean Cuisines, and if he uses his club card, then each meal will end up costing only $1.50. He can't resist. He loads up his cart. He then wheels down the aisle, makes a left, and after passing a few lanes, makes another left: cat food. He buys six cans.

IV

Turning the key to open the deadbolt and then pushing the door open, Martin feels relieved by a sense of privacy and ownership. He intuits that his place has had no interlopers, and he enters it calmly. He immediately takes the grocery bags into the kitchen, and as he unpacks the cans of Fancy Feast, a part of him hopes that a cat will appear. After filling the freezer with his latest nutritional acquisitions—and when no cat has appeared—he heads to the bedroom to change his clothes.

"Goddamnit!" Martin says, with a resigned bitterness.

There's a cat turd on his bed. Not just *on* his bed—rather, smack-dab in the *middle* of his bed. Because... when a cat shits on a bed, it aims for the middle. (It's just so much more meaningful that way.)

"What the fuck did I do to piss *you* off?" Martin asks anyone who might be within earshot.

V

Martin has returned to the laundry room, hoping his stuff is dry. He knows, though, that it probably needs ten more minutes. He sits in the plastic chair and waits. He closes his eyes (as if that would help), but when he hears the elevator doors open, he feels anxious. Yesterday's break-in is apparently on his nerves.

"Hey!" says the tattooed girl, bouncing into the room.

"Oh. Hi."

"I'm Brittany," she says, briefly making eye-contact.

"Martin," he says, extending his hand.

The hand overture is wasted, however. Brittany's primary interest is in the availability of a washer, which is indicated by its opened lid.

"Thank fucking God!" she exclaims. "Can you believe this place? What? Like forty apartments and only two fucking washers? What's that about?"

That's about twenty apartments per washer, Martin wants to say.

"I mean," Brittany continues, as she upends her laundry bag into the machine, "I realize we're lucky. I mean, I have so many friends who have to go to the Laundromat, and that's gotta suck."

She digs quarters out of her pockets, and Martin notices that the top of her jeans digs with her. He wonders how many inches exist below her pierced bellybutton and the things he shouldn't see. And because he doesn't want to know the answer, he stops looking. He closes his eyes. (Maybe she'll think he's into some form of meditation...)

"Another fucking awesome evening," he hears Brittany utter unconvincingly, as she apparently plops down on the floor beside his chair.

Martin opens his left eye to confirm his assumption. "Hey!" he says, standing up. "You know what's worse than this place having only two washers?"

Brittany looks up at him as if there is a great deal of direct sunlight in her eyes.

"This place having only one chair," Martin explains, attempting a smile. "Here," he says, offering the plastic chair to her. "Please. Sit."

"It's okay," she says, waving off his gesture. "Really. I'm just in a bug-ass mood tonight. And I don't think a chair's going to fix it."

"You sure?"

Martin is now in a quandary. She not only has rejected the chair, but in doing so, she also has prevented him from having a good "out." She has taken away his opportunity to wander in and out of the room, to not engage in conversation. Martin is quite certain that if he returns to the chair, Brittany will keep talking.

Martin doesn't return to the chair. Rather, he opens the dryer door to see if his sheets are done. They still feel a little damp. He might even have to put in another quarter. And he hates this. He hates this scene of potential conversation.

"So," Brittany starts, as Martin feeds the machine another quarter, "when'd'ya move in?"

"I've been here almost three months," Martin answers, returning to the chair.

"Ya like it?"

Martin can't answer this. In fact, he doesn't.

"I think it's a pretty good place," Brittany offers. "You know, as places go. Oh! Scuse me..."

Brittany's cell phone is singing a dancing song, and she responds.

"Ben. What's happening?"

Apparently, Ben replies with a question.

"Just sitting in this goddamn laundry room," Brittany states. "On the fucking *floor.*"

You were offered a seat, Martin thinks.

"Yeah, I don't know," Brittany says. "The people who go there are kinda over-the-top. I don't know... Yeah, I should be ready by nine-thirty or so. Wanna hit the place down the street? Yeah, let's do that, then.... Cool. See you later."

"Aw, jeez." Brittany says, after closing her phone.

Martin turns from his throne on the one laundry room chair. "You don't sound too excited about the plans you just made," he comments.

"I don't know. Sometimes I'm not sure about the scene in this town. Do you get it?"

"I don't know how to answer that," Martin says, replying in all honesty.

VI

Martin returns to his apartment and tosses the clean sheets onto his bed. He didn't bother folding them downstairs because he knew he would only have to unfold them later. He sneers at his logic—realizes it's another instance of allegedly not having the time...

After popping a Lean Cuisine pot roast in the oven, he wanders into his bonus room. Checks his email. Just spam. *Boy,* he thinks, *if I had an inch for every time I accepted an offer for penis-enlargement...*

"I'm such a prick," he tells his monitor.

It occurs to him that his self-designation has changed. Yesterday he was a loser. A "fucking loser." Tonight he is a "prick." Regarding his self-esteem, he doesn't know whether this is a demotion or a sign of improvement. Martin then remembers the "fucking loser" Google search he had bookmarked. He calls up the page and opens the first hit. The dialogue therein appears to have taken place in a chatroom. He begins to read the entries. He's in no particular hurry to find that place where the computer has wisely highlighted his self-deprecating search phrase. He just starts reading.

The virtual conversation recorded on the page apparently took place four days ago, when "Sus323" wrote:

```
I'm just so tired of it, but I don't want to
go with any of the prescription stuff. I just
don't trust the pharmaceutical companies. They
seem to wait a few years before finding out all
they should know about side effects and other
stuff.

ginny5:  i guess i understand your concern but
its hard for me to agree. my husbands a doctor
and he swears by hrt.
```

With the lower-case "I" and a clear disregard for punctuation, Martin pegs "ginny5" to be in Generation X or something further down the alphabet. But he can't figure out the typo at the end.

```
Sus323:  You're not on it, though, right?

ginny5:  im holding out. it seems to be bad
just some of the time and i figure it might
be a little early for me. but when the time
comes.
```

"What are they talking about?" Martin asks the screen.

```
Sus323:  How old are you, if you don't mind my
asking…

ginny5:  i dont mind - 56
```

"Well, I got that wrong," Martin comments, curious that a woman his older sister's age cannot bother to hit the shift key or throw in an occasional apostrophe.

```
Sus323:  Wow. Lucky.

ginny5:  what do you mean?
```

"A question mark," Martin interjects. "Nice touch, little-g."

```
Sus323:  I'm forty-eight.

PT999:  Still there, huh?

Sus323:  Hey. Where'd you go?

PT999:  I'm such a fucking loser.
```

"Ah," says Martin, regarding the statement and its yellow highlight. "My soulmate has arrived."

And in that moment, as if on cue, Martin hears a feline chirp. He looks to the floor at his left and sees the cat.

"Hey, buddy," he says. "Thanks for the gift."

The cat nuzzles Martin's shin, and then looks up at him and yawns.

"Don't let me keep you up."

Just as he returns his gaze to the screen (he is curious as to whether PT999 will reveal the reason for his or her statement), the cat jumps on his lap, and Martin immediately and reflexively begins stroking it.

"I'm eavesdropping," he explains to his visitor. "The Internet lets us do that."

The cat begins to purr.

Martin looks below the phrase that has created a bond between him and PT999.

```
Sus323:  Why do you say that?

PT999:  I just had a conversation with my
daughter - on the phone - she called - and I
really pissed her off. I didn't mean to - I
just couldn't listen to her complaining about
her roommate.

Sus323:  College roommate?

PT999:  Yeah. Such stupid problems.
```

"Stupid problems," Martin echoes.

VII

The sound of the kitchen timer gives the cat a jolt, which, in turn, causes Martin to wince as a couple of claws get caught in the legs of his sweatpants.

"Nice," he says to the animal, as he closes the chatroom. "You are completely shifting my mess and pain paradigm. Quite an accomplishment for one day."

He holds the cat as he stands. Then, he puts it on the floor. "Care to join me for dinner?"

The cat follows him into the kitchen.

Before Martin opens the oven door to retrieve tonight's entrée, he takes the can off the top of the stack of Fancy Feasts. "Mmm...," he says. "Tender Beef in Gravy. That's a natural for you, I bet. If you were wild, truly wild, you'd no doubt be stalking cattle somewhere in the Fresno Valley."

He reaches into the cupboard, where an odd collection of dinnerware represents his weekend forays into yard-saling. When he and Lisa split, she was relatively magnanimous regarding the potential distribution of tangible household goods. She even insisted that he keep the sterling silver serving tray that was one of their more valuable wedding presents. After all, she had reasoned, it was *his* grandmother who had given it to them. So in the instance of the tray, Martin acquiesced. But he didn't want any of the good china, and he didn't even want the "everyday" stuff. Everything seemed to belong in a set, for some reason. It was bad enough that he and Lisa were breaking up. Why break up the dishes?

If Martin still had the serving tray, he would probably let the cat eat off of it. That would look ironic: a small can's worth of tender beef on a tray that could hold a leg of lamb. (The size relativity might even cause the cat to feel more hungry, as it might assume more courses were in the offing.) But, Martin got rid of his grandmother's gift. He sold it on craigslist, just after he'd moved. He didn't need some reminder of nuptials-gone-bad taking up half the cabinet space in his bachelor-size kitchen. He also didn't really need the fifty dollars that represented probably one-tenth of the tray's value. But it was kind of fun spending that money at the yard sales.

VIII

As he walks home from Rite Aid, lucky to have made it only moments before they closed, Martin is not altogether surprised by the relative crowd he sees just ahead at Vermont Avenue's new margarita watering hole. Sure, it's late for him, but for the younger folks who seem to own this little section of Los Angeles, he believes that "bedtime" is probably a concept associated only with a parent's scolding glance.

He feels self-conscious as he nears that part of the sidewalk that shares its concrete with the outdoor tables. And when he hears his name called, he has no reason to believe that the person cheerfully yelling "Martin" is speaking to him. Still, though, he can't help but look toward the crowd that is imbibing, and when he sees Brittany, and she is waving at him as if they were the oldest and dearest of friends, he smiles for some reason.

"Hey," he says, approaching the small table where she and a handful of friends, all sipping through straws, share a common ethereal smile.

17

"That's a damn big Rite Aid bag," Brittany comments. "What'd ya buy?"

"Uh," Martin fumbles, even starts to open the bag (as if he needs a reminder). "A-uh-kitty litter pan. And some... kitty litter."

"The manager let you have a cat?" Brittany asks.

"I didn't ask," Martin says. "I didn't know."

One of Brittany's friends—a guy who apparently has a budget for weekly trips to the nail salon (and who seems to favor the darker end of the color wheel)—gives Martin an eye that is neither rude nor friendly. "Dude," he says, smiling through his attitude, "you got some explaining to do!"

Manicure man then kicks out an available chair, adding: "If I buy you a drink, will you tell me why you didn't know you had a cat?"

"Join us, why don'tcha," Brittany says, with a sincerity that is slightly compromised by a faint slur. Her wink and her smile are hard to resist. "Hey!" she adds, shrugging her shoulders, "It's not like you have to *drive* home." (She is clearly the queen of this table.)

Martin, self-conscious in his sweats, sneakers, and relative years, accepts the offer. And for the next two hours, he drinks margaritas and mostly listens.

CHAPTER THREE

I

When his alarm goes off at 6:30 the next morning, Martin's will to live is not within reach. He does, however, have just enough strength to put a stop to the electronic noise. He stretches for the clock and stifles the sound. As for the other noise—the pounding in his head—there is no snooze button for that.

"Fuck!" he says, lying back in the bed. "Fuck!"

He closes his eyes for a moment, and takes a few deep breaths. He knows there is no way he can get to work. The freeway is no place for his hangover.

The cat, apparently, has sensed Martin's anguish, and it is now kneading his chest, which—fortunately for Martin—is protected by at least three layers of bedding.

"Dude, you wanna go to work for me?"

The cat doesn't change its kneading rhythm. The cat is on a self-serving mission that will probably continue for nine lives.

II

Martin tells Brenda that he must have got food poisoning. He tells her he was up most of the night. Her response is kind. "Take care of yourself," she says, "and, hey, it's good it's Friday, huh? You've got the weekend to make sure you recover fully."

"Thanks, Brenda. Yeah, I should definitely be better by Monday. But... you know, if anything comes up today, please feel free to call. I'm laying low, obviously, but I'm here."

"We'll be fine, Martin. Rest up."

Martin returns the phone to its cradle and works his way into the kitchen. *Coffee,* he is thinking. *Coffee...*

About six feet down, the cat is thinking about something other than coffee, and it serpentines between Martin's legs to convey its deepest wishes.

"Alright, Dude, just a minute. Let me at least get some water going."

Martin fills the tea kettle and puts it on the stove, turns on the burner.

"Mao?"

"I'm coming! Jesus! Who fed you three days ago, anyway?"

Martin opens a can of Fancy Feast. This one is Savory Salmon. "Mmm...," Martin says, as he and his headache lean to deliver the contents onto the plate that is still encrusted with yesterday's remaining morsels of Tender Beef. "Once again, right up your alley. If you were wild, Dude, truly wild, you'd probably be living on some riverbank right now, just scooping those sharp-ass claws of yours into the water and catching every sucker that happens to be swimming upstream."

It occurs to Martin suddenly that he has named the cat, and the name is "Dude." He also realizes that this name will stick, regardless of the cat's gender. If he learned nothing else from his margarita experience with the thirtynothings, he came away with this: "Dude" is an androgynous name. And where the cat is concerned, this name is convenient, as Martin has not yet bothered to lift the cat's tail.

III

Pulling two "coffee bags" out of the box, Martin makes a mental note to buy a coffeemaker this weekend. He won't plan to replace the fancy espresso machine that was a staple in the large kitchen he and Lisa shared, but anything will be better than this Folgers product that is barely a notch above "instant."

He heads for the living room and the comfort of its couch. He sits, and he hates the way he feels. He never could hold liquor very well. He also never tried to. Never wanted to, really. That was part of the problem with Lisa. Seems she could drink until the cows came home. She claimed it was her Kentucky upbringing. Bourbon. Mint juleps. Martin's headache gets worse as he thinks about it.

He remembers that trip they took to visit her folks. They had been dating for only six months or so, and they were enjoying being a young couple in Chicago. The advertising firm where they'd met was huge and kind of stuffed-shirt. Neither of them felt like a fit. She constantly complained of the marketing department's unwillingness to take artistic risks. As for Martin, he couldn't speak of artistic risks. He worked in the accounting department, and numbers are numbers.

But he liked Lisa's sense of joy and adventure, and when they'd go out to dinner, and she'd have a few drinks, he liked how she softened. He didn't feel like the odd man out, nursing his one beer or whatever. It was cool. Their turf was somehow equal.

But, God, that trip to Kentucky. Why didn't he see it then? Why didn't he realize that her legacy included something to which he could never relate? It wasn't a weekend of special-occasion partying, he later understood. It was just... a weekend. The kind of weekend she was used to having. The kind of weekend she would continue to have—with, or without, relatives.

IV

Later that day, Martin's headache has lifted, and he feels the need for some fresh air. He decides to go for a walk—maybe he'll check out more of the shops in his neighborhood; maybe he'll venture beyond the half-a-square-mile that has become somewhat familiar.

When he enters the small elevator, he notices two signs that were not there yesterday. One is a flyer entitled "Missing Man." Apparently composed without a computer (or, with a font meant to look as if one has no computer), the sign features a fuzzy reproduction of a photograph. The words that follow it get right to the point: *Mr. Lonzo Lazarra is missing from his apartment on*

21

Vermont Avenue in Los Feliz. He has not contacted his family since March 10th. We don't know where he is. If you see him, or if you have any information, please call 213-655-2993. Thank you. We are worried about our uncle.

Next to the family's sign is another flyer. This one is typed, and has the added official quality of being formatted as a memo would be:

```
Date: Friday, 3/26
To: Tenants of 1773
From: David Ferguson, Building Manager
Re: Lonzo Lazarra

Dear Fellow Tenants:

You'll see signs like this around the neigh-
borhood, and I'm just adding one here because
Lonzo is a long-term tenant of this building.
He's lived in Unit 412 for 20 years. He's a
nice guy. Always paid his rent on time. Rarely
had any company, from what I could tell (but I
haven't been here that long). Anyway, if you
know anything or have any clues, knock on my
door. It doesn't seem like anything happened
in his apartment. Everything looks the same in
there. I hope we can help find him. His family
is really upset. Thanks, DF
```

When he realizes the missing man's unit is just below his own, Martin feels strangely sad. He can't recall ever having seen Lonzo, but there's some bizarre affinity there.

The elevator doors open, and he quickly heads out for some fresh air.

V

Having walked in an inattentive daze down Vermont and onto Hollywood Boulevard, Martin is invigorated by the new sights around him. Although he is somewhat off the beaten path (where the concept of "Los Feliz Village" is concerned), he is struck by the neighborhood's consistent capacity to present a new idea with every shop. He is initially intrigued by the name

Ozzie Dots, but WACKO, which is just a door or so east, intrigues him more.

After thirty minutes perusing the bookshelves, Martin is beginning to feel more relaxed. He appreciates the distractions of this store, and he knows that they will go on forever. He's not even an eighth of the way in.

He looks at the collection of action figures (Jane Austen, Crazy Cat Lady, Moses), and he thinks of more possibilities: What about a New Bachelor action figure, whose props might include one set of everything, a freezerful of frozen dinners, and a tiny checkbook... the word "alimony" written on the memo line of each individual check. Or, a Thirtynothing action figure, complete with margarita mix, bottles of dark-colored nail polish, and an at-home piercing and tattoo kit. Or... a Missing Man action figure: a box containing possessions, an empty apartment, but no actual "figure."

Passing the spinning tops and toys, Martin feels that he's being thrown back in time. When he sees record albums on his way out the door, the sense of nostalgia and innocence is all just a little too overwhelming.

As he heads home, stopping at the bank along the way, Martin keeps looking into the faces of passersby. He keeps looking for Lonzo Lazarra.

CHAPTER FOUR

I

When Martin decided, late Sunday morning, to head over to the most retail-oriented section of Glendale, he didn't expect to run into the rest of the world there. But there it was—the sea of humanity, grabbing every bargain available, filling their carts, and creating interminable lines at the registers. The errand turned into a three-hour ordeal, and now, as he fumbles to unlock his apartment door, Martin can hear his phone ringing. Finally inside, he races into the living room and picks up the receiver.

"Hello?" he says, breathless.

"Uncle Marty!"

"Zac! How ya doin?"

"I'm fine, but, Dude, you sound stressed. Don't you know it's the Sabbath? Shouldn't you be resting?"

Martin chuckles (perhaps for the first time in weeks). "I was just at Target. Not exactly a house of worship."

"Or maybe it is, in a way... So, whad'ya get?"

"A coffeemaker. And... a set of sheets."

"Nice."

There's a moment of silence. Neither is praying.

"So..." they both say at the same time.

"Zac, I'm sorry. I owe you an email. The end of last week was kind of rough for me—"

"It's okay, Uncle Marty. I don't know, though, I kind of felt self-conscious. I mean, asking you about visiting and then not hearing..."

"Oh, God, no! I mean, don't be self-conscious. I actually haven't given it a lot of thought. And, I don't mean that in a bad way. I just—"

"Not to worry. You know, if this isn't a good time—"

"It's not a *bad* time, Zac."

"I'm just trying to figure out my summer."

"I understand," Martin says, gleaning that his nephew is starting to sound a little down (and wondering if he has exacerbated that mood). "I, uh, need to think about it."

"Cool. You know? Totally cool. Really. It was bold of me."

"It's okay."

"Anyway, you probably need to put your stuff away, and I gotta study, so... can we touch base in a week or so?"

"Absolutely," says Martin.

"Cool."

Martin feels sad as he returns the receiver to its cradle. As if there's something about pecking order when it comes to lost souls. He is Zac's uncle, for God's sake. He is Zac's *elder*. Shouldn't he also be wiser? More happy?

He is reminded of his "fucking loser" soulmate in that weird chatroom: PT999, who inadvertently pissed off her college-age daughter.

Stupid problems, she had said.

II

Martin finds the bookmark and enters the chatroom uninvited. It's past midnight, and he knows it's foolish to be doing anything relatively active at this hour. But, lately, he's had the worst insomnia.

```
710KAT: I know what you mean about the mood
issues. Sometimes I am amazed where my mind
goes.
```

ginny5: im not sure about that. you know my husband thinks a lot of that is just built up in the literature.

Sus323: This is frustrating for me. I'm tempted to sign off.

710KAT: I wish we could meet in person. Any of you in the L.A. area?

ginny5: im in utah.

Sus323: Kat! Are you in L.A.? Really? Where are you?

710KAT: Pasadena. You?

Sus323: Silver Lake. My God, could we PLEASE have this conversation off line?

What conversation? Martin wants to know. *What are they talking about?*

He looks at the header at the top of the page: **PowerSurge-Panel**, it says. "What the hell?" Martin says to the sleeping Dude, curled on his lap. "I don't get it. I'm not picking up power from any of them. Except little-g's husband maybe..."

CHAPTER FIVE

I

When Martin arrives at work on Monday morning, Brenda is more friendly than she has been for the past several weeks. She immediately makes eye contact when she hears him approaching, and she conveys kind concern when she asks him if he is feeling better.

"Much better, thanks," he replies.

"New thermos?" she asks, noticing the large receptacle in his hand.

"Yeah, I was starting to realize how much I was spending on lattes. Seemed like a good investment."

Brenda smiles and nods. It's been such a long time since they've had an inconsequential, congenial conversation, returning to the small talk of yesteryear isn't something either of them can do on command.

"Well," Martin says, breaking the silence. "Guess I should see what happened while I was away."

Entering his office, he rolls his eyes at his own lame command of dialogue. And figuring no one wants to experience it at the moment, he shuts his office door.

Martin puts his thermos down on the coaster—the one that matches all the other desk accessories. Combined, they represent the first Christmas present he ever received from his in-laws. It was actually a thoughtful gift, and he remembers being touched by it. He always figured Lisa and he would receive a "couple gift," not something he himself could enjoy after they had split (not that he had anticipated the parting-of-ways). The blotter, the pencil holder, the pen and pencil set, and the small notepad holder are all so... fifty years ago. But they're nice, and they give his desk a certain class that he sometimes thinks is above and beyond him.

He spins in his chair, takes in the view of the Hollywood Hills—as seen from the western edge of Studio City. Spinning in his chair reminds him of the soda fountain at the drug store back in his hometown in rural Maryland. It was a different era—before the chain stores took over completely. Back when a humble pharmacist could rent his little piece of property and make a decent living filling prescriptions, selling school supplies, and offering kids a milk shake for less than a dollar. He remembers spinning on the soda fountain stool while his mom scanned the shampoo shelves, caught up with a neighbor or two, and was permitted to be a woman whose primary function was to raise her family.

When he's done spinning, Martin sits back. He wishes he had a headrest on his chair. He wonders when that little perk kicks in. He smiles then, but it's a sad smile. He's remembering one of his earlier dates with Lisa...

They were in a restaurant one block from Chicago's trendy Michigan Avenue shops. They had gone out a few times at that point, and the chemistry was growing. Taking her to Rosebud on Rush was raising the ante a bit, in terms of his budget. But, he wanted to let her know she was worth it. He wanted her to feel special.

She was about halfway into her second glass of wine when he shared with her his theory regarding the hierarchy of office chairs. Although he had given this theory some thought, he had never actually articulated it. Now, though, with her alcohol buzz following a geometric progression whereby two glasses of wine brought three times the buzz of one glass, he couldn't resist the opportunity to make her giggle.

"So, yeah," he had said. "I was walking by the office mail-room the other day, and you know what I noticed?"

"What," she asked, leaning in with curiosity as she anticipated a bit of office gossip—perhaps of the prurient variety.

"One stool."

"Okay," Lisa replied, curious as to why this might be of interest.

"One cold metal stool."

"Okay," she said again.

"How many guys do you think share that stool?"

"Don't be sexist, Martin! One of the mailboys is a girl, remember?"

"Right," he agreed, laughing at her cleverness. "Anyway: in the mailroom, probably about five or six employees share a stool. Which, when you think about it, is not altogether inappropriate. Their job, after all, is not about sitting down."

"No it isn't," Lisa had said, smiling at him through the rim of the bulbous crystal stemware.

"So that's the bottom of the corporate food chain," Martin went on to explain. "One cold metal stool. After that, of course, we have the secretarial pool. Their chairs, as you may have noticed, have seats and backs. They also swivel, but there's a risk of bodily injury if one pursues that swiveling function with too much aggression. You also might note that while they swivel, they do not lean back."

"Interesting."

"Now," Martin continued, "the administrative assistants have it a little better. Their chairs not only swivel, they also lean back. What's more, those chairs have arms! *But*, and note this please: the backs of those chairs don't go above shoulder-blade level."

"I'm just so amazed by how deeply you've studied these things," Lisa said, her smile at once teasing and flirtatious.

"Just wait, little lady. It gets better."

Lisa leaned forward and glanced seductively at Martin. "I'm waiting," she said.

"Okay," Martin said then, at risk of revealing the type of broken voice that occurs when a boy is in that special phase of puberty, "So... we've pretty much covered the folks who are in the corridors and the cubicles. Now, let's talk about private offices."

"Ooh, yeah," Lisa responded, her tone sultry. "Let's go into some private offices."

"Chairs in private offices," Martin went on, "have a few nice features. They roll on wheels that never get stuck. They have the armrests, of course, and the swiveling and leaning-back features. And it's all so much more safe and smooth with those chairs. I mean, they *really* swivel. They *really* lean back. Of course, the chair's additional height—I mean, the part of the back that goes just up to the neck—that helps. It's not a headrest, of course. That doesn't come yet—"

"Why not?"

"That comes with promotion. But...there's just enough there. Just enough of an added back to make the leaning function really enjoyable."

Martin looked across the table and reflected Lisa's smile. So playful and self-assured. Her presence made him feel special. He almost forgot where he was going with his story.

"You stuck?" she asked.

"No," he replied. "Just imagining you and me on some incredible chair."

"So? Where is this incredible chair?"

"That's what I'm getting at," Martin replied, regaining his storyteller's composure and nodding affirmatively. "I'm thinking it's in the corner office."

"Sounds right to me," Lisa commented.

"Of course," Martin continued, "before I get into that—the full description, I mean, I should do just a little sidebar about windows."

"Windows?" Lisa asked.

"Well, yeah, 'cause windows are kind of relative. I mean, think about it, back in the mailroom? No windows. The secretaries on the corridor? No windows. The administrative assistants in their cubicles – maybe one window per eight."

"I see, yes... windows..." Lisa then drained her second glass of wine, and all she had to do was raise her eyebrows to give Martin the cue.

"Waiter?" he called, before completing his theory.

"So," Martin said, as Lisa pointed to her empty glass and the waiter nodded cordially, "the corner office has corner windows and therefore a one-hundred-eighty degree view. And accordingly, it just has to have the one-hundred-eighty-degree chair."

"The one-hundred-eighty degree chair?"

"Correct," Martin replied.

"So, tell me about it," Lisa said then. "That is, if you don't mind."

"I think that the one-hundred-eighty-degree chair exists actually just a few inches above the ground. It doesn't have wheels because it doesn't need them. It just...hovers."

"Mmm... and I assume it also swivels?"

"I wouldn't say it swivels," Martin answered, smiling along with his date. "Rather, it hums an arc."

"Hums?"

"Yes, and on the subject of humming, it is completely in tune with the mind of that Senior VP who is sitting in it. It's like it knows. It just knows. Like when that VP wants to lean back? The chair just somehow *knows* it. Its contours change."

"Wow," cooed Lisa, taking a sip from the wineglass that the waiter had just delivered. "I bet this one, then, has a headrest."

"A headrest? Oh yes—like a mother's cradling hands. It even has *massage* features. The chair *embraces* the person sitting within it..."

Martin realizes, when Brenda buzzes him from outside, that he's been spinning again.

"Yes," Martin says, stopping (and a little dizzy).

"You got that meeting with Barry in ten minutes. His office."

"Thanks," Martin says.

Like a kid at a soda fountain, he spins one more time. Then he prepares... to put on his thinking cap, go up to Barry's office, and talk the talk.

II

When Martin gets in his car that night, he doesn't head for the freeway. Instead, he drives into Valley Village. He has no interest in seeing Lisa. (In fact, a part of him never wants to see her again.) But he misses the house. He misses—anyway—that sense of property. Four walls. A roof. A lawn.

It was a nice little plot of land, and even though it took her parents' rather generous donation to make it all happen, he actually believed, for the first couple of years, that he had a right to it. That it was his, too.

Martin makes the left onto La Maida, and he immediately gets a queasy feeling. "What the fuck am I doing?" he asks the dashboard. "This is stupid."

He creeps along, at a pace that is probably suspiciously below the speed limit. But: it's the best he can do. And: as soon as he can get off this street—he will.

Martin doesn't live on La Maida anymore.

And he needs to deal with that.

III

Upon entering his apartment, Martin hears a "Mao."

"Dude!" he replies, putting down his briefcase and scooping the cat into his arms.

"You know, Dude," he says, stroking the cat's neck, "I may not have a roof or a yard anymore, but I got you."

"Mao."

IV

Dude seems particularly excited as Martin opens the can from the top of the stack.

"No kidding," Martin says to his new buddy. "And damn right you should be excited. Tonight, it's Ocean Whitefish and Tuna."

He begins to scoop the contents onto the plate (still encrusted—still waiting for some cleaning routine). "You know, Dude,"

Martin says, "if you were wild, truly wild, you would be living on Catalina right now. The *west* coast of Catalina. Splendidly rustic. And everyday, you'd swim out just a bit, gather a fish in your jaw, and swim home. Ocean Whitefish, Dude. It's a natural for you."

As Dude begins scarfing down the Fancy Feast, Martin opens his freezer. He opts for the Chicken Florentine Lasagna, and he is relieved to see that it will take less than thirty-five minutes.

After turning on the oven and placing the container on its rack, Martin returns to the packaging and notices the microwave instructions. There is something ironic there. On La Maida, the microwave was such a "given." They had it, but they hardly ever used it. After all, they weren't *bachelors*.

It's not that he wishes he had a microwave now (as he has discovered lately, his alleged "time constraints" are all bullshit). It just strikes him: sometimes the tools you could use are the ones you give up in the settlement.

V

Martin puts his dinner on a plate, grabs a fork, and heads into the living room. Upon making that entry, he realizes how totally spaced he is. He had anticipated turning on the television. But he hasn't had one in almost a week.

"Oh, well," he says, plopping into a place on the couch.

"Mao."

Dude has entered the room from the middle hallway, which means, Dude probably just used the litterbox (a welcome routine).

"So, what are your plans?" Martin asks the cat, as he ingests his first forkful of the healthy cuisine.

Dude walks by. Apparently, he has business to attend to in the kitchen.

Martin shrugs his shoulders.

VI

It is 12:30, and Martin is really frustrated. He's been tossing and turning for more than forty-five minutes. He has no idea what's keeping him up these nights. When Dude leaps off the bed, Martin knows he shouldn't even try anymore. Trying to sleep is pointless.

He throws off the sheets and blankets and stands beside his bed. "This sucks!" he says to no one. "This totally sucks! Why can't I sleep?"

He turns on lights as he wends his way into the kitchen. He grabs a bottle of water out of the fridge and nearly trips over Dude as he heads out of the room. "Sorry, buddy," he says to the cat.

In the bonus room, his computer is sleeping, but Martin doesn't feel bad about waking it up. If computers had to choose, they would probably be nocturnal. There is something about them that is sneaky. They can go anywhere at anytime. They don't need to live by the majority's nine-to-five schedule.

The chatroom's most recent dialogue was posted three hours ago. He doesn't recognize the handles, and that disappoints him. There's something about Sus323 that intrigues him. He's assuming, of course, that she's a woman. In fact, he's starting to think all the chatters at this particular site are women, but he has no way of knowing for sure. That's the thing about the Internet: it's anybody's game. Anonymity is the one thing everybody can have in common—if that's what they want.

The most recent string was begun by "Fab@55," who wrote:

```
I just want to encourage all of you! I'm about
inspiration! I believe it's my gift and I am
driven to share it.

Beverly: I'm happy for you, Fab, but if you're
in such a good place, how did you come upon
this site?

Fab@55: Because I feel it! I understand it!
And I believe we can all embrace it and make
it part of our daily lives!

Beverly: Right, sweating profusely every hour
on the hour - part of my daily life. This is a
good thing?
```

```
Fab@55: Think of it as the bad energy just
streaming out of your pores!
```

"Oh, Jesus!" says Martin. "Fab is a fucking freak."

"Mao?"

"I mean, she's obviously one of those over-the-top happy types. I don't believe her for an instant. I'll bet my next paycheck she's a miserable mess. It's blatant overcompensation."

Dude stretches out his left front arm, revealing the claws that are slowly rearranging the texture of Martin's upholstered furnishings. Martin makes a mental note to drop by the pet store on Hillhurst and pick up some clippers.

He looks again at the dialogue he'd just read, and he homes in on "sweating profusely." *Hmm,* he thinks. *Is this about... Hmm...*

He scrolls down to see what any previous dialogues might reveal, and he sees the handle that he's been drawn to: Sus323. She's the one in Silver Lake. And 710KAT is there, too. Was that the Pasadena person? It seems that, earlier this evening, they followed up on their plans to meet off-line.

```
710KAT: I have an elderly aunt who lives in
Atwater. I'll be visiting her on Saturday. Are
you available late afternoon?

Sus323: Yes. In fact, that's perfect. Where do
you want to meet?

710KAT: Well, I'm open to suggestions, but
if you don't have any preferences, there's a
great little place right there on the main
Atwater street. I think the street's called
Glendale at that point. Anyway, it's at the
intersection of Larga. On the Griffith Park
side. Sorry, I can't remember the name of the
place.

Sus323: Not to worry. Anyone on this site is
lucky to remember her own name. (LOL)

710KAT: I'm with you on the LOL! Thanks for
giving me a smile. Anyway, you'll see the
place at that intersection. There are no other
restaurants or cafes in that block, I don't
think.
```

Sus323: Sounds great. What time?

710KAT: Is 4 too early? I'll be going to my
aunt's at 2:30, and 90 minutes is generally
about all she has energy for.

Sus323: 4:00 sounds great. We won't have to
worry about not getting a table.

710KAT: Right. So, let's meet out front. I'm
tall, slim, short grey hair, glasses. You?

Sus323: 5-8. Long dark hair (washing out the
gray roots later tonight!). No glasses. And
probably no make-up.

710KAT: You're in the book! See you Saturday!

Sus323: I'm looking forward to it.

Martin reaches for his blackberry and opens the calendar app.
It doesn't surprise him at all to see that he's totally free on Saturday. He enters the info regarding the little restaurant in Atwater.

CHAPTER SIX

I

Just before pulling into his reserved space in the underground parking garage, Martin notices Barry, getting out of his Lexus in the far corner. Given the route to the elevators, Barry will probably be walking by Martin's space in about twenty seconds, thereby putting them on a potentially common itinerary that could afford five to seven minutes of conversation. And Martin doesn't have five minutes in him, let alone seven. So he remains in his car, moves very little, and just in case Barry notices him, he reaches for his cellphone and holds it to his ear.

Sitting there, in faux conversation mode, Martin questions his reaction and the motivation behind it. It's not that Martin doesn't like Barry. And he certainly doesn't feel intimidated by the man who is just a notch above him on the org chart. He actually finds Barry quite congenial, remarkably approachable. So, as Martin essentially "hides" in his BMW, he wonders what the hell is going on. He wonders why he can't do the back-slapping routine that he mastered early on and perfected throughout his thirties and forties.

What's happening to me? Martin thinks.

II

Settled into his office and only halfway through his thermos of fresh, inexpensive, home-made coffee, Martin is grateful for the day's deadline. He has to have the report on Barry's desk

39

before he leaves that evening, and if that means staying until seven o'clock or eight, that's fine with him. There's nothing to do at home, and he can avoid the rush-hour traffic.

The report is easy enough. He just needs to consolidate some numbers from the active accounts, figure out the bottom line, and make some projections. It's basic, and it relaxes him.

Martin loves math. And he appreciates the timing of the affair that has lasted for more than three decades now. When he was in elementary school and even in junior high, he sucked at math. He couldn't wrap his brain around it to spite his face. But that shortcoming also was never an issue. Given that his Dad was a newspaper columnist and his mother an ace craftswoman, there was an expectation in the family: no math gene. So when he came home with that ninth grade report card, and the D in Algebra stood out quite glaringly from the grades that would otherwise place him in some national honors society, his parents just laughed.

"Well," his dad had said, "at least we know your mother didn't have an affair with some agent of the Internal Revenue Service!"

Martin finished out his ninth grade year with a C in Algebra—practically a gift from his teacher. But when his parents sent him to private school, beginning in his sophomore year, something changed, and within a few short weeks, he revealed a remarkable understanding of geometry. It helped, of course, that class sizes were relatively small. And it didn't hurt (where attentiveness was concerned) that the classrooms were filled only with boys. He no longer had Georgia Marshall's sassy blond braid to stare at when he should have been looking at the blackboard and comprehending the concept of a tangent. He no longer felt compelled to steal sidelong glances at Penny Ricketts' thighs, which seemed to go on forever on their way to the bottom of her remarkably short mini-skirts. He just had... geometry and the completely unsexy schoolmarm-type who was teaching it. Suddenly, there was logic in those processes and numbers and angles. And he really enjoyed solving the problems.

By the end of his junior year, his command of Algebra 2 was so acute and apparent that his classmates sought his help as they studied for finals. He ended up leading spontaneous tutorials in one of the classrooms that was located in the main building. He worked patiently with his peers to help them get through the problems. He spent so much time, in fact, being the reliable helper-friend, that when he sat down to take the final, a scary thought crossed his mind: he had forgotten to study! But, all the work he had done with his classmates proved a resourceful studying tool. In the end, he not only aced the exam; he received the highest mark of anyone in the class.

And a year later, at graduation, he received the Math Award. His parents, sitting proudly in the auditorium—about halfway back—told Martin later that they just about fell over when his name was called.

At the time of his embracing of math, Martin didn't give a lot of thought to the turn-around in his competencies. But he understood it several years later, when distance had afforded a perspective on his adolescence. He realized that the confusion of puberty had created too many gray areas, and his inability to find answers exacerbated that confusion. With math, there were no gray areas. Every problem had a solution.

CHAPTER SEVEN

I

"Dude! It's Saturday! Can you chill for a minute?"

Having been in Martin's keep for ten days, the cat apparently prefers the eating schedule that reflects Martin's Monday through Friday routine. Which is to say, Dude expects a rendezvous, in the kitchen, no later than six-thirty a.m. Because it is now a full hour after that assigned time, the cat is making its needs known. It is digging into the blanket on Martin's chest, as if there's an opened can of Fancy Feast somewhere between that blanket and the sheet that is just under it.

Martin looks at the cat. "You know the definition of expectation?"

The cat stares at him.

"Pre-meditated resentment."

Dude begins to dig again.

"At least, that's the human definition," Martin says, inching his way to the edge of the bed.

"In the feline dictionary," he continues, putting his feet on the floor, "it's probably something else."

Dude jumps down from the bed and looks up at him.

"I can't believe you're so intrigued," Martin says to his fur-lined roommate.

"So, anyway," the human continues, as the two walk together to the kitchen. "In the feline dictionary? I'm guessing in that good book, expectation is defined as just being really obnoxious until you get exactly what you want."

Martin is too tired to read the label. He simply opens the can, scoops it onto the plate, and throws the empty tin into the garbage.

"Bon appetit," he says, meandering out of the kitchen and back to bed.

II

Martin approaches the little café at the intersection of Glendale and Larga and peruses the menu in the window. The cuisine appears to be French/Mediterranean. There's a woman standing on the sidewalk—she's wearing glasses and she has short, gray hair. Martin guesses she's 710KAT.

As he studies the appetizer list (or pretends to), it occurs to him that he should probably wait until Sus323 has arrived, and he should probably wait, for that matter, until the two of them are seated. If he gets a table first, he may end up across the room from them. And he doesn't want that. He is here to continue his eavesdropping, and just as Sus323 was anxious for their conversation to take place off-line, so is he.

He decides to walk south, to pretend that he's undecided as to where he's going to have his late afternoon meal. And after about five or six minutes of looking in store windows, reading the occasional menu, and acting like a relaxed guy with no apparent agenda, he takes a quick glance back in the direction of the rendezvous café. The presumed 710KAT is no longer on the sidewalk, which means, Martin hopes, that Sus323 has arrived. He wanders back up the street and enters the restaurant.

The two women are sitting at a table by the window, and there is another small table adjacent to it. It is the only other window table, and Martin views that as fortuitous. It is logical to prefer a window table. (It is not logical to prefer the table that is as close as possible to the only other occupied table in a restaurant.)

Martin heads for the chair that will give him the best view of their table. He'll be looking at the back of Sus323, who is sitting across from 710KAT. Before he takes his seat, he puts his laptop on the table (in the space made available by the removed second place-setting). After he sits, he casually opens the laptop. Martin has no intention of doing any computer work during this meal, but he wants to appear to have a project.

He has been listening as he's made these maneuvers. He has been listening to 710KAT and Sus323 conversing. Unlike anyone else in this restaurant (which, at the current time, refers only to those who *work* in the restaurant), he knows that this is the first time these two women are meeting in person. He is struck by their energy and sense of camaraderie. They are already speaking like two old friends. Martin has always admired women's ability to do this—to bond so effortlessly.

Martin looks at the menu and listens.

"I know," says Sus323. "Don't you just want to smack her?"

Martin suspects they are speaking about ginny5.

"Yes," replies 710KAT, "and I also want to smack her husband. I was curious when she mentioned she was from Utah. It made me wonder how many wives that doctor-husband of hers has... how many wives are being told that menopause is a myth."

"Well, if she *is* married to a polygamist," Sus323 says, "he's probably had the good sense to wed a span of ages. I know I wouldn't do a husband any good right now. It's so frustrating!"

Just as 710KAT asks Sus323 if she's currently single, the waitress approaches Martin. He doesn't want to lose a moment of the dialogue at the next table, so he points to a random item on the menu and asks for an iced tea. Regarding his entrée selection, the waitress makes a facial expression that is somewhere between being impressed and dumbfounded. She takes the menu and walks away.

"...and it was great, so great, for a while," Sus323 is saying. "But, then, I don't know, the sex just changed for me. I used to love it. I used to pride myself, in fact. I mean, you know, when a woman's a good lay, she knows it. And it's a pretty powerful tool. But... as soon as my libido bolted, he did too."

"It sounds like you're well rid of him."

"I realize that. I mean, clearly, he wasn't in it for the long haul. And now, I don't know. I can't imagine finding someone at this point. I also don't know if I care," Sus323 adds, with a tired hint at resignation. "What about you?"

"I'm lucky," 710KAT replies. "I've been married to the same wonderful man for thirty-eight years."

"Wow. You mind my asking how old you are?"

"I just turned sixty in January."

"Congratulations," says Sus323, holding up her glass of wine.

"Thanks," responds 710KAT, as she engages in the ceremonial clinking of glasses. "And you?"

"I'm forty-eight."

"Too young to be freaking out, my dear."

"I know. I know."

III

When the waitress delivers Martin's entrée, he has to work very hard not to look completely shocked. There are tentacles on his plate, and he has no clue as to how he is supposed to negotiate them.

For a split second, he considers calling the waitress back and claiming that she had misread the direction of his finger— the finger that pointed to something random on the menu and therefore ordered on his behalf. But he also knows that this dish, whatever it is, is probably one they rarely serve. (God knows he'll never order it again!) And so, it would be wrong to put the burden of his arbitrary selection on the restaurant. He also doesn't want to make a fuss. He doesn't want to distract 710KAT and Sus323.

Fortunately, there are items on the plate that Martin recognizes. There's the rice (or, at least, he thinks it's rice), and there's a rather large array of vegetables, mostly green and not completely slimy. He'll do what he can to get through this meal. It doesn't matter, anyway. He didn't come here for the food.

"One thing that has helped me," 710KAT is saying, "is just to try to get out of my norm. I actually talked Stephen into taking Salsa dance classes with me. You should see us! We are so spastic in that group, but it's been fun, and it's given us something to share. For two hours every week, we are equally awkward together!"

"That's sweet," Sus323 responds (and while Martin cannot see her face, he senses that she is smiling). "Actually, I—um—am about to step out of my 'norm.' In a big way."

"How's that?"

"I recently applied for a job at Trader Joe's on Hyperion. They hired me, and I start next week!"

"Great company to work for. A couple of my kids worked at some of their stores. The benefits package alone is remarkable. At least, it was fifteen or so years ago."

"Well, I think the state of the economy has changed that a bit, but—"

"So?" 710KAT asks, "What are you leaving? Where have you been working prior to Trader Joe's?"

Martin watches the back of Sus323's head. The newly colored hair that is hiding the gray roots seems to sparkle as she nods.

"You're probably not gonna believe it," she shares with 710KAT. "I—um—just recently resigned from a law firm. Downtown. I was an attorney with them for twenty years, and five years ago, I made partner."

"Wow!" says 710KAT, smiling broadly. "You are really giving it the finger then, aren't you?"

Sus323 joins her new friend in some conspiratorial laughter. "I guess," she says. "I don't know, though, I just don't want that crazy routine anymore. And I can afford to make the change. I don't have the financial worries other people have. My husband—I, um, did once have a great husband—he was a cop." Sus323 pauses for a second. "Anyway, he was killed twelve years ago. On duty."

"I'm so sorry."

"Me, too," says Sus323, her tone taking it down a notch. "Anyway, there was a settlement there, which I didn't really need. But, the house—the one we bought in Silver Lake—it's been paid for for years now. And, about eighteen months ago, when my mom died, well, there was, you know, money from her estate. So... I don't know, I'm in some ways fortunate in that I don't have financial worries. But: I also am a widow and an orphan. And... at the tender age of forty-eight, I can't have an orgasm to save my ass."

IV

Martin returns home with the largest doggie bag he has ever brought out of a restaurant. When Dude greets him with a "Mao," Martin can only say, "You have no idea."

Once he's in the kitchen, Martin opens the bag. The waitress wrapped his leftover tentacles in foil, and as he unwraps her construction, he wonders if she was aware that the amount of tentacles left on his plate was absolutely equal in portion and size to the amount she delivered when she served him the entrée he had ordered. He didn't even try to taste them at the restaurant, and he also neglected to check the window menu once he had left the establishment. He still doesn't know what he ordered.

Dude is getting feisty on the floor—walking more quickly and in seemingly smaller circles. Martin expects that the smell is appealing to the cat. Martin wonders if this will be the spoiler. After this doggie bag, will Dude find Fancy Feast too pedestrian?

With the leftovers in front of him, Martin still is unsure what to do. So he decides to just wing it. He grabs a knife, cuts off a tentacle at about three inches, and sportingly throws it over his shoulder. Dude immediately dives in for the catch. Within a few seconds, the cat has made a toy of the seafood. Dude flings it and chases it, while Martin stands there, bewitched by the conversation he overheard in the Atwater café.

After a minute or two in a trancelike state, Martin realizes that he should probably re-wrap his doggie bag contents and put it in the fridge. He also realizes that he is hungry. Rice and some green, not-too-slimy vegetables did not do the trick, particularly since—in anticipation of a "meal out"—he ate almost nothing earlier in the day.

He opens the freezer and immediately smiles at the thought of a French bread pepperoni pizza. That is so what the doctor ordered right now. He sets the oven on three-fifty.

He can hear Dude in the living room, making a major game of the tentacle. Martin has a feeling that the cat is as clueless as he was regarding the intended purpose of this culinary offering. Martin has a feeling that the tentacle will entertain Dude for a few too many hours. It may even end up sharing the bed with them later that night...

CHAPTER EIGHT

I

Opening his door to retrieve the Sunday paper, Martin looks down the hallway. Such a weird place. Such a weird quiet, and it seems to be quiet much of the time. There are no other papers waiting outside the doors of his neighbors' apartments, and Martin knows—or believes, rather—that this is because he is the only tenant on this floor who gets the paper. After all, it's eight o'clock on a Sunday morning. It is highly unlikely that his thirtynothing co-tenants are already up and working out that Sudoku puzzle.

He feels like a judgmental prick for having this thought, but he also feels justified, somehow. Because he is certain that among the residents who traverse the extremely tacky, burgundy and black, oddly-Harlequin-patterned, ancient goddamn carpeting, there is probably not one whose marriage ended because *he* was deemed the one who could not conceive.

"What a crock of shit," Martin utters, beginning to entertain some hurtful memories as he goes back into his apartment and shuts the door.

"What a crock of shit," he repeats, as he enters the kitchen, tosses the paper onto the counter, and reaches for a coffee mug.

It doesn't surprise Martin to realize how much he is still pissed off at Lisa. When she got that "mommy" virus, well into her late thirties, she seemed to assume a completely different personality. Then, when she continued never to get pregnant, she went on a mission of fact-finding that Martin believes, to this day, ultimately revealed few actual facts.

It was weird how the process was never one they pursued together. It was just Lisa. Lisa, learning—through some tests—that there was nothing wrong with her eggs. Lisa, learning—through some research and consultations—what Martin should do. Lisa, scheduling his appointment and reminding him not to miss it. Lisa, not bothering to accompany him to the appointment.

"Hey," she had said that morning, "it's not like you came with me for my tests!"

"I didn't *know* about your tests, Lisa!"

A few weeks later, it was Lisa again. Lisa... telling Martin that the test results had come in. That his sperm count was low, really low. That, in terms of their status as a couple, he was the infertile one.

"Can I see?" Martin had asked, referring to the tests.

"I was so upset, I tore them up."

Over the years, Martin has learned that when he is feeling ire toward Lisa, it is best just to leave the house. Now, of course, he doesn't have a house. *Lisa* has a house. Lisa has *the* house. But still, Martin needs to leave. He needs to leave his measly apartment. Because, what he also has learned—in the three months since he left his wife—is that his contempt for her can stay with him for a very long time. And it is in his best interest to walk away from its lure.

Martin turns off the coffeemaker that has been preparing his morning's fix. He picks up the newspaper he has just tossed on the counter. And, with no further ado, he heads for the Starbucks down the street.

II

The crossword puzzle's 6-down clue is likely to be a deal-maker (at least, in that northwest quadrant of the grid), and so when Martin is confident with, and enters, EURIPIDES, he sits back to enjoy a long sip of the large triple espresso-whatever he ordered for an astronomical sum of money.

"I know you," Martin hears then.

Martin looks up.

It's manicure man. It's one of the "Dudes," from the night of margaritas...

"Right," Martin says, extending his hand.

"Martin, right?"

"I'm surprised you remember," Martin replies, as they shake hands.

"Hey, it's not a common name these days. Mind if I join you?"

"Umm... Sure! Yeah, please. Have a seat."

Manicure man settles into the other chair that is assigned to the table where Martin's crossword puzzle is taking center stage.

"You like puzzles, huh?" manicure man asks.

"Well, yeah."

"I never could take to them myself."

"Right."

Martin is feeling remarkably self-conscious, as if someone from his office might happen into this establishment and guess that he and manicure man are at the end of a long-night's journey into day.

"So!" Martin says, "you're up awfully early."

"Just getting done with the night, actually."

"Oh?" says/asks Martin, furtively looking for traces of white powder around the nostrils of his table-mate.

"Yeah," says manicure man, "I just got off work."

"Oh?" says/asks Martin.

"I do outreach for a runaway shelter."

"You do," asks/says Martin.

"Yup," replies manicure man, a hint of exhaustion in his voice. "You know we're living in the runaway capital of the world, don't you?"

"I guess I didn't know that," Martin responds. "But, I'm also not surprised. Um, I've forgotten your name."

"It's Jason."

They shake hands again.

CHAPTER NINE

I

When Martin emerges from his car on Monday morning, Barry is just walking by.

"Martin!" Barry says, with his old-world avuncular energy.

"Morning, Barry." (Martin manages a smile, and there's a part of it that is remarkably genuine.)

"Good weekend?" Barry asks, patting Martin on the back.

"It was okay. And you?"

"The wife kept me busy," Barry responds, sharing an expression that is at once bedraggled and non-complaining.

"How so?" Martin asks, beating his boss to the punch of hitting the Up arrow at the elevator banks.

"Margaret is crazy for flea markets," Barry answers, "and this weekend was the monthly Rose Bowl madness."

"Oh, yeah," Martin says, nodding, as the elevator doors open, and as Barry's arm gesture tells him to enter first, "I've always heard about that, but I've never been."

Barry presses the L button and turns to his colleague. "It's just madness," he says.

"How so?" Martin asks.

"People. Booths. Wares. Bargaining. Buying. Selling..."

The elevator doors open, depositing them on the main floor, where they'll turn the corner and catch a second elevator that will take them to their office floors—the eighth, for Martin; the ninth, for Barry. As they walk the walk, Martin notices that Barry is looking down. The exit from the first part of the ride allowed him to end his flea market monologue. Now, he seems to be within himself. And Martin doesn't know what to do. He feels awkward. He feels as if he is witnessing a part of Barry that the generally gregarious Senior VP doesn't usually reveal.

When they reach the elevator banks for Floors 2-14, Martin presses the Up arrow. "I'll have to check it out," he says to his colleague.

"What's that?" asks Barry.

"The Rose Bowl."

Barry shakes his head and smiles in a way that creates a frown. "It's madness," he says. He chuckles to himself as the elevator doors open and the two head up to work.

II

Martin pounds the steering wheel in frustration as he waits his turn. He is in the hell of hells. It is Monday evening, and along with half the population of the free world, he is in the parking lot of Trader Joe's on Hyperion.

What is it about Trader Joe's? he thinks, as he watches a small SUV nearly back over a denim-clad, extremely pregnant woman whose cart is undoubtedly filled with items as organic as her Birkenstocks. *Who is the sado-masochist that the ultimate Joe hired? And why did he do this to us? We are nice people who frequent Trader Joe's. Why do we have to go through this hell every time we want to shop here?*

Behind him, a fellow "nice person" honks loudly.

"Fuck you!" Martin yells, safely protected within his closed windows. "I'll move when I can!"

He sees some white back-up lights emanating from a Camry that has been parked against the retaining wall. He inches forward.

III

As Martin pushes his cart down the first aisle, he is painfully aware of his ulterior motive. Sure, there are things to buy, and the juice to his right is a good place to start, but... more than anything, he's hoping that Sus323—the former law partner; the widow; the orphan—is somewhere in the store, baptizing her new career as part of the evening's crew.

He scans the refrigerated shelves of fresh vegetables and opts for a bag of Spring Mix. He passes on the frozen food aisle, though he knows there are items there that would grab his attention.

Frozen desserts? No...

Martin realizes, as he continues to push the cart he probably won't fill by a long shot, that this exercise could get old.

At the tasting kiosk, the incredibly friendly crew member is offering an empanada in three-pepper salsa. Martin takes a sample, and it is good. For about twenty seconds, it occupies him. But, when he's disposed of his little Dixie Cup, he is back where he was: heading toward the southernmost aisles of Trader Joe's on Hyperion, with two items in his cart: a bottle of juice and a bag of greens. There's only one thing to do: lose the cart.

This is madness, Martin thinks to himself, echoing Barry's description of the Rose Bowl flea market.

Holding his two items, one in each hand, he makes his way—as fluidly as possible—to the least busy cashier.

When the lane's shelf for the next grocery basket becomes available, Martin places the juice and greens on it. And when the cashier—who's probably nearing the end of his shift and has achieved a certain rhythm—reaches for the next load of groceries, he is thrown off by those items' having no container.

"Wow," he says to Martin, "you clearly knew exactly what you wanted tonight."

"I did," agrees Martin. "I did."

After receiving his change, Martin heads for the door. But he stops when a sound distracts him. It is the sound of Sus323's soothing voice. She's there—two steps up in the office area. She's talking to a co-worker.

"Not a problem," Martin hears Sus323 say, her tone cool and confident.

IV

Martin feels lucky to find a parking space on Rodney. In a neighborhood as popular as his, leaving his car within easy walking distance of his apartment isn't something he takes for granted. Strolling the block-and-a-half back to his building, he realizes he's gaining a slow appreciation for his environment. It is somewhat refreshing to be living where there is pedestrian traffic into the night and the vague sense of a constant party. In Valley Village, it was more valley than village. To pull into the driveway at night after work was to confront adult life and nothing else.

Brittany happens to be returning to the building just as Martin is, and so they exchange "Hiya's" as they each fumble for their keys. She wins the fumbling race and opens the door for both of them.

"Good day?" she asks, as she indicates that he should enter ahead of her.

"It was okay," Martin responds.

They walk together up the wide hallway.

"And you?" he asks.

"Aah," she says noncommittally, shrugging her shoulders.

Martin presses the elevator button. "Did you work today?" he asks, noticing a blue portion of her hair that he is sure was pink last week.

She rolls her eyes in a way that says *yes, and I hate my job.*

After they enter the elevator and each has pressed the appropriate button, Martin asks the logical question (which is backed by a genuine sense of intrigue): "So where do you work?"

"It's a mortuary company," she replies, her eyes toward the heavens.

The elevator stops at the third floor, and as the doors open, Brittany says, "Well, this is me. Good night, Marvin."

Martin (who has always been especially glad his name is not Marvin) is still wearing a completely dumbfounded expression when the doors open on his own floor. He emerges to find his building manager—David—throwing a bag down the trash shoot.

"Martin!" David says, with an enthusiasm that is rare in an apartment manager.

"Hi," replies Martin, who is still a bit perplexed from learning of Brittany's employment.

"Everything going okay?" David asks.

"Yeah," says Martin. "Things are fine."

As it happens, in large apartment buildings, crossed paths lead to common routes. At the moment, Martin and David are happening to walk down the hall together. And because of that, Martin feels compelled to make conversation.

"Too bad about that guy. Lonzo—" Martin offers, referring to the missing man. "Any developments?"

"Not really," David replies. "No news of any sightings. I had the saddest talk today, though, with his niece. God, the family's just torn up about it."

"I'm sure they are," Martin comments, slowing as he approaches his own apartment door.

David stops walking at this point, rubs the heel of his hand on his brow, "Yeah," he says, "the niece I talked to today was asking about Lonzo's cat. She just remembers her uncle having a cat."

"I thought this was a no pets building."

"Well, technically, it is, but, you know—the grandfather clause."

"An old cat?"

"I'm not sure the cat was old. Anyway—"

"And..." Martin asks/says, "she's worried about the cat?"

"I don't know," David shrugs. "Anyway, Martin, let me know if you need anything."

V

After scarfing down a Healthy Choice roasted turkey dinner, which he eats almost as quickly as Dude eats the canned Turkey and Giblets, Martin grabs the phone and relaxes into the couch.

It was good to come home to the message from Rachel, and he's glad she let him know that she would be up late and he could call until 11:00 her time. He'll make it just under the wire.

"Rachel!" he enthuses, after hearing her meek and—to him—sadly charming voice.

"Oh, Marty, I'm so glad you called," she states, almost inflecting. "I hate this time difference."

"So what's three hours between sibs? And, hey, it's not like it hasn't been this way for a while."

"I know," she says.

"You sound down," Martin comments, hoping that she'll use the opportunity of their conversation to unload whatever needs unloading.

"Yeah, well, I just don't know what I'm doing these days. I feel so lost, and I don't know, I think Jack is getting tired of me."

"How long have you two been together?"

"Three years."

"So what makes you think he's getting tired?"

"I don't know. It's like the spark's gone. Sometimes I think we should move in together just to shake things up, but that doesn't seem like a solution really."

There's a pause.

"And then," Rachel continues, "I just get all sad because I forgot to have kids, and I'm way too old for that now, and I don't even know what my purpose is."

Martin loves his younger sister, but her existential crises always throw him. He never knows what to say.

"I mean," she goes on, "I suppose if I had *wanted* kids, then I would have had them, right? And it's kind of an unrealistic thing to be thinking about even. Jeez, remember my apartment? There's not even room for my shoes!"

"Brings to mind a nursery rhyme..."

"Right," says Rachel. "Right... There was an old spinster who lived with her shoes. Boy, I feel so much better now," she states facetiously and in a tone that is dulled by resignation. "Thanks for making the connection there."

"So how's your job?"

"It's not bad, you know? It's challenging. They respect me. And I just scored a six-figure grant from a foundation they've never received funding from before, so that's pretty cool."

"It's an environmental nonprofit, right?"

"Yeah. Clearly in a good place to get funding these days. And I had fun, too, with the grant. They let me design the project pretty much."

Rachel's voice is beginning to lighten up. Martin wants to hear more, and he knows that he will.

"Yeah," she says, continuing in that tone of hers that is at once droll and childlike, "they wanted to create a project for middle school kids, so I thought about, you know, how they behave, you know, how mean kids can be at that age, and I came up with this project called 'Green with Envy'."

"That's great!" Martin responds, laughing.

"Yeah, so it's this sort of competition thing. And the kids, you know, develop their own environmentally friendly ideas, specifically reflecting behaviors in the everyday household, and after the semester, they'll all gather at our annual middle school conference, they'll present their projects, and we'll award prizes. It's pretty cool."

"You'll have to keep me posted. I probably could use some of their ideas around my new place."

There's a pause, and during that time, there's a part of Martin that would love, more than anything, for Rachel to inquire about his new place.

"Yeah," she says, instead. "So, we'll see."

Martin shrugs to himself and to the air. There's nothing cruel about Rachel. She just seems to find comfort in a certain degree of sadness, and she has to stay very close to herself to feed that need.

"So how's New York?" Martin asks. "This is a great time of year in the city, isn't it?"

"Well, it's been kind of rainy the past couple of days."

"Have you talked to Mom and Dad recently?"

"Last week, I guess," Rachel says. "They sound good."

"And Reggie?"

"Not lately. You?"

"No," Martin responds, "but I got an email from Zac. He suggested he might spend some time out here with me this summer."

"So, are you going to do that?"

"I don't know."

"How's your new place?" Rachel asks.

Finally... some inquisition.

"It's okay," Martin says. "I'm getting used to it. I like the neighborhood a lot. It's busy. It's got a nice urban feel."

"Los Feliz, right?"

"Right."

"Yeah, that's supposed to be a pretty cool place."

Another pause, and Martin begins to feel antsy. This would be a good time to have a call coming in, but few people ever call him.

"You miss Lisa?" Rachel asks.

Suddenly, Martin has follow-up questions regarding the "Green with Envy" project.

"I don't know how to answer that, Rache."

"It's okay," she says, with the audible equivalent of a hand gesture that shoos something out of the room. "It's none of my business, anyway."

"But I will say," Martin adds, "it was sweet of you to ask. I appreciate that."

"Hey," she says. "I care about my big brother."

"I care about you, too."

"Well," Rachel exhales, her voice an animated sigh, "this is probably a really good note on which to say good-night."

Martin chuckles. "It's a positive note!"

"That's my point exactly."

"Let's talk again soon, Rachel."

"Absolutely. Goodnight, Marty."

"Goodnight."

"Mao," Dude chirps, just after Martin hangs up the phone.

"Dude, hey! I didn't even get to tell her about you! Do you think that would have cheered her up?"

"Mao."

"I know. Me neither."

Martin looks at the cat then. He realizes his impulses are selfish and wrong. "Dude" might be here only because Lonzo Lazarra disappeared. "Dude" might have a name (and a gender, for that matter) known to the nieces of the missing man.

"You know what, Dude?" Martin says to the cat, not altogether convincingly. "You might have relatives. And, they might have a yard."

VI

"Hey!" David-the-manager says, opening his door only partially.

Martin can smell the marijuana, and while he doesn't make any judgments about it, he acknowledges that David's responses might be influenced by what he's been doing up until two seconds ago.

"Sorry to bother you," Martin says.

"No prob," David replies, keeping the door opened at half-mast. "What's up?"

"Uh, you mentioned a cat earlier. One that Lonzo's niece was asking about?"

"Right. Right. You seen it?"

"Well, I think it might be living with me."

CHAPTER TEN

I

Brenda is whispering into her phone as Martin walks by. "I know, I'm a little shook, too. Let's talk later."

It's Thursday morning, and so Martin can only assume Brenda is talking about the *American Idol* results show. He knows, because he has listened, that every Wednesday night, some wannabe is sent packing. It's the reality genre. Whittle them down. Whittle them down.

He enters his office and rolls his eyes at the masses. He cannot believe how much he knows and understands about aspects of pop culture in which he does not directly indulge.

But when Brenda walks in, a few minutes later, Martin doesn't see a pop culture gleam in her eye. He also notices that she has arrived without a prop. She is not carrying a folder or a document or even a pink slip from some higher-up. She has simply entered his office.

"Martin," she says quietly, as he stares at her intently, "we got some bad news this morning."

"What's up?" he asks, tilting his head and hoping that his half-smile will somehow lighten her mood.

"Barry's wife died."

"What?"

"Yeah. And, apparently, it was a suicide."

"What?"

II

Driving home that evening, Martin feels shaky. The whole day at work was such a weird trip. The sense of disbelief was palpable. Martin had never met Barry's wife, and he had to assume few of his co-workers had met her either. But, it was as if everyone had a *sense* of her. Barry's wife. You couldn't help but look at Barry and do the math. He was gregarious, jovial, a back-slapping throw-back to a previous time. You couldn't help but assume, knowing Barry, that his wife—the Margaret he spoke about—was also a throw-back. You envisioned her in June Cleaver clothes, playing bridge with the girls, keeping a lovely house, raising the kids with cookies and crafts. Doing all the right things. Until... she offed her life.

Barry's wife?

Martin exits the 101 on Highland. He knows he's going to be sitting in traffic forever, but he doesn't care. He can't deal with the freeway right now, even if his usual exit is only two miles away. He'd rather sit in traffic waiting for lights than be on a freeway where the speed limit of sixty-five is a rush-hour joke.

As he inches toward that opportunity to make the left onto Franklin, Martin reaches over to the passenger seat and opens his briefcase. The post-it is in there. The Trader Joe's post-it.

Ever since his trip to the store on Monday... ever since his embarrassing lack of immediate need for the retail venue's extensive inventory, he started to make a list. Last night, he even surveyed the kitchen stock, hoping that one item would inspire the need for another. When he saw the jar of marinara sauce in the cupboard, he jotted down pasta. And, in the bathroom, he noted that a package of toilet paper might be a good investment.

III

Martin makes the left onto Hyperion off Griffith Park Boulevard. And after he's inched past the southern entry to the overcrowded lot, he smiles at the availability of the perfect spot.

It's the meter closest to the main parking entrance. He is able to settle into it with the driver's equivalent of three keystrokes.

He checks the meter and sees a thirty-two minute gift from the previous patron. More time than he will need.

There's a cart right there, leaning into the newspaper dispensers, and he grabs it. It's a good one. No sticking in the wheels. No autonomous desire, on the cart's part, to make a sudden left turn.

The store is crowded, of course. But the first aisle seems to be relatively unoccupied during this brief moment in time. He grabs a few apples and works his way to the other side of the free-standing bins, picking up a can of Bay Blend *en route*. He knows that he should buy some of the fresh, pre-washed vegetables, but he also knows that if he does, they will become not-so-fresh before he is even halfway into the bag.

He makes his way to the frozen food aisle, and while taking in the variety of pizzas, Martin realizes that he's smiling. It's an odd feeling, but also a good one. Following the day of morose haze at the office, it feels good to be among the denizens of Silver Lake and Los Feliz. They are an easy crowd, and at Trader Joe's, he has the pleasure of mixing (albeit anonymously) with people who actually might be old enough to remember when the Beatles landed in the States.

Nothing on his list directs him to scope the offerings in the next aisle, but when he sees the cereal, he realizes that his list is incomplete. He picks up a box of something that looks quite fibrous and tosses it into the cart.

He returns to the post-it and sees that he only needs pasta and salsa. An easy roll down the next aisle or two and he'll be ready to choose a check-out. He's feeling anxious now. He hopes she's there.

After completing his grocery tour, he starts to wheel slowly to the check-out lanes. He's scoping the backs of the cashiers' heads. He's looking for the dark hair that kindly distracted him from that pile of tentacles at the Atwater café. Is that her, at the third register in?

Each cashiers' line seems to be equally available, and so he passes a more obvious option on his way to the third cash register. He sees her easy smile as she speaks to the customer who is in the process of paying. It's her. It's Sus323.

Martin realizes that his nervousness might be noticeable, and so he puts his hands in his pockets. He rolls back on his heels and closes his eyes. He takes a few deep breaths.

"Damnit," he hears the woman in front of him say.

He opens his eyes. The woman is looking at him, and her expression indicates that she is probably engaged in a bit too much multi-tasking. "I just realized," she says to him, "I forgot an entire meal! You can go ahead of me." She takes her cart off the line, and Martin is face-to-face with Trader Joe's newest cashier: a forty-eight-year-old PowerSurge panelist who says "Hello" with calm warmth and pulls his cart forward.

"Did you find everything alright?" she asks, as Martin reads her nameplate and is not surprised to learn that her name is Susan.

"Yes! Everything was just where I left it!"

Susan laughs as she continues the scanning process. Martin notices the way she pays attention to the details of her task. And because he knows that this is her first week, he realizes she is still on a learning curve. It touches him to think of a former law firm partner *learning* the register at Trader Joe's.

"You need to grind this here?" Susan asks, holding up the can of coffee.

"No," he replies, smiling and feeling his face flush. "Thanks for asking, though."

She smiles back at him, and as she takes the last few items out of his cart, Martin swipes his debit card and enters his PIN. When the total appears, he accepts it, and they complete their transaction. He thanks Susan; he thanks the colleague who bagged his goods; and he rolls out of the store. He's still smiling as he puts the groceries in the trunk of his car. He's also making a mental note: buy a coffee grinder.

IV

Relaxing into his bonus room chair, a fresh can of diet soda just popped and still fizzing, Martin checks his e-mail. A few

Forwards from Aunt Betty, of course. (Delete, delete.) And, hmm... a message from Lisa.

The Subject is "just following up," which could mean anything. Martin realizes that a few weeks ago, he would have opened this message immediately. He would have opened it with expectation (and not the "cat" kind of expectation). He might have opened it expecting her to apologize or promise to change or ask him back or tell him he's worthy of living somewhere other than an advanced dorm on Vermont Avenue. And whatever it was that would have taken him into that email, he would have regretted opening it.

He leaves it there. Doesn't delete it. Just leaves it. It can remain bold forever, as far as he's concerned. If there's something important for him to know, he'll hear about it through his lawyer.

Feeling empowered by this non-action, Martin decides to send a message to Zac. He hits the Write button and enters Zac's name. His nephew's email address comes up automatically. In the Subject line, Martin types: **Life in L.A.**

```
Dear Zac:

Hello, my friend. Sorry I've been out of
touch. Just making the adjustments to "bach-
elor life." It's been a rough transition,
but I feel like I'm clearing some hurdles. I
wanted to follow up on your proposition re
coming out here this summer. I don't know what
you're thinking about, time-wise, but a few
weeks might be doable. You need to know that
my place is small. Just a one-bedroom apart-
ment in a building that houses a lot of young,
hip folks. (Actually, you'd probably enjoy
my neighbors more than I do!) So, more than
a few weeks wouldn't work. There's just not
enough space.

And, guess what, I have a cat! At least, I
think I do...
```

(Martin realizes he hasn't seen Dude since he came home from Trader Joe's.)

```
Hold on a minute...
```

As Martin leaves the bonus room and makes his way down the middle hallway, he calls out "Dude!" so as to make it a three-syllable word.

Dude is in a remarkable stretch on Martin's bed, and the high curve of the animal's back tells Martin that Dude has probably just come out of one of those ten-hour cat comas. Dude un-arches its back and puts one arm out, then the other. The cat then moves into its forward reach and works the back legs – one goes back and *stretches;* then, the other... "I can't believe it," Martin says. "Cat yoga. Dude, I think we should do a YouTube."

Before returning to his computer, Martin heads for the kitchen, where he opens a can of Fancy Feast and scoops it onto the plate. Dude's face is in the food just as Martin returns to a standing position.

"You worked up an appetite, I see," Martin comments, as he leaves the kitchen and returns to the bonus room.

He picks up the email where he left off:

```
... yeah, so, I have a cat (for now anyway). I
don't remember if you're allergic or anything.
Just wanted to let you know.

Let's see... what else... Work is okay. Weird
thing happened today, though. (Actually, it
didn't happen today, but today was weird.)
Found out that my supervisor's wife died—a
suicide, apparently. I'm still trying to wrap
my head around it. And while I'm not close
to Barry (my supervisor), I just feel for him
in a big way. I can't even imagine what he's
going through.
```

Martin sits back. He remembers that his nephew is only nineteen—maybe twenty by now. He wonders for a minute if he should be sharing this. But Martin also knows this: In terms of exposure, nineteen or twenty is the new forty-five. Zac has probably seen more shit than Martin ever will. He keeps typing.

```
Intrigue here, too. A man who's lived in this
building for 20 years is missing. His family
is missing him, anyway. The cat might be his.
```

Don't know yet. And did I tell you my place
was burglarized? No big deal, and in a way, my
fault. I forgot to do the top lock. Anyway,
I'll replace the stolen television before you
arrive.

So, how's the homestretch going? I'm guessing
you've got finals in about six weeks or so.
Everything cool? Do you know what you want to
be when you grow up? (You can insert a smiley
face here, if you'd like.)

Let's talk some more in the next few weeks
about summer plans. I have to ask, though,
if you've run this idea by your mom. I don't
mind being the cool uncle, but I won't play
that role if it also makes me the bad brother,
you know? Make sure it's okay with her. Also,
I guess I should mention… I'm not sure what
I have accrued in terms of vacation hours.
Which is to say, I don't know how much time
I could take off while you're here. We'll
figure it out. Just make sure it's okay with
my-sister-your-mother.

Write me back soon!

Uncle Marty

V

That night, as Martin tries to fall asleep, and as Dude tries
to help him by creating a grounding weight smack-dab in the
middle of his chest, he keeps leaving the realm of relaxation with
thoughts of Barry and his wife. Martin thinks of that morning
the week before when he ostensibly hid in his car, when he
didn't want to walk with Barry to the elevators. That morning,
while he held his cellphone to his ear in a faux conversation,
Martin viewed Barry as a happy, settled man. He viewed Barry
as the ultimate sit-com Dad. He imagined Barry's life as one that
was easy. Martin imagined that any problem Barry encountered
could be solved. For that matter, the solution would be clever,
and it would occur within thirty minutes (with commercials).
    "Poor Barry."
    "Mao."

"Poor Lonzo?"

The cat doesn't respond.

"Right," Martin says, before closing his eyes again and hoping he can fall asleep.

CHAPTER ELEVEN

I

On Saturday morning, as he goes through his kitchen routine, something occurs to Martin: he has no friends. At least, he has no friends in L.A.

"How'd that happen?" he asks Dude, as he empties a can of cat food onto a clean plate that the cat quickly approaches with no regard for Martin's rhetorical (yet quite emotional) question.

"How'd that happen?" Martin asks again, standing now at full posture, the empty can still in his hand.

Pouring some nonfat organic milk onto his cereal, Martin is perplexed by his own query. He takes his bowl of cereal and a cup of coffee into the living room, sits on the sofa, and chomps away on the flakes and clusters, trying to figure it out.

Women amaze Martin, he realizes. They have this way. They have this way of incorporating socializing into all that they do. Women make sure they have friends. He guesses they must work at it, and yet they never appear to be doing so. So maybe, Martin thinks now, as he scoops another dried blueberry into the spoonful of twigs, he just got really lazy these past twelve years or so. He let Lisa set up the friendships and so he forgot to create any of his own.

It was kind of a natural dynamic, Martin supposes. Party girl that she was, Lisa always had a plan for the weekend. And because she also loved entertaining, a month would rarely go by without a gathering at their house. Whether it was a cocktail party or a full-on dinner party, Lisa made it work. She made it work that Martin believed he had friends.

But he didn't. The men he got to know—the men he "partied with"—were no more than the significant others of Lisa's friends. These men were never Martin's friends.

Martin's self-pitying revelation is interrupted by the doorbell. In a way, that revelation is also confirmed by the doorbell, as this is the first time he's heard it ring.

II

"Hey," says the friendly manager, David. "Hope I'm not interrupting anything."

"No, no," answers Martin. "I'm just having some coffee. Um. Would you like some?"

"Wow, sure, that'd be cool. Thanks."

"Cool," echoes Martin, a bit thrown off by the fact that he is entertaining his first "guest" in his pajamas and robe.

David follows Martin into the kitchen. "So everything going okay in here?" he asks.

"Everything's fine," Martin responds evenly, finding a mug from the eclectic post-marriage assortment and filling it with the freshly brewed coffee.

David grabs the cupful before Martin has a chance to offer milk or sugar. "Thanks," the building manager says, and then he studies the mug. He turns it, taking in the *Greetings from Chicago* iconography.

"Trippy," David says.

"What's that?"

"I used to have a mug just like this."

"Oh yeah?" replies Martin, "I bought it at a yard sale over on Edgemont."

"Really? How long ago?"

"I don't know. Within the month, I guess."

"That's wild," David says. "I think I *sold* it at a yard sale three years ago, when I was living over on Kingsley."

74

"So what you're saying is it really should say *Greetings from Los Feliz.*"

David laughs. "What goes around comes around, I guess." He lifts the mug, toast-style, before taking a gulp.

"'Scuse me," Martin says, "I'm gonna go get my cup."

"Yeah, oh, and by the way," David says, raising his voice a little as Martin rounds the corner. "I wanted to let you know. I finally got a chance to speak with Lonzo's niece yesterday."

Martin returns to the kitchen, hoping there's a poker face just above his neck.

"I mentioned the cat," David says.

"Oh?"

"Yeah, and she didn't seem to care so much this time. At least, not about the cat."

"Well, they've got other things on their minds," Martin comments. "And no word on Lonzo?"

"Nothing, apparently."

"How old was he—Or," Martin shakes his head, "Boy, that was wrong. How old *is* he?"

"Sixty-eight," David responds. "But he looked a bit older, in my opinion."

"Know his story?"

"What do you mean?"

"What he did, for instance? I mean, for a living."

"Not a clue. You know, I'm just the rent collector and the go-to guy. And there are forty units in the building."

"I understand," says Martin, "I guess I figure with his tenure in the building, there might be a story to tell."

"Well," David says, "if you're seriously interested, you might want to drop in on Myra."

"Who's she?"

"Second floor tenant. Unit 207. She's been here almost thirty years."

"Jesus. Thirty years... And she pays, what? Five-fifty a month?"

"She *dreads* five-fifty a month." David takes a final gulp of coffee from the Chicago souvenir mug he probably once owned and places it on the counter.

"Thanks for the coffee, Martin. I gotta run. Really just wanted to tell you about the cat conversation"

"So," Martin says, following David to the entry hall. "Okay if it stays here, then?"

"Hell, it's lived here probably longer than you and I put together," David replies. "This is its home. So, I don't see a problem with it."

David opens Martin's apartment door, "Just, uh, you know, don't flaunt it around the other tenants."

"Got it," Martin replies, standing at his door. "No crazy cat parades in the hall."

"Right," says David, over his shoulder, as he heads back to his own unit where he'll probably make a beeline for his bong.

As soon as Martin has closed the door, there is a "Mao" at his feet.

"Hey, buddy," Martin says, smiling as he reaches down and picks up the cat. "Dude, we may be roommates for a while. Is that okay?"

Dude nuzzles Martin's cheek and begins to purr loudly.

CHAPTER TWELVE

I

Brenda looks up as Martin arrives on Monday morning. He catches her glance. "Good morning," he says, with a bit more friendliness than he has offered over the past few months. "Good morning," she replies, looking a bit stressed. "Um, Martin, FYI, there's an all-department meeting in the big conference room at ten o'clock."

"Okay," he says, feeling for some reason that he should have a deeper comment to make.

"I'll be there," he says next, with strange pseudo-cheer, as he passes her desk and enters his office.

Martin shuts his office door and immediately sits in one of his guest chairs. He pours a cup of coffee out of his fresh-from-home thermos and beckons the Hills outside his window to help him relax.

He hates "all-department" meetings, especially those that are not on the monthly schedule. He hates them because, the minute he learns of their interruption to the workday routine, he knows they will be run by someone from Human Resources. And, from Martin's experience, the folks in H.R. are bizarre. If Martin were recruited to draft the definition of folks in H.R., he would write this: "they are relentlessly cheerful people who happen to know a lot about rules, regulations, and benefits."

It is because of Martin's definition that he has issues with H.R. people. Frankly, he finds the personality type to be somewhat incongruous. If a person is relentlessly cheerful, Martin thinks, shouldn't she or he (and, nine point nine times out of ten, it's a she) be... say... working at a weird hybrid shop in a mall, where folks can come by and watch cooking demos, buy fabrics, and partake of affordable on-site childcare? Shouldn't this cheerful person exist somewhere *outside* of an office? To Martin, it seems odd to expect this relentlessly cheerful person to understand all the facets of HMOs, 401Ks, workers compensation, and OSHA requirements. To Martin, it seems odd that a relentlessly cheerful person can remain cheerful when knowing all that information.

II

Entering the big conference room at one minute before ten, Martin is relieved to see that all of the twenty or so chairs that are "at-one" with the almighty conference table already are occupied. As he takes a chair on the periphery (one that is very close to the door), he scopes the inner circle. Those who are sitting *at* the table are not necessarily higher-ups. Rather, they are the indisputable Type-A's of the company.

... There's Mary Jane, the self-appointed "kitchen-witch," who—rather remarkably—set into place a system by which no one's fridge food would ever get stolen or spoiled, and the fridge would always be clean. Granted, it took her a year to set up the system, and it included all kinds of coding and the assignment of specific tasks to monthly monitors, but... Mary Jane did it. More power to her.

... There's Cody, Mary Jane's boss. No surprise that those two work together so beautifully. Martin takes a furtive glance at Cody—his equal on the food chain; one of four other Los Angeles-based VPs who reports to Barry. Hungry Cody, Martin thinks to himself. Their product is probably the same, but the effort is different. When presenting a report to their common boss, Cody isn't satisfied simply to hand over a folder of charts, graphs, and comments. He has to go the distance. He can't just do the work for Barry. He has to hump Barry's leg.

... There's Vivian, the one and only female among the Senior VPs of this old boys network; Barry's equal at the Western Regional office. Martin is, in some ways, surprised to see her sitting among the meeting's early-arrivers. But, she's definitely Type A, so her self-designated seat assignment is appropriate.

Vivian, looking up for a moment, meets Martin's glance. He immediately looks down. It was not his intention to be staring at her.

... There's the door. Opening. And the cheerful H.R. officer, Justine, followed by a man whose handlebar mustache is an outright fire hazard.

This must be the suicide expert, Martin guesses.

Sure enough...

While handlebar guy shares statistics, warning signs, and community services, Martin writes on his little post-it pad. He makes a list for Trader Joe's.

III

"Martin!"

He hears his name called out not ten seconds after bolting the room. He couldn't wait to get out of what had become a two-hour meeting. He couldn't wait to flee the scene of FAQs that were laced with tears. He couldn't wait to leave the room so that he could stop imagining the moment when someone, without a Kleenex box in front of her/him, would be forced to use the shirt sleeve of a co-worker. He couldn't wait to leave the room.

"Martin!" Vivian calls again.

He turns, makes eye contact with the Senior VP who is not his boss, and then walks toward her as the other meeting attendees—many sniffling—are slowly filtering out into the hallway.

"Vivian," he says, "What's up?"

"I need to meet with you," she replies, quite officiously. "Have you got lunch plans?"

"No."

"Good. Can you meet me in the lobby at one o'clock?"

IV

Martin is somewhat perplexed by Vivian's choice for a lunch venue. The Smokehouse seems so anachronistic. Were he Judy Garland and were Vivian Louis Mayer, it would make all the sense in the world, but... wouldn't Mo's have sufficed? Regardless, here they are. Vivian drove (of course), and she managed even to make small talk (albeit small talk about international politics and global warming) all the way to the restaurant.

Vivian's even managing to talk small now. She's even managing to talk a whole lot smaller. As she reaches for a slice of the famous garlic toast, she asks Martin, "So, are you settled in at your new place?"

"Yeah," replies Martin. "It's fine."

Martin doesn't know what else to say on the subject. He's also surprised Vivian knows about the recent changes in his personal profile. But, office grapevines are what they are, and while he doesn't participate, his mere existence places him among the potential subject matter.

"I'm glad to hear you're settled, Martin. I'm really glad.

"Martin," Vivian says next, just as the waiter approaches with their lunch orders, "we need to talk about what happens next, following Barry's early retirement."

Hearing Vivian's statement, Martin realizes that he must have tuned out that morning at a particularly informative part of the presentation. This is the first time he's heard of Barry's early retirement. Martin is grateful that his processing of this information is simultaneous to the delivering of their entrees.

"So what's the plan?" Martin asks, once the waiter has moved on.

"The plan," Vivian states, "*should you choose to accept it...*" (Vivian is trying to be light at this point, and Vivian really sucks at being light. She also probably realizes this and so, as if to retrieve her attempt, she straightens her back and squares her shoulders.) "Martin," she says then, "the plan is to groom you for Barry's spot."

V

On his way to Trader Joe's that night, Martin stews over the "grooming" possibility ahead. Vivian let him know that he could think about it for a few days, and she probably said that simply because it is the thing to say, not because she expected Martin to do anything but jump at the chance. What might surprise her is that Martin is not particularly thrilled with the idea of a promotion. He knows that if this grooming possibility had occurred a year or two ago (that is, if he were still a groom), the idea of being lifted into a higher tax bracket would have been greatly appealing. It would have pleased Lisa, and so it would have felt right.

At this point in his life, though, he's not so sure. The fact of the matter is, he's sick of his job. He's sick of the place, the people, and the broader generic world of accounting and personal finance. Were he to accept the promotion, he not only would have to convey a larger commitment, but he might even have to feel that commitment genuinely.

But can he turn down the offer? More specifically, can he turn down the offer and still remain employed by the firm? If he declines, will he be revealing his inner truths so clearly that his co-workers (and particularly those above him on the org chart) will start to notice the degree to which he has mastered the concept of "phoning it in?" Ever since he left Lisa, the fact has become increasingly clear to Martin: he really only needs about twenty-five hours a week to get his job done. The rest of the time, he's pretty much spinning in his chair.

VI

While waiting in Susan's check-out line, which goes by the name "Rowena," Martin wishes he could ask her out. Right here. Right now. Just as soon as her shift is over. But not because he wants to jump her bones. No, he wants to pick her brain. He wants to understand the process she went through that took her from a law firm to this friendly grocery store. He wants to understand her courage.

"Hey there," she says smiling, as she pulls his cart forward.

"Hey back 'atcha," says Martin. "How's it going?"

"So far, so good," Susan replies, smiling as she looks at the clock. "Just a few more hours."

"I bet this is a great place to work though, huh?"

Susan nods as she scans the cereal. "It definitely is," she replies, smiling as she makes eye contact.

Martin loves her face. It has a slightly weathered quality that conveys intelligence and depth.

"So," he says, "are you kinda new to this crew?"

"Actually," replies Susan, as she moves the organic milk over the scanner for the third or fourth time, "I'd say I'm 'very' new. This is just my second week."

"Well, you definitely have the vibe."

"What's that supposed to mean?" Susan asks, her expression indicating that she's intrigued and not offended.

"This is the Joe's!" Martin responds, not aware that he's getting increasingly red in the face as he rocks on his heels, balanced by the hands in his pocket.

"This is the Joe's?" Susan asks.

"It's the coolest one in town," he offers, shrugging.

Susan grins at him as she begins to bag his groceries. "I guess I'm flattered, then," she says.

"Did you swipe your card?" she asks next.

"Oops," says Martin, as he takes his hands out of his pockets and begins the process that will bring this little date to a close.

CHAPTER THIRTEEN

I

The restaurant just north of Colorado in Oldtown Pasadena is very high-end, and Martin is not surprised that Barry chose it. Even in grieving, and even though he seems an informal man on so many levels, Barry is also elegant. His self-respect is a source of pride.

It's been only a week since Martin and his co-workers learned the news. Services are planned for the weekend. So Martin was somewhat taken aback when Barry suggested dinner. When he called Barry, Martin's intention was to begin by offering condolences. His plan was to see if the conversation could go elsewhere, and if it could, he wanted to share with Barry the offer that Vivian had made. But Barry quickly made it clear that he knew of the firm's plan, and—in a way—he also conveyed an understanding of Martin's need to talk about the prospects.

"Barry!" Martin says, approaching his former boss from the bar area where he has been waiting.

They shake hands, and Martin absorbs the tired sadness that Barry cannot possibly hide behind his jovial outer persona.

"Sorry I'm late, Martin. I've got some family at the house this week. Lots of distractions."

"I imagine distractions are good at this juncture," Martin comments, immediately (and silently) chastising himself for choosing the word "juncture."

"I'm not sure what's good at this point," Barry replies, as the hostess takes them to their table. "Except some single-malt scotch. Will you join me?"

II

Martin has had all of two (painful) sips of his scotch when Barry orders another round from the waitress.

"I'm fine, Barry," Martin says. "Just get one for yourself."

"Nonsense!" Barry replies. "Two more," he says to the waitress.

As the waitress walks away, Barry leans in. He seems to be flirting with a buzz, or it is flirting with him. Martin has never experienced this aspect of the would-be sit-com Dad.

"Ask me anything you need to ask, Martin," Barry says. "I realize you may not want this promotion, but I think you're the best man for the job."

Martin is shocked and somehow touched by Barry's insight. Martin also realizes that Barry's buzz might work to an advantage (at this juncture). He goes for it:

"You're right, Barry," Martin says, "and I'm glad you mentioned it first. I'm not sure I *do* want this promotion. I'm going through some changes these days, you know? And I'm just not sure that taking on more responsibilities is the best thing for me or the firm."

"It's a tricky road, my friend. It's a tricky road."

Whatever Barry was going to say next is upstaged by the delight with which he greets the waitress and her small, round tray. She places the two scotches on the table, the first in front of Martin and the second in front of Barry. When Martin sees the millimeter's difference between his first drink and the one on deck, he predicts—accurately—that his second drink will become Barry's third.

"You were saying?" Martin asks, his eyes widening when Barry returns the glass to the table and it is already half-empty.

"You have to think about the options, Martin. You also have to think about perceptions. If you accept the promotion, then everything is great, as far as the other people are concerned. You're a team-player and you have ambition. They'll like that. They'll like *you*. If you don't, well—then, you're basically telling them to fuck off, and that won't go over very well."

"So you're telling me I need to accept it or I'll lose my current job."

"It's possible."

"Hmm..." Martin thinks for a second. "There's another thing that doesn't feel right."

"What's that?"

"I don't understand why they haven't filled Alan's spot."

"I don't either," Barry agrees, referring to the Regional Vice President position, that box on the org chart that hovers above the two Senior VP's. "Alan certainly gave them ample notice before he left."

"Yeah, and it's been more than a month. Do you think they're considering Vivian for that position?"

"I doubt it. I think if they were, we'd all know that by now. On the other hand," Barry adds, staring sadly into his drink, "when the top brass are three thousand miles away, it's hard to know a lot."

III

Driving home, Martin is glad he put up such a fight. It took some reverse logic and the help of some of the restaurant staff, but he was able to get Barry to surrender his cell phone and its speed dial features. Martin was able to contact some of the family that are currently camped out in Pasadena, and Barry's daughter—Maggie—agreed to come to the restaurant and retrieve her scotched-up father. Maggie's exchange with Martin was cordial, at best. She probably didn't appreciate adding embarrassment to grieving.

Driving home, Martin is thinking about the stuff Barry talked about as they worked their way through their steak dinners. It wasn't a conversation so much; more, a monologue—delivered by a man whose wife had committed suicide just eight days

85

ago. Barry talked about dreams... about the dreams of young couples, newly married. Barry talked about raising children and making sure their needs were attended to. Barry talked about balancing home life and work life, and how work life sometimes has nothing to do with home life. Barry talked about his wife's interests, the intensity with which she approached projects, and how, when that intensity was used up, she'd have to shut down for a while. He'd had to provide a balance when they were raising their kids, Barry said. During those kids' "wonder years," he often had to do a lot of the parenting that Margaret had somehow overlooked.

"Margaret," Barry said, in a manner of summing up the personal history that had poured out of him, "never had any interest in routine. And part of me was always envious that she knew that about herself."

Driving home, Martin realizes that Barry's subliminal advice was really to not take the promotion. But Barry's advice also was to understand that not taking the promotion was occupational suicide. In other words, if Martin turns down the offer, he will be as good to the firm as Margaret now is to her marriage with Barry.

Done. Over. History.

Services this weekend.

IV

When his building's tired and ancient elevator doors open, Martin is surprised to see a person occupying the small cell.

"Hello!" comes the deep-voiced, friendly greeting of the woman who, by all appearances, is also opposed to routine. Given her garb—the focal point of which is a fuschia cardigan decorated with turquoise bird appliqués—Martin cannot help but wonder what articles of clothing just had a spin in the laundry room.

"Hello," Martin replies, entering the cage. Martin immediately guesses that this is Myra, the woman David mentioned—

the tenant who has lived here for thirty years. The illuminated "2" on the elevator's itinerary backs his assumption.

The doors are still closing as he extends his hand and realizes immediately that, because of her laundry, she has no hand available to meet it.

"Not to worry, dear, but I appreciate the gesture. You are a gentleman." Her vocal intonations, which could be described as having a Merchant-Ivory quality, don't blend well with her dental situation. Martin guesses that her mouth probably once housed a greater quantity of teeth.

There is a ding, indicating their having arrived at floor two.

"May I help you?" Martin offers, extending his arm to retrieve at least one of the three pillowcases that is currently weighing her down.

"Why would you want to?"

"I don't know," Martin says, as they step out onto the second floor together, he carrying more than half her laundry weight. "You called me a gentleman. I guess I want to validate that before you change your mind."

"Far be it from me to strip the cape off of Prince Valiant. Just three doors down here, on the left."

While turning the key, she warns, "You might get a whiff of cats. I have three."

"Grandfathered from the previous pet-owning policy?"

"Exactly," she says, opening her door. "And those of us who *have* cats are old enough to be grandparents. I just hope Lonzo's cat found a home."

"Not to worry," Martin says. "I happen to know it did."

"Really? Please, come in."

Once Martin is inside, his eccentric neighbor kicks the front door shut with her batty old laced-up boots. She then heads for another room, carrying a bag of laundry with her. Martin takes in the bohemian rhapsody that is written in a very sharp key. A great deal of fabric in conflicting patterns creates a sort of clutter, and that clutter is such that actually noticing two of Myra's three cats is synonymous to winning a game of *Where's Waldo*.

As for the webbing that exists between the tops of the curtains and the crown molding, a cleaning crew would have a field day.

When Myra returns to the room, Martin wants to say, "Who's your decorator? Miss Havisham?" But he just smiles instead.

"You can toss those on the chair," she says, regarding the two pillowcases he was hesitant to place on the floor.

"So what do you know about Lonzo's cat?" she asks then.

"It's with me. It came in through the window one night."

"Hmm... A cat burglar."

"Funny you should say that. I was burglarized the day before the cat showed up."

"You were? Please. Sit."

Martin acquiesces as if she had been his trainer at obedience school. She joins him on the couch and stares at him intently through her bejeweled cat's-eye glasses that are probably first generation.

"Did you report the burglary?" she asks him.

"No."

"You should have. It might have been an inside job."

"You think?"

"There's a shady guy on this hall," she shares, raising one eyebrow a full inch from its original position. "I don't trust him for anything. Besides, an outsider is unlikely to pull that off in this building and on this street. Think about it."

"Good point. Well, it's probably too late to report it, and nothing's happened since. It was my fault anyway. I didn't set the top-lock."

"You shouldn't say it was your fault. What did you say your name was?"

"Martin."

"Martin. And did I tell you mine?"

"I don't believe so."

"It's Myra. Myra Agnes Davis Newsom Everett Simon Stevenson. MADNESS. An appropriate monogram for someone who exchanged wedding vows four times, don't you think?"

"You might have stopped with the third and called it a typo."

"Pshaw! That's a good one, Martin, my boy. That's a good one. Would you like some tea?"

"Thank you, but no," Martin replies, standing up. "I should get back to the cat soon. It's probably hungry."

"I'm glad it's okay," Myra says. "I hope Lonzo is, too."

"Did you know him?"

"We were very close friends for a couple years, but that relationship ended in oh-four."

"You had a falling out?" Martin asks.

"You might say that," Myra replies, as she audibly rises from her well-worn seat in the couch. "Nothing that prevented us from being cordial when we ran into each other. It's just that I got to know too much about him, and you know, sometimes it's better when you don't dig too deep with a person."

"What do you think happened?"

"I'm guessing he went to Vegas and got in over his head," Myra suggests.

"Do you think he's still alive, then?"

"I don't think he's dead."

"But what about his place?" Martin asks, as he watches Myra amble over to one of her hanging plants and begin to study the leaves. "What about his family?"

"He never cared for his family much, and I was under the impression they didn't care much for him. Frankly, I'm not even sure why they went to the trouble of putting up flyers. I certainly don't get the narrative of those little signs.

"As for his place," Myra adds then, turning to renew the intense eye contact of moments ago, "I don't suppose you've seen it."

"No," says Martin.

"Well, suffice it to say, my dear, the only possession he had that was worth having came in through your window. And thank God for that."

"So, except for the cat, he wasn't really leaving anything," Martin concludes.

"No."

"Why did he even have a cat then?"

"Because someone gave it to *me*," Myra explains, "and I didn't want another one."

"So he wanted to appease you."

"You're a quick study, Martin," Myra responds, walking him to the door.

V

Martin is sitting in the television-free living room that should be a social focal point of his life. He's petting Lonzo's one possession, and he's glad this cat isn't in Vegas right now, performing in some Siegfried and Roy side show.

"Oh, Dude," Martin says, having returned from the distraction of Myra to the distraction of his professional future, "I don't know what to do."

Dude rolls over and lets Martin scratch its tummy.

"What would you do?"

Dude curls into a full-body smile.

"I guess in cat-world, there aren't any real promotional issues. I mean, you're all at the top of the org chart, right?"

Dude doesn't need to talk to answer that question. The cat's body and attitude both say "Right."

CHAPTER FOURTEEN

I

"I'm glad to hear it," Vivian says, standing and extending her hand. "Welcome to the Senior VP level."

Vivian comes around from behind her desk and sits in the available guest chair, next to Martin. She opens the folder that she's carried along for the ride.

"So!" she begins, perusing the page in front of her, "we need for you to go to Chicago next week. Just a two-day trip. No biggie."

In an effort to resist Chicago memories, Martin immediately thinks about Dude. David-the-manager can probably assume feeding duties. Or maybe Myra?

"And you'll need to do a New York trip as well. Another short one. Plan on a week between them just to keep everything balanced."

Martin accepts this prospect more readily. It'll be good to see Rachel.

"As for the homefront," Vivian says next, "there are three VPs to supervise. Three for the moment, anyway, until we fill your position. You should plan to meet with them weekly. Cody, Phil, and Debora."

In addition to wanting to roll his eyes at Vivian's need to *list* the names of VPs with whom he once shared a boss, Martin wants to challenge her directive regarding their meeting as a group. He wants to challenge it because he knows it is Vivian-specific. Barry never brought his VPs together for weekly meetings, but the group seemed to get the job done.

"Any questions so far?" Vivian asks.

"No," Martin replies, knowing the questions he has are of no genuine interest to his colleague. "I just hope there's a bit of a grace period here. You know, to make it seem like your collective decision was a wise one."

"We are confident in our decision," Vivian states, smiling through her much-too-narrow power eyeglasses.

"Now," she continues, "you'll be taking Barry's office, which will be ready for you on Monday."

"So soon?"

"Yes. So, you'll need to get Brenda to help you today with organizing that move. As for Brenda, we need to discuss that."

"Okay."

"You may or may not know that Alice is on a short leave. She was very upset about Margaret's death, and she's, of course, very upset about Barry's decision. She was his assistant for twenty years. But, of course, Barry's retiring does not translate to Alice's retiring, and she knows that office. We'd like for you to accept Alice as your assistant."

"What about Brenda?" Martin asks, surprised by his sense of concern for the assistant to whom he's never felt any strong allegiance.

"We thought we'd assign her to the VP who replaces you."

Martin doesn't respond.

"It's really not debatable, Martin. Alice has seniority over Brenda, so we need to honor that."

If this isn't "debatable," Martin wonders, why did Vivian suggest they "discuss" it? Aren't those words relatively synonymous?

"But what we'll do," Vivian goes on, "—until Alice gets back and until we've hired a new VP—is have Brenda work temporarily with you on this floor."

Great, Martin thinks, *give her a bigger, better chair and then whip it out from under her when Alice gets back.*

"She can make your Chicago and New York travel arrangements," Vivian continues, "and she can be your point person here while you're on those trips. Alice should be back in three weeks, which squares well with your having completed your business jaunts."

"It sounds like everything has been thought through," Martin says (though, if he had been permitted to do the thinking, the word "jaunt" would not have come up).

"This was unexpected and, for many of us, emotional," Vivian states, placing her hands in the middle of her lap and looking at him intently.

This is Vivian, being emotional, Martin thinks.

"We simply need to move forward," she says.

"Okay... Well, is, uh, Brenda aware of these plans?"

"I wanted to wait until we had discussed it. And, I think the decision would be best coming from you."

Although Martin nods, his current mood is not agreeable. It strikes him as more than ironic: he is now Vivian's equal, and yet he has never felt so far below her on the org chart. He hopes that once the transition is made, and once he is also housed on the ninth floor, the extra fifteen feet of altitude will put him on a level equal to hers. Maybe then, Vivian will convey a truer understanding of the meaning of the word "discuss."

But she is and will always be Type A, and Martin knows that, too.

II

Brenda is slamming desktop articles into packing boxes, and while Martin understands her ire, and even empathizes, he is sick of having to witness it.

"Brenda," he says, in a pleading tone, "why won't you believe that this was not my decision?"

"It's okay," she responds, unconvincingly. "I believe you."

"Then why are you taking it out on me?"

"I'm not!" she fumes, her teeth clenched.

Martin reaches into the box she has been packing and retrieves the largest component of the leather set he received from his in-laws. "You bent my blotter, Brenda."

But because he really doesn't care, he has delivered the statement with a smirk. And because of his smirk, Brenda is able to suspend her hissy-fit and smile.

III

"Frankly, I can't believe you accepted it," Brenda states rather loudly, apparently liberated by the first kick of her second margarita.

Martin takes a swig from his Corona, warm now because he's been nursing it for an hour and a half. "I didn't feel I could turn it down," he states matter-of-factly.

"I don't know," says Brenda, "you just don't seem the Senior VP type to me. No offense or anything."

"No offense taken."

"So are you going to become like a Vivian?"

"What? You mean, start wearing skirts and power pumps?"

Brenda laughs, as she reaches for a chip and dips it in the salsa. "She's just so uptight!"

"I don't think I'll get to that place," Martin states, nodding to himself and wishing he were in some other life. "I think I'm just about as uptight as I want to get."

IV

Martin smiles as he walks toward the elevator area. He hasn't seen Brittany in a few weeks, and the site of her hair's primary color is refreshing to him. "Hi!" he says, as he approaches her and unconsciously gives the elevator's up-arrow key a redundant push.

"Hey, Marvin."

"It's Martin."

"Oh, Jeez. I'm sorry," she says, rolling her head around. "And thank God, by the way," she adds, stopping the roll and looking at him with an impish smile. "I mean, who would name their kid Marvin?"

"Not me, certainly."

"Me either." She looks at the panel above the elevator doors. The indicator lights are apparently not working.

"Fuck!" she exhales. "What's taking this thing so long?"

"Maybe one of the hunchbacks is on a break."

Brittany so does not get this.

"So how's the mortuary gig?" Martin asks then, feeling playful because he's away from the office and living in a building where most tenants don't fly to Chicago on business.

"Not bad, I gotta say. I got a promotion this week!"

"Congratulations!"

"Yeah, I'll be the first main point person for a portfolio of customers. You know, talking them through the process, the products, that sort of thing.

"It's nice," Brittany says, nodding so as to agree with herself. "I like talking to people, you know? I like being able to help."

"That's sweet," Martin comments, genuinely.

As if to punctuate Martin's sincerity, the elevator dings.

"Thank God!" Brittany says.

V

Dude is scarfing down his food. Martin is relieved to see that the cat likes the Trader Joe's cheap fare just as much as it likes the Fancy Feast. In the long run, the TJ's cans will be cheaper, and Martin will have more excuses to see Susan.

After grabbing a Diet Coke out of the fridge, Martin wanders into his bedroom to change into more comfortable clothes. As he takes off his tie and hangs it on the rack in the closet, he thinks about the wardrobe he has seen on his fellow tenants of 1773 Vermont. It occurs to him that he's probably the only one who doesn't wear leather to work. This reality begs a question: if he's wearing a tie, why is he living here?

But the comfort he has begun to develop in this building begs another question: if he's living here, why is he wearing a tie?

VI

Tie off and sweats on, Martin goes to his computer. He hasn't checked his email in probably two days, and so there's a possibility there might be something there he actually wants to read.

Once the system has received seven of seven messages, he quickly deletes six of them: two Viagra ads, a mortgage offer, and three forwards from Aunt Betty. With that house-cleaning done, he opens the message from Zac, which bears the telling subject of **TIME TO PLAN!**

```
good news uncle marty. mom is cool with the
idea of me hanging with you this summer.
just two weeks though. so lemme know about
timing. i'm thinking early to mid june. does
that sound good? (mom thinks i'll be able to
get 2 months worth of summer work in july and
august. i told her not to hold her breath.)
things are okay here. spring break was good -
spent it with my roommate matt at his family's
place in nags head. nice time, though his
parents are kinda weird. the beach was nice.
how are things with you? i should go study
now. let me know about this summer. and let me
know what's new. see you really soon, i hope. Z
```

Just as Martin hits the "Reply" button, the cat jumps on his lap.

"Hey, Dude," Martin says. "Looks like you're going to meet my nephew in a few months."

Dude responds with a yawn, followed by a bath.

Martin makes a mental note to follow up with Myra. He should probably have the name of a reliable local vet. He should probably know, for that matter, if Dude should go to a vet. *Do cats get annual check-ups?* Martin wonders.

He has no idea. Growing up, his mom made all that knowledge look innate.

CHAPTER FIFTEEN

I

Per their agreement, Martin and Brenda both arrived early on Monday morning. Now, it is just after nine, and Brenda is heading back down to the eighth floor for another load of files. When she leaves Martin's new office with the handcart, he takes a moment to breathe. Everything has happened so quickly. He walks over to the fridge/coffee area and pours himself a cup of the French roast that Brenda made an hour ago. Then, he sits down on the couch. It's so strange that this is no longer Barry's office. It's so strange that this couch is no longer the spot where he'll casually sit with his boss on an as-needed basis. This is the couch where *his* staff will sit. *His* staff? The VPs under *his* watch? Martin still doesn't get it. He doesn't understand why they promoted him.

Martin has no idea how long he's been sitting here—taking it in, processing the change. But when Brenda returns with a fully-loaded cart and announces, "This is it," Martin is relieved to have something other than career advancement on which to focus.

"Damn," he says, getting up from the couch and taking stock of the precariously balanced piles of files. "You made sure that was the last trip!"

"Yeah, well, this moving stuff is pretty tedious. And it's weird for me."

"I know," Martin says. "And I appreciate your helping me out."

"It's okay," Brenda says.

For a few moments, they work in silence, Brenda quietly orchestrating the direction of the file folders and Martin understanding her suggestions.

"Oh, by the way," Brenda says at one point, "I checked my email while I was downstairs. You're all squared away for the Chicago trip."

"Leaving Wednesday?"

"Yeah," Brenda responds. "A mid-afternoon departure. And a mid-evening arrival."

"Out of Burbank?" Martin asks.

"Right. So... have you made plans for the quote-unquote down time?" Brenda asks.

"Well, I got a call in to an old friend. Hank Lawson."

"Hank? Who names their kid Hank?"

"His parents, for one."

"Weird name."

"It's a nickname for Henry."

"Okay, so who names their kid Henry?"

II

"So!" Vivian says, conveying an enthusiastic team-building tone as she walks into Martin's new office later that Monday morning. "How's the transition detail going?"

Martin turns his head for a moment. He and Brenda are currently struggling with some pendaflex files that do not want to change offices.

"Be with you in a minute!" Martin says to Vivian, returning to the project at hand.

"It's exhausting, I know," Vivian says, at a distance and with an audible grin. "Anyway, Martin—Welcome to the ninth floor."

Martin stands to accept the handshake that seemed likely to have followed that statement, but Vivian has left the room.

"Boy," Brenda says, now standing beside Martin and looking at the doorway through which Vivian just came and went, "and you think that *I* bent your blotter!"

III

When the phone rings, Brenda runs for the door. "Might as well grab it from out here," she says, "and get used to the routine."

A few seconds later, a button on Martin's console begins blinking. He intuitively depresses it.

"Mr. Sheffield," Brenda says, in a facetiously officious tone that Martin appreciates, "there's a Hank Lawson, from Chicago, on line one."

Martin releases the button, "Thank you, Ms. Falconer. Keep up the good work."

When he depresses the button again, he hears her giggle.

Martin crosses the room to the entryway, where he exchanges mischievous smiles with Brenda. Then, he closes his door and returns to his new desk. He sits back in the chair that knows more about corner offices than he ever will. He picks up the phone and hits the button for line one.

"Hank!" Martin says enthusiastically, leaning back and hoping the chair won't take him for some ride he's not anticipating.

CHAPTER SIXTEEN

I

"Hank!" Martin says, enthusiastically rising from the comfortable settee in the Chicago restaurant's foyer. He greets the friend he hasn't seen in seventeen years.

"Martin!" Hank exclaims, giving his former colleague a "man-pat" on the shoulder, "Damn! You look good! Shall we get a table?"

The maître d', who already got the reservation details from Martin, leads them to the spacious deuce that is just off the servers' beaten path. They both sit.

"Yeah, you look really good, my friend," Hank says again, delivering the comment in his signature way: head a bit downcast; always seeming to be suppressing a smirk.

"It's such a trip that you're here," Hank adds. "I can't believe how long it's been since we were pushing papers together over at the firm. Congratulations again on the promotion. That's quite a coup."

Hank immediately follows this last statement with a wink and one of those handgun gestures that males use to indicate their approval of the accomplishments of other males. The gesture does not make Martin feel either approved or accomplished.

He just watches with bemusement as Hank reaches for the wine list, where his apparent interest in its content suspends further conversation for at least a minute.

II

"That's perfect," Hank says to the wine steward, after tasting a sip. "Martin?"

"I don't need to try it."

Hank doesn't argue with Martin, but simply says "Fill 'er up!"

As the steward follows instructions, Hank leans in toward Martin. "So, you've returned to bachelorhood."

"Well, it's like I told you on the phone..."

"I'm not surprised that you and Lisa split, Martin, and I just gotta say, I am *so* sorry.

"Cheers, by the way," Hank adds, holding up his glass.

Martin meets the clink and is not sure where to go with Hank's tone.

"Cheers, and what are you talking about?" Martin says, taking a short sip, "I mean—really—I'm not looking for anyone to be sorry about anything."

"That's commendable, Martin. I gotta hand it to you there."

"You know, Hank, it's like I said on the phone. Things end."

"But," Hank says, "you're not pissed? You're not, at least, pissed at me?"

"What are you talking about?"

"You mean, you didn't find out? Lisa didn't tell you?"

"Tell me what?

"Martin: Lisa and I had a huge affair fifteen years ago. I figured you must have learned that. I figured that was why you two split up."

III

"Oh my God!" (At her end of the telephone conversation, Rachel is cackling.) "So he thought you had divorced because of an affair he had with Lisa fifteen years ago? What a narcissist! I hope you made him pay for the dinner."

"There was no dinner. I took my leave before the entrees had arrived."

"So you mean you stuck around long enough to order them?"

"Yup."

"But you left before they arrived?"

"Yup."

"Then, Dude, you made him pay for dinner. I love it."

"Rachel, you used that word. That androgynous word."

"What's that?"

"Dude."

"Oh, yeah," Rachel says, turning her tone down about five notches. "Sorry about that. That's from hanging around with the kids."

"No, Rache. Don't apologize. It's a great word. Did I tell you I have a cat named Dude?"

"You have a cat? Oh, I'm so jealous. I can't have cats here."

"Too many shoes?"

"Damn you, Marty. I can't wait to see you. I can't believe you're going to be here in two weeks."

"Just don't tell me you had an affair with Lisa, okay?"

"Marty? I gotta tell you—Even if I liked women—you know, in that way—I would never have gone for Lisa. I don't mean any offense, dear brother. She's just... not my type."

IV

A few minutes after hanging up the phone, it occurs to Martin that he never had dinner. A roll or two—to soak up those four sips of wine—but that's not going to carry him until morning. He finds the room service menu and scans the offerings. He knows that his expense account would cover it, but he's going to pay for it with his personal card. No way he wants Vivian—or anyone back at the office—thinking he spent precious team-building time holed up in his hotel room.

Steak sounded good about an hour ago. It still does.

After placing his order, Martin stretches out on the bed, grabs the remote, and begins to surf the two-hundred-plus free channels. The big screen's content is nothing more than moving wallpaper, a visual backdrop to his constant thoughts. He wishes he had a way to turn off the questions and the worries and the remorse, or at least put them on Mute. He wishes he were in another year or another city or another life.

Yesterday evening, when he deboarded the plane, he had a glimmer of hope. Entering through Gate 39 with the other passengers, he felt like a responsible business man. Even after he had checked into his room, hung up his suit, and filled a small dresser drawer, he thought he might be able to pull it off. He started to think that maybe this promotion would be the ticket. He began to wonder if it were possibly divine intervention, giving him the life he was meant to lead and backing that provision with a generous executive benefits package. After a late-night snack, he slept well, probably better than he had in a few months.

But then the morning came.

The firm's regional office is close enough to the hotel, so Martin was able to maintain his fantasy during the brisk fifteen-minute walk down streets and across intersections that represented his young adulthood. It was "Martin the man" doing the walking now. Martin, Senior VP. Martin, worthy of promotion and likely to do the job as no one had done it before. He would wow them all. He would even play in Peoria.

He isn't sure of the exact moment when the bubble burst, but about thirty minutes into that first meeting with the Regional Vice President and his three Senior VPs, Martin got that feeling again. That *I don't belong here* feeling. Of course, he didn't let on to the others. Rather, he did what has become rote back in L.A. He listened. He nodded. He threw in comments that were indisputably correct (and to him, obnoxiously obvious). He even made jokes. His humor, in fact, was so well-received by the collective that Don (the Regional Vice President; the firm's *grande fromage* for Chicago) commented on it more than a few times.

"Martin," Don had said at lunch, which was an *entre nous* affair, "Vivian didn't even tell me what a witty guy you are!"

"Well, humor is a taste issue, isn't it?" Martin had replied.

"I suppose. Anyway, it's refreshing. I'm glad you're on the team."

As he continues to channel-surf, it strikes Martin that the "team" comment was rather odd. Isn't the entire department a "team?" Isn't that what they give lip service to on a regular basis? Maybe, in the long run, they aren't. Maybe the levels are teams, and the entire department is some sort of ongoing intramural event...

When the phone rings, Martin jumps. He hopes it's not Room Service, announcing an absence of steaks.

"Hello?" Martin says into the receiver.

"Martin."

While Hank's voice has always been distinctive, Martin decides not to acknowledge that.

"Who's calling please?" asks the guest in Room 911.

"Martin, it's Hank, and I am so sorry. Really, buddy."

(*Buddy?*)

"I, uh, don't blame you for bolting," Hank continues. "And thanks for ordering your steak the way I like it. I got a doggie bag. Tomorrow night's dinner."

"And did you get a doggie bottle for the wine?"

"Nah, I finished it there."

"No wonder you and Lisa got along so well."

"Look, Martin, about that. I have a good friend here in town who is an amazing shark of a divorce attorney. I know you said, when we talked on the phone the other day, that you're in the process, so you've got an attorney, but this guy—I mean, Jesus, he's a shark."

"All divorce attorneys are sharks, Hank."

"Right, right, right."

(Martin can picture Hank's dismissive hand gesture, his facial expression, that almost semi-smirk that hints at condescension.)

"Anyway," Hank says next, "I'm just thinking you should talk to this guy. See about the infidelity aspects. Might get you a better deal. And... I'd be happy to be your witness."

Martin rolls his eyes just as the doorbell rings. *Thank God for room service,* he thinks.

"Hank, I gotta go. Someone's at the door."

"Listen, I, uh—"

"Hank. Get over it. I have."

V

Later that night, when he is unable to fall asleep, Martin is grateful for the plasma screen and its seemingly infinite channels. As he surfs, the truth becomes more apparent. He's not "over it." And maybe he never will be.

He stops on an animal channel, just in time to hear the voiceover: "In the wild, it's just a matter of surviving through another day."

CHAPTER SEVENTEEN

I

Dude is a sight for sore eyes.

"Hey, buddy," Martin says, in reply to the "Mao" that greets him. Martin immediately hangs his suit bag on the frame above the front door, puts his briefcase on the floor, and picks up the cat.

"Hey, Dude," he says, stroking the happy cat's neck. "Did Myra take care of you alright?"

With Dude in his arms, Martin enters the kitchen. He notices the long note on the counter. He notices particularly the concept of penmanship. *Ah, the "Palmer" method,* he thinks.

Placing Dude on the floor and reaching for a can of cat food, Martin wonders why he remembers these things. The *Palmer* method? Martin wonders where this information is stored. He wonders *why* it is stored.

After unloading half a can's worth of the Trader Joe's fare on Dude's plate, Martin stands and reads Myra's missive:

```
Martin!

Welcome back, dear boy. I hope you had a
good trip. Safe and successful and all those
things. "Dude," as you call him, was a dear. I
think he remembered me from his kittenhood! (I
didn't visit him much once I passed him along
to good old Lonzo.)

I fed him twice a day and spent some time
with him, too. We sat on the couch and talked
together about the old days. (HA!) Really, it
was lovely to do this favor for you, Martin,
```

```
and I hope you will call on me again. For me,
it's nice to spend a little time in someone
else's lair. I enjoy taking in the energy and
being away from my own beasts for a bit.

Speaking of energy, I have to share something
with you, Martin. I don't think you know this
about me, but I have keen intuitive skills. I
got a vibe while I was here, Martin. I think
you are about to embark on an incredible jour-
ney. (Did you ever see that film, or is that
before your time? A wonderful tale about two
dogs and a cat! Highly recommended, but... you'd
need a TV for that. Why don't you have a TV,
Martin?)

Please pop in after your return so I know
that you are safe and that "Dude" has his new
dad back. (God forbid I should see a Missing
flyer with your picture on it! Enough with the
elevator art, if you know what I mean!)

Your friend and neighbor,

Myra (aka MADNESS)
```

"Dude!" Martin says, having taken particular notice of the pronouns in Myra's note. "Congratulations! You're a boy!"

II

Returning from a very brief, "I'm back and thank you!" trip down to Myra's on the second floor, Martin is smiling. He is smiling at the sour attitude she brought to the door when he knocked lightly. He is smiling at the fact that she apparently felt no pressure to change that attitude. He is smiling at the missive that was left on his kitchen counter.

She is madness, Martin thinks, entering his apartment. *And she is also refreshingly sane.*

III

Martin is still musing over the "incredible journey" predic-tion as he approaches the computer in his bonus room. It has now been three days since he last checked his email. He expects a lot of Viagra offers, and possibly a personal message or two. He opens his In-Box. Twelve deletes later (the usual), he is looking at three messages that are looking back—boldly—at him. One is from Lisa (it will remain bold). One is from Zac. And one is from his sister Reggie (Zac's mom). Although Reggie's message came after Zac's, Martin decides to open it first. The subject is **Really?**

Dearest Brother!

Lord, Marty, it's been ages, hasn't it, since we talked?

Martin immediately envisions a "Palmer" method inside his sister's brain...

You're a good man to agree to have Zac with you for two weeks this summer, but I just want you to know that you need not feel any family obligation. I don't know if you real- ize this, but watching over (okay, "hanging with," as they say) a college student is not exactly a day at the beach - even if you go to the beach, which, I realize, you can do there in Los Angeles. I just don't want to create a burden for you, Marty.

I appreciate your offer, and if you want to stick by it, then Richard and I will certainly buy him a ticket and send him off on his merry way.

Please, though, Marty, don't feel obligated!

Talk soon? The number I have for you is 818- 504-2030? Is that current? (I really don't want to get involved with Lisa again... not that I didn't love her; we all did. So sorry about that.)

Let's talk, Marty. Please?

Much love to you,
Reg

"Really," Martin states, in answer to his sister's subject line. He begins to wonder if Reggie and Myra were separated at birth. But, that doesn't compute exactly. Myra's too old. Myra's too... hip.

"Myra's hips are too old," Martin states out loud and to no one, laughing at his own joke and realizing that Don in Chicago may have actually been genuine in welcoming Martin's humor onto the "team."

Dude jumps up on Martin's lap. "How are *your* hips, buddy?" Martin asks the cat.

Dude responds with a rather penetrating stare.

"Whatever," Martin offers, reiterating the one-word subject line of Zac's email—the one he opens next.

```
uncle marty! how ya doin? i just got off the
phone with mom. she thinks i'm imposing with
my plans. i don't know. so tell me dude and
please be honest. i don't want to make the
trip if it's not convenient for you. i mean,
whatever, right? fuck, i just feel so confused
right now... Z
```

Martin feels bad. Zac sent this message on Wednesday night, when Martin had just arrived in Chicago. The fact that Zac hasn't heard back yet—the fact that Reggie has fed his head with doubt—couldn't be good.

Martin looks at the clock. Eight in L.A. is eleven in Pennsylvania. And, it's a Friday night. Martin doubts he'll reach his nephew, but he goes for the phone anyway. Martin feels compelled to nip this little problem in the bud.

"Hello?" Martin hears a tired voice on the other end of the line.

"Zac!"

"Yeah, yeah, Zac as in studying. Who's calling?"

"Dude! It's your Uncle Marty!"

"Marty? No way!"

"Yes way. And I just want to tell you I'm sorry for not replying to your email immediately. I was in Chicago on business. I just read your message tonight."

"Okay. Yeah, so did you hear from my mom, too?"

"Yes," Martin says, "and forget her worries. I look forward to your visit. I really do."

"Really?"

"Zac. The next time I want to hear from you is when you have a flight number, an ETA, and some ideas about what you want to do out here. Now, as I shared a while back, I may not have a lot of days off, but we can work it out. So: are we on?"

"Damn, Uncle Marty, we are so on, and you are so cool!"

Martin strums an air guitar with his phone-free hand.

"I'm glad you think so, Zac. I'll see you in June."

"So cool! Love you, Uncle Marty!"

"Love you, too," Martin says, as he returns the phone to its cradle and he puts away his air-guitar. (For now, at least.)

CHAPTER EIGHTEEN

I

As he inches his way through this late Saturday morning traffic that is heading north on Hyperion, Martin makes the admission: "I'm crazy," he says to the dashboard. "I'm fucking crazy."

He's starting to hate his obsession, and even more than that, he's really hating the slow motion of the right-hand lane. He pulls out of it, and by choosing the left lane, he also knows that he's saying "no thank you" to both entrances of the main parking lot.

Not surprisingly, the traffic thins out just after the light at Monon. Martin is able to return to the right lane quickly and then pull into the Trader Joe's parking annex—a lot just up the street; a lot that is new to him and, for some reason, equally as annoying as the one he just avoided.

II

Martin skips the carts and goes for a basket. Today, he doesn't need all that much.

Having already selected some fresh fruit, Martin makes his way past the next couple of aisles. He stops—because he's tempted—at the tasting kiosk, but he immediately recoils. He doesn't know what they're offering today, but it appears to be something that children like. At least, there seem to be a lot of children around the kiosk.

Martin acknowledges, as he strides past the kiosk with his basket, that he's never actually had anything *against* children. They just always seem to be "too short," particularly when they are in crowded places where adults are shopping.

After sauntering past the salsa and chips, he happens upon pet-central. He grabs eight cans of TJ's finest and a bag of pine litter.

At this point, Martin's completed his mental list, and he can only hope that Susan is on duty.

At the check-out station called "Griffith Park," he sees her beautiful long hair. He moves there, and he stands in line. It is busier than usual, and so there are two people ahead of him.

Within a few minutes, a crew member calls out from the "Hyperion" station.

"Dude!" the crewmember says, "I can take you over here!"

Martin realizes that the crewmember is speaking to him.

Immediately remembering the about-face of that frazzled fellow customer with whom he had shared Susan's line a few weeks back, Martin adopts a confused expression, quickly looks into his basket, and then smiles at Hyperion-guy. "Thanks anyway," he says. "I just realized I forgot a few things."

III

Having dumped the contents of his basket into a cart, Martin is revisiting all the aisles. And he is throwing into that cart things that he doesn't immediately need, but that also will not "go bad." Paper towels and tissues from the west wall, and liquid soap from one of the aisles. From another aisle, some cans of chili and a jar of mustard.

He's going to spend more money than he had planned to spend, but that's okay. He's filling his cart, and he's making his way back to...

IV

Susan's aisle.
It's like a miracle.

When Martin approaches the holding pattern that is "next?" in Trader Joe's land, there is no "next." Susan is simply waiting for him. His cart slides into her station without missing a beat.

"So how ya doin today?" Susan asks, as she begins to scan his items.

"I'm good," replies Martin, smiling at her as he always does.

"Lucky for you," Susan says next, moving the contents of his cart through the check-out process. "Your cat or cats obviously accept the Joe's version of wet food."

"Yeah," Martin says. "Yours don't?"

"My cats are prigs," Susan says. "I think, actually, that they are direct descendents of ratters that came over on the Mayflower."

"Ooh," says Martin, entering his PIN into the keypad. "You mean they have attitudes? I can't imagine a cat with an attitude!"

"Go figure, huh?" Susan is bagging at this point.

"So how many ya got?" Susan asks.

"Cats? Just the one. And you?"

"Two old geezers," she replies. "They don't have a full set of teeth between them."

She smiles and looks at Martin directly, her own full set of teeth revealing a smile that is calming and warm.

Martin is compelled to look down in this moment, to busy himself with an alleged task that involves his wallet. He cannot maintain the eye contact. He cannot maintain it and not give away everything he thinks, knows, and hopes.

V

Leaving the store, with his cartful of goods, Martin is smiling. He likes knowing that Susan has cats. If Susan has cats, then Susan is not allergic.

As Martin pushes his cart up the sidewalk's small incline, approaching that auxiliary lot, he realizes that Trader Joe's probably had some socially conscious motivation for creating this parking annex that is several doors away and up a (sort of) hill. Because: for the dozens of shoppers who do this routine daily—pushing their carts in a direction that counters gravity—this experience, however brief and however subconscious, provides the feeling of being at one with the homeless.

Martin is glad that his car will be waiting for him. He's glad he'll be able to empty the contents of the cart into its trunk, and that he can then drive home. Martin is glad that the cart itself is not part of his worldly possessions.

VI

When he has to park on Melbourne, only about two houses in from Hillhurst, Martin is starting to rethink the benefits of owning a shopping cart. This is going to be a pain. He should have thought it through. It's Saturday, after all, which explains why he had to park so far from home. Anyone who wasn't at Trader Joe's is in his neighborhood, and they all brought cars.

He peers into the opened trunk and begins to dig through the bags. He'll consolidate only those things that can't wait a day or two in the trunk. Doing so, he can get home in one trip.

"Hey, Martin," comes a mellow voice, approaching from the sidewalk.

Martin looks up and sees manicure man, whose hair appears to be newly dyed and whose tee shirt features rips that seem a bit too symmetric. This week, his nail polish is an electric blue.

"Hey," Martin says. He smiles as he extends his hand, and he wishes he could remember the name of Brittany's friend.

Manicure man peers into Martin's trunk. "You went to Trader Joe's on a Saturday morning?" he asks incredulously.

"I'm going through this masochistic phase," Martin explains spontaneously. "I also forgot temporarily that my apartment building doesn't have curbside valet."

"I can help you. That's where I'm heading."

"Oh yeah?" Martin responds. "God, that'd be great. We don't have to take it all in, but..."

"Why not? I'm counting two bags, two large items, and four hands."

"You're a math genius!"

Manicure man smiles as he grabs one of the bags and the trio of paper towel rolls. Martin grabs the other bag and the kitty litter. He closes the trunk, and they head west toward Vermont.

"So how's your job going?" Martin asks.

"Dude, it's pretty gnarly these days. Lots more runaways this time of year."

"So there's a season?"

"Well, you know," manicure man says, "when the weather gets better across the country, kids are more likely to hit the road."

"They come from all over the country?"

"Yup."

"Why L.A.?"

"Hollywood. Dreams. Weather. Drugs. Tricking."

"Is it sad?" Martin asks. "I mean, your work?"

"Of course it is. But there are also success stories, and I like being part of that. I know where the kids are coming from and what they're going through."

They walk in silence for a few seconds. Martin wants to ask all kinds of questions, but the ones he is thinking of now all seem much too personal. And, since he can't even remember the guy's name, asking him personal questions seems particularly inappropriate.

"You going to see Brittany?" Martin asks instead.

"Yup. We're gonna have coffee up at Psychobabble. Hey, if you'd like to join us, I'll see if she wouldn't mind."

Martin surprises himself when he immediately says, "That'd be cool. I'd like that."

VII

Martin has just finished putting away all the groceries when his doorbell rings.

"Hey!" he says to Brittany and manicure man, "Come on in! I just need a minute to change my shirt. It's about fifteen degrees warmer than it was when I went to the store."

Brittany and manicure man enter the living room as Martin walks further to the bedroom.

"Oh my God!" Martin hears Brittany say next, "your cat is beautiful. Jason! Look!"

Jason, Martin thinks. *Thanks, Brittany!*

"So no one ever claimed it, huh?" Brittany asks, speaking loudly enough for Martin to hear her in the next room.

Returning in a cooler (but not necessarily hipper) shirt, Martin fills them in: "As it turns out, this cat belonged to the guy who's missing—Lonzo."

"Oh yeah," Brittany says quietly, sitting next to Dude on the floor. "The flyer. It's so sad."

"I don't know about that. You know Myra? Second floor?"

"Are you kidding!" Brittany exclaims. "I love Myra! She is the real deal. She has cats, too."

"Right. Three of them."

"So what's the story?" Brittany asks. "Did she say something about Lonzo?"

"She thinks he's in Vegas," Martin replies. "And apparently, with the exception of this beast, he didn't have much to leave behind."

"Hmm..." says Brittany, the conversation apparently leading her to other, personal thoughts. She pets Dude lovingly, and he offers her his belly.

"You're a lucky little runaway," she says to the purring creature.

Then she looks up to smile at Martin and Jason. The tears sit just on the top of her eyes, creating a glossy film while defying gravity.

VIII

Not surprisingly, Psychobabble is filled with a lot of wacky types who are talking incessantly. By the time Brittany, Jason, and Martin have their orders filled and find a table outside, they've already engaged in about fifteen minutes of conversation. While much of the content was a bit surprising to Martin, he was grateful for the context of standing in line and placing orders. It allowed him to take in the information without giving away the naïveté of his Norman Rockwell upbringing.

He has learned that, twelve years ago, Brittany was a sixteen year old runaway who spent a full six months literally living on the streets of Hollywood. He has learned that she and Jason met there. Jason was a local kid, and while he had a home, his parents' drug-using lifestyle translated into no disciplinary tactics. Jason spent his nights with the street kids and occasionally brought one home for a shower.

Martin has learned that Brittany received tremendous benefits from a nonprofit organization in the community. She ultimately got housing, and she got her GED. She took a few courses at L.A.C.C., too, but because she liked working more than anything, she spent more time earning money than she did earning a degree. Up until two years ago, her jobs generally were minimum wage. Still, though, she loved to work. She gave it her all.

Martin has learned that the nonprofit that once served Brittany is the one where Jason works, doing outreach. Martin also has learned that the organization is holding its big annual event at the end of May. Brittany is going to be the alum-of-honor.

IX

When Jason returns from his cigarette run to the 7-11, he looks with feigned shock at his filled coffee cup.

"Martin bought us another round," Brittany announces.

"Good thing I've got tonight and tomorrow off," Jason says, smiling as he takes his seat. "This is normally bed-time for me."

"I don't know how you do that shift," Brittany comments.

"Hey, in the runaway business, it's the equivalent of nine to five. Besides, it's only four nights a week."

Jason lights a cigarette and sits back in his chair. "So Martin, I was just thinking."

"Thinking? But this is your day off!"

Brittany reaches out and squeezes Martin's arm. "You're funny," she says, giggling.

"That's 'cause it's my day off," Martin retorts glibly, offering a brotherly smile to Brittany and wondering what sort of parents would drive such a charming girl out of their home. Then, he turns to Jason, "So you were thinking."

"Yeah, but I just stopped about a second ago."

Jason gives them both a teasing glance as he takes a slow sip of his second latte. Returning the oversized mug to the wobbly table, "Yeah," he says, "I was thinking. Martin, you should come to that dinner event. At least buy a ticket. And I don't know where you work, but if it's a corporation of some kind, maybe they could buy a table."

"How much?"

"Individual tickets are one-fifty, I think. Tables start at three thousand and they grow astronomically from there.

"Here," Jason says, reaching into his back pocket and pulling out a small pad of paper and a pen. "Write down your email address. I'll send a note to the development director when I get home later, and she can provide you with the details. She'll get my email on Monday."

"Cool," Martin says, recording his email address on the pad. "And, uh, you can count me in for at least one ticket. I'm not sure about my firm. I'm, uh, never sure about my firm."

"So where do you work anyway?" Jason asks.

"I don't want to talk about it," Martin replies.

"Top secret?"

"Top bullshit."

CHAPTER NINETEEN

I

"Martin!" Vivian says, in that cheerful tone that he doesn't trust for a nanosecond.

He looks up to see her entering his office. He immediately realizes he made a mistake in not closing the door. Vivian is carrying what is probably her favorite mug: it features a Van Gogh reproduction. And, for some reason, seeing it gives Martin this incredible urge. Seeing it gives Martin this urge to lop off one of Vivian's ears.

"Mind if I sit?" she asks, casually, as if this were a typical Monday morning for both of them.

Martin responds with a combination facial/hand gesture that says "of course" while still allowing him to retain his inner disdain.

"So," Vivian says, after settling into one of his guest chairs. "How was the trip?"

"It was fine. You know, a meet-and-greet basically. It was good to be with the Chicago team. They're a nice bunch."

Vivian nods, smiles, and looks through her power glasses. "And isn't Chicago a great town?"

"Actually, Vivian, I lived there for fifteen years, so—"

"I had no idea," she replies, showing the slightest hint of a dimple, but only on the left side.

"So?" she asks next, "Did you paint the town red?"

"Red's not my color."

"Good one," she responds, winking, as she takes another gulp from Van Gogh's caffeinated sunflowers.

"Vivian, I'm glad you dropped by, actually. I, uh, learned this weekend about a nonprofit event."

"Oh?" she sits back and crosses one leg over the other. This is the power woman's "I-might-be-interested" stance.

"Yes," Martin continues, fully acknowledging—to himself, anyway—the bullshit in her stance. "There's an organization in Hollywood that helps teenage runaways. They do really good work. Anyway, they're holding their annual benefit in late May, and I was thinking it might be nice if the firm—or, if a handful of us—bought a table."

"Hmm." says Vivian, uncrossing her legs, leaning forward and holding her mug in both hands—cradling it, essentially. (She gives the impression of "thinking," but Martin doesn't buy that for a minute.)

Nevertheless, he gives her a minute. (Hell, he'll give her all day.)

After pretending to consider his suggestion, Vivian places her mug on his desk, clasps her hands, and erects her posture. "Martin, you know that Haley-Mitchell-Phelps has a strong credo about corporate philanthropy. There's an entire department in New York that handles our work in the area. But, it's all quite established. We do the United Way campaigns every year, and we have our long-term commitments with RIF and MADD. And I think that places us in a credible position of being good citizens."

"Right. Well, I, uh, am not really looking to upset the corporate philanthropy fruit basket, certainly. I just thought that those of us who are local might want to support something that is local."

"We do support local," Vivian replies, smiling tightly. "And we do it through the office in New York."

Martin and Vivian observe a moment of silence.

"Moving on," Vivian says, clapping her hands once. "Are you meeting with your VPs this week?"

"Brenda and I will work on that scheduling today."

"Wonderful," Vivian says, standing up. "And again, great to have you on the team, Martin."

Vivian's exit is synchronistic to Brenda's entrance.

And Brenda's crossing-of-the-eyes, accompanied by a tongue sticking out, is mirrored by the same facial expression on Martin.

"So?" Brenda asks, whispering, "is she your boss or something?"

"I have the feeling that Vivian is the boss of everyone in Vivian's life."

"Are you going to be able to handle this?"

"As long as I don't have to go home with her, I'll be fine."

II

When Dude has finished his dinner that night, he comes into the living room and joins Martin on the couch. The timing is right. Martin wants to get up and check his email, but he also just wants to sit. He just wants to ... tune out. Without a television to distract him, a cat is the next best (or probably a better) thing.

Rubbing the cat's tummy, Martin also gains permission from the presence of another being in the room. He gains permission to talk out loud.

"Oh, Dude," he says, "you would not believe where I work. You would not believe what I work with! Dude, my God, Vivian? Not a cat person. No way."

Dude curls and rolls, enjoying his tummy-rub.

"I can see her, though—" Martin continues, staring across the room and getting a smirk on his face. "Yeah, I can see her training Schnauzers. –Sit. –Heel. –Stay. –Fetch. –Meet with your VPs once a week. –Go to Chicago. –Go to New York. ....And don't pee on our corporate philanthropy."

Dude nips at Martin's hand, but it's a gentle nip. Playful, friendly, and non-lethal.

"Oh, Dude. I just can't wait for take-your-cat-to-work day."

Dude rolls some more.

"Will you bite her hard for me? I mean, really hard?"

Dude suddenly leaps from the couch and bolts out of the room.

III

When Martin sees **HRHY's May Event** in the subject line, he knows it isn't spam. In fact, he opens the email right away. It is from a woman named Laura Galancid.

```
Dear Mr. Sheffield,

Our outreach worker, Jason, let me know of
your interest in attending our event on
Wednesday, May 20th. He also suggested that the
corporation where you work might be interested
in buying a table. We would welcome any and
all support you can provide! I am attaching a
copy of the event invitation. Please disregard
the deadline for tribute journal entries. We
are still accepting them.

For more information about our work, please
visit our website at www.hrhy.org. And you may
certainly feel free to call me if you have any
questions, etc.

We welcome your support and hope to see you on
May 20th!

Warm regards,

Laura Galancid
323-555-2030 ext. 23
```

Martin opens the attachment. The invitation is both hip and elegant, and as he peruses its details, he is a bit amazed by the potential levels of giving. With tables selling for as high as $30,000, he realizes that if he buys a ticket for $150, his contribution is but a drop in the bucket.

As for the tribute journal, the price levels also run the gamut. It's philanthropic real estate. The inside front cover, the back, and the inside back cover seem to be as valuable as the homes up the hill—the ones he might pass on the way to the Observatory. And within the cover's boundaries are other options. A full journal page seems the equivalent of those single-family homes between Franklin and the Boulevard, while a half-page might be represented by one of the craftsman houses on Melbourne. A quarter-page could be like a condo in that twin tower complex at Los Feliz and Hillhurst.

His apartment? A joke. For the value of his little rental, he could maybe put his name on one of the three staples that holds the whole baby together. Don't even go there.

Martin sees that he can pledge a business card-size tribute for five hundred dollars, and he thinks he might do that. He wouldn't submit his business card, though. Rather, a little message to Brittany. A message of congratulations.

He thinks, too, that he'll just go ahead and buy two tickets at one-fifty each. He can swing it. Hell, he just got a raise.

Martin closes the attachment, but he doesn't immediately send a reply. He hasn't given up just yet on recruiting more supporters. After all, he's got the meeting this week. The meeting with the VPs who will be reporting to him. Maybe he can generate some interest.

CHAPTER TWENTY

I

"How ya doing, boss?" Brenda asks, as she enters Martin's corner office and catches him spinning in his chair.

Martin manages a full stop just when he should. "It's Thursday, right?"

"Yup," Brenda replies. "Big meeting day. And, also, I've finalized your travel plans for next week."

"Did you swing another Wednesday through Friday?"

"Yup. Got you on the Tuesday night red-eye, so you can have a day to chill before the bogus team-building on Thursday."

"Good. That gives me five full days out of this joint."

"You know what, Martin? I'm kinda glad you got this promotion."

"Why's that?"

"Because I feel I know you better now. And... I, uh, like what I know. You're one of us!"

"I don't know who I'm one of, Brenda, but if that's a compliment, I'll take it."

Brenda smiles as she walks around his desk. Then, after putting a folder square in the center of his workspace viewing area, she sets his chair on a serious spin.

"Whee!" Martin is saying, as she leaves his office giggling— as she shuts the door behind her so as to allow him his privacy before the big Vivian-dictated VP meeting.

II

Martin, Cody, Phil, and Debora are all gathered in the small, ninth-floor conference room. Brenda is there as well. Martin asked her to join them. He has come to realize, in the past week or two, that the "support" in "support staff" can mean a whole lot more than simply maintaining files, relaying phone messages, and running general interference. "Support" can mean having an intuitive understanding regarding what makes one's "boss" actually come to work in the morning.

Martin also has come to realize, in the past week or two, that he will be turning to Brenda for support probably long after Alice—his designated eventual assistant—returns from her leave.

"So—" Martin says to the group gathered ("his staff," as it were), "thank you for setting aside this time today. I, uh, didn't write up an agenda for this meeting, because I didn't think it was necessary. I just thought that we should gather, share whatever we feel like sharing, and maybe see what we can do to help each other out."

Martin immediately notices that Cody is frantically jotting some notes on his pad. *Why?*

"Um, Cody?"

"Yes? Martin?" Cody replies anxiously.

"Well, I just noticed that you were scribbling rather hurriedly there. Do you have some thoughts to share?"

"Oh. Oh. Um, no. No. No, I, uh, was just, you know, writing down some stuff."

"That's fine," Martin says, stretching his arm into the middle of the table (the best he can do for a halfway point, where Cody is concerned.) "Really," Martin smiles, "that's fine.

"Anyone else?"

Debora raises her hand in a casual way.

"Debora?" Martin says/asks.

"Martin," she begins, in her remarkably mature voice, "I just want to tell you—and I know I can't speak for everyone and of course we're all shook up about Barry—but I want to tell you that I think you were the best choice. I think they got it right."

"Thank you, Debora," Martin responds, feeling his face redden a bit. "I appreciate the vote of support.

"So," Martin continues, "I, uh, don't know that we'll need to have meetings every week. I mean, we didn't with Barry, and that seemed to work fine. Also, of course, my door is always open, and I hope each of you will feel comfortable about dropping in when you have a question or a concern."

As he looks at each of them, Martin cannot believe he's actually saying things like "my door is always open." Another promotion, and he'll be a walking cliché. As he looks at each of them, Martin also realizes that Phil is as enigmatic as ever. His shark eyes give away no emotions or interest. He's just *there*.

"Anyway," Martin says next, "I asked Brenda to update a spreadsheet with all your accounts on it."

(Brenda takes this as a cue to pass around the spreadsheets.)

"Thanks, Brenda. So... we've got the usual format: the accounts on which you perform lead duties and the accounts for which you are the back-up person. I don't think we need to go down anyone's list, line-by-line, but does anyone here have any updates that could benefit us all? Does anyone have any issues that we could brainstorm together?"

Cody raises his hand.

Nodding at Cody, Martin smiles. "You know, folks," he says then, in a friendly tone, "I don't think we need to raise our hands in these meetings—"

Cody immediately withdraws his hand and assumes a position that can best be described as "sitting fetal."

"It's okay, Cody," Martin says, reaching his arm toward the middle of the table again. "I appreciate the show of respect. Really. I just want everyone to relax, okay?"

III

The group's spreadsheet review doesn't send up any red flags for Martin. Everyone seems to be doing his or her job, and unlike earlier in the economic downturn, there are no unprecedented surprises. Martin is reflecting on this assessment while they all wait for Debora to return from the Ladies' Room.

It's a rather awkward moment during a meeting that Martin never intended to hold. It's a moment when four co-workers have a little unscheduled break, when co-workers should be bantering or talking about their homes or their pets. It's a moment when Martin realizes just how absurd the firm's climate is...

"Thanks, guys," Debora says cheerfully, as she returns to the room. "Did I miss anything?"

Cody furtively shakes his head, answering for all of them.

"Well, we can wrap this up soon," Martin says. "Actually, the only other item I wanted to bring up is not really business. It's just, I guess, an announcement of sorts. And, by the way, if any of you have 'announcements of sorts,' please feel free."

"What is it?" asks Debora, sounding genuinely intrigued.

"I, uh, recently learned of a very good, very worthy nonprofit in Hollywood."

(Brenda takes this as a cue to pass around the copies of the email attachment Martin received from Laura Galancid.)

"Thanks, Brenda," Martin says.

"Anyway," he says to the group, as he watches them peruse the documents in front of them, "this is a 'no pressure'—and I mean that, folks—moment of simply sharing with you an opportunity to support a very worthwhile organization. It's a group that serves runaway youth in Hollywood, and they're having their annual event on May 20th. So, take a look at the information there. Take a look at their website. And if you're interested, purchase a ticket."

"Wow, cool!" says Cody, responding to a detail on the invitation copy. "Conan is the Emcee!"

"I can't believe you shared this, Martin," Debora says, looking up from a quick review of the information at hand and smiling broadly. "My husband's on their board!"

"He is?"

"Yes. Len is a doctor at Children's Hospital – with the Division of Adolescent Medicine. They partner with this organization all the time. I'll have to check my calendar, but I'm pretty sure I'm already scheduled to go. Len usually buys a table."

"Well then," says Martin, surprised to learn of Debora's connection to the runaway center. "I'll probably be seeing you there as well as here.

"Anything else, anyone?" Martin asks, allowing a few seconds to pass after that last, lame statement.

"Alright, then! Meeting adjourned!"

"This is great, Martin," Cody says, standing on anxious legs. "I'm really glad you brought this event to my attention."

"Good," Martin replies, watching Phil's quick exit from the small conference room. "And if you can make it, great! But again, this is not about work, and this is definitely not a work-related favor I'm asking for."

IV

That night, Martin needs to do a load of laundry, and rather than go up and down from the basement to his fifth floor apartment, he decides he'll just spend the hour or two in that room in the building's depths. Although he has brought a book with him, he knows he'll probably not open it. He knows too well the hypnotic effect that laundry rooms have on him. The sounds help him think in ways he doesn't think when he's in his own apartment.

Martin sits in the laundry room's one and only chair. He smiles ironically as he looks around him—at the exposed piping that is noticeably rusty; at the walls that are desperate for a coat of paint; at the dusty corners of the cracked cement floor. He wonders about his staff, the people who report to him. He imagines their laundry rooms are a lot nicer...

Debora's husband is a doctor. Martin only learned this today. Moreover, he is a doctor who serves on the board of the runaway nonprofit. He buys tables every year for the event. Are they three thousand dollar tables or thirty thousand dollar tables? Either way, Debora undoubtedly has her own washer and dryer, and she probably has household help whose responsibility, among other things, is to manage the laundry. There are no quarters involved—except maybe maid's quarters.

With Cody, Martin is not so sure. Cody doesn't wear a wedding band, and so Martin assumes he is not married. Still, he might be living with someone, and they might have a condo. They might have one of those stackable units. Martin cannot envision Cody either in a laundromat or in a basement laundry room. He cannot envision Cody having the patience to deal with the task of doing nothing but laundry.

As for Phil, Martin shakes his head in a sort of jerking way. There is something about that guy... something he just doesn't trust.

The elevator door opens in that moment, and Martin looks to his left. The man who emerges is unfamiliar. Skinny and wearing a cap, he doesn't smile immediately. But, why should he be smiling? He is spending a part of his Thursday night doing laundry in the basement of an old apartment building.

Martin nods a hello. Cap man, who has an odd apparatus slung over his left arm, nods back before approaching the available washer and dumping a load in it. When's he's done feeding the machine, he approaches the area where Martin is sitting.

Cap man then opens the apparatus to reveal a portable chair. He sits.

"Wow," Martin says, nodding. "Smart move."

"What, the chair? Yeah, well, Rite Aid was having a sale. Mind if I smoke?"

"I don't care," says Martin.

Cap man lights up a Marlboro and sighs after his first exhale.

"I'm Martin, by the way," Martin says, extending his hand.

"Scott," cap man replies, offering a handshake that is reluctant at best.

"Been in the building long?" Martin asks.

"Mm, a year or two."

Martin nods his head, as if he might agree. But he doesn't. Cap man Scott has been in the building either one year or two. How could anyone be so indefinite? The second option is a one hundred percent increase over the first.

"What floor you on?" Martin asks.

"Second."

"Lucky you. You don't have to depend so much on that antique they call an elevator."

Scott shrugs and takes another drag from his cigarette.

It becomes apparent to Martin that Scott is not interested in "shooting the shit," and for Martin, that's fine, really. But, there's something about this guy—some creepiness... Martin then remembers what Myra said about a man on her floor—a man she didn't trust. Martin wonders if this is the man. Just then, his washer stops, indicating that he can move on to the dryer stage of this basement routine.

V

It's been probably ten minutes since Martin fed quarters to the dryer. It's been probably ten minutes that Martin has been sitting side-by-side with cap-man Scott, and neither has spoken.

But Martin has been thinking. And Martin has been formulating.

"It's funny," Martin says, speaking just as Scott lights up another Marlboro. "I feel like I'm watching TV sometimes. You know, when I stare at the dryer."

"If that's the channel you like," Scott offers, his monotone indicating a lack of amusement.

"I gotta get a TV," Martin says, shaking his head as if he is berating himself for some reason.

"You don't have one?"

"No. Mine died about two weeks ago, and I just haven't got around to it. And, you know, these days, the way technology is changing. I don't know, I just feel like if I wait another week, there will be some hybrid TV that runs on french fry grease!"

Martin knows that his attempt at humor is wasted on cap-man Scott. He's really only saying this stuff to entertain himself.

"I might be able to help you," Scott says.

"Really?"

VI

Martin doesn't stop at Myra's that night, because he doesn't want to have a chance meeting with Scott on the second floor. But, he can't wait to tell her. He can't wait to tell her that on Saturday, he'll be visiting Scott in the cap-man apartment. Apparently, Scott has a "spare TV." He upgraded recently, and he has been unable to sell his old set on craigslist.

CHAPTER TWENTY-ONE

I

Finishing up his first mug of coffee, Martin feels a little anxious. There's a part of him that doesn't want to visit weird capman Scott's apartment. But, they agreed on ten in the morning, and so Martin will head down to the second floor. He decides, because it seems more neighborly, to refill his mug and carry it with him.

II

"Oh, hey," says Scott. His tone sounds anxious, particularly coming several seconds after Martin's third knock. Scott opens the door slowly and only so much, managing to block Martin's entrance just as he says, "Come in."

"Did I get the time right?" Martin asks, feeling like he's some sit-com character about to enter an otherwise B-level slasher movie.

"Yeah, sure, sorry." Scott replies. He opens the door a bit further—just enough to let Martin in.

"I'm a bit of a tech geek, as you can see," Scott offers, nervously.

"Wow," Martin comments, coffee mug in hand. "And I thought Circuit City went out of business!"

"Huh, yeah," Scott says, his energy alarmingly frenetic, "I'm constantly buying, selling, trading. It's just kind of a hobby of mine."

Martin notices that Scott is scratching his arm rather furiously. Scott also is staring at Martin's coffee. In fact, he's staring in such a way that Martin feels rude for having arrived with only one mug.

"So..." Martin says. As he takes in the stock, his disbelieving smile allows him to buy a bit of time. He uses that time to notice, through a peripheral glance down the hall, that the television in Scott's bedroom—currently showing what could be a porn film—looks remarkably like the very plasma screen that once graced his own space on the fifth floor. *So,* Martin thinks, *Scott stole my TV.*

"Anyway," Scott says, his eyes and body jumping as he speaks, "uh, this TV here is pretty good." He's indicating a Toshiba that shares a tabletop with several stereo speakers.

"Digital?"

"Of course."

"How much?"

"I'll let you have it for one-twenty-five."

Martin looks at the nineteen-inch flatscreen. There's a part of him that wants to make the deal and get the hell out of this apartment. There's another part of him that just wants to get the hell out of this apartment.

Scott's state of being, Martin realizes, is nothing that he can cure. "You know," he says to the man who appears to be warehousing stolen goods, "I'm really looking for something bigger."

"Cool," says Scott, anxiously scratching an unknown itch.

"That one down the hall looks like the right size," Martin comments, directing a glance toward Scott's bedroom. "That your new one?"

"Yeah, that's my upgrade," Scott replies, becoming increasingly jittery.

"What's the make?"

"Panasonic. Forty-two inches, I think."

"Remember what you paid?"

"I think it was about eight hundred."

I think it was about nothing, Martin wants to say. *I forked over the eight hundred dollars.*

"I guess that's the going rate," Martin states, sharing an insincere smile that is nevertheless convincing.

"Thanks, anyway," Martin adds, "for showing me what you got. I should probably continue my shopping in more traditional locations."

III

Upstairs, Martin rifles through his papers. Before he left for Chicago, he had written down Myra's number. Now, all he wants to do is call her and get her up to his place. This conversation can't possibly take place on the second floor...

IV

"I knew it!" Myra exclaims, her emphatic hand gesture nearly causing an injury from the too-hot tea that Martin prepared for her.

"Wasn't I right?" she then asks Dude, rhetorically. (Dude is stretched out on the couch beside her, offering his belly for a rub.)

"He's a creepy guy," Martin agrees. "And he was really weird today. I mean, when I met him the other night in the laundry room, he was quiet—kind of lethargic, even. This morning, though, he was weird—frenetic and itchy."

"He's an addict, Martin. A junkie. Get with the program!"

"What are we going to do?"

"I think we should have a talk with our building manager."

V

David is grateful for the mug of coffee that Martin offers him. "Ah," David says, regarding the Chicago tourist montage, "my old mug!"

"Hi, Myra," David says next, entering Martin's living room and taking a seat in the straightback chair beside the desk.

"So," the reluctant manager then says to the tenants, "what's going on?"

Martin is glad that Myra jumps in. Martin is glad, because she seems to have such a better sense of cap-man Scott's idiosyncrasies.

After listening to Myra's accusations, David grabs a gulp of coffee. Martin senses that he's buying time; that listening to such stories and then possibly doing something about them is well beyond what he signed up for.

Looking first at Martin and then at Myra, David shrugs. "I don't know. I don't know if there's anything I can do."

"My God!" Myra blurts out, "Doesn't it concern you to have such a freak in this building?"

Martin watches as David takes in this question. He watches as David gives Myra a quick once-over. There she is in her leopard skin top, her emerald green leggings, her batty boots, and her old grey hair tied up in a macramé whatever that might have been designed to hang a plant. Martin wonders how David can respond to his most tenured tenant's query.

"It's not just that he's a freak," Martin offers. "He's a potentially dangerous freak."

"My God, man," Myra says next, looking pointedly at David. "He broke into Martin's apartment!"

"We don't know that, actually," Martin states.

"Oh, please, Martin!" Myra responds, still stroking the cat. "You saw your TV in his bedroom just this morning! He's the burglar!"

"Did you call the police?" David asks Martin.

"When?"

"When you were burglarized."

"No."

"Guys," David states, standing up, "I hear what you're saying here. Maybe Scott's a thief; maybe he isn't. Maybe he's an addict; maybe he isn't. I'm just a manager, you know? If there's some stuff going on here that you think is illegal, then I suggest you call the police."

"See you later," David adds, as he heads out of Martin's apartment and back to his own.

VI

That afternoon, Martin decides to take a walk. Maybe see what's playing at the movie theatre across the street. Maybe drop into some of the shops that grace his little section of Los Feliz Village.

The elevator arrives quickly, and he hopes it will descend quickly as well. He needs to get out of the building for a while. After pushing the button for the first floor, he notices a new sign taped on the wall. A sign from David.

```
Date: Saturday, 5/2
To: Tenants of 1773
From: David Ferguson, Building Manager
Re: Security Issues

Dear Fellow Tenants:

It has been brought to my attention that one
of our apartments was burglarized recently.
Please protect your belongings and yourselves
by remembering always to lock both locks on
your front doors. Also lock windows that are
accessible via the fire escapes. If anyone
needs any repairs in order to take those
steps, just let me know. Thanks, DF
```

"Oh, fuck!" Martin blurts out, in response to both the sign and a strong sense of fear.

He hopes that Scott has not used the elevator today. He hopes that Scott has not seen this sign. Martin knows that, by writing and posting this little missive, David was probably trying to be responsive. But David clearly wasn't thinking. With so few hours having elapsed between Martin's visit to Scott's apartment and the public announcement of a recent burglary, the connection is much too evident.

Martin rips the sign off the elevator wall. No way he's going to have some jittery freak addict thinking that a fellow tenant, ostensibly shopping for a television, put two and two together and shared the result.

VII

After studying the line-up at the Los Feliz 3 Cinemas, Martin surmises that there must be some chick flick festival that no one told him about. He heads for Skylight, where he knows the bookstore perusing routine will help him calm down a bit.

He walks past the establishment's original venue and enters the arts annex. He is immediately drawn to the racks of chapbooks and eclectic periodicals. Whenever he visits Skylight and takes in its contents, he appreciates his neighborhood and its true connection to the world at large.

He picks up a copy of the *Utne Reader* and begins flipping through the pages.

"Well," he hears then, the voice familiar but the context confusing. "There's my favorite customer!"

Martin turns and sees the friendly, smiling face of Susan.

"Hello, favorite customer!" she says.

Martin fakes a turn to look behind him, playfully pretending to assume that Susan must be talking to someone else.

"No," she says, when he turns back and looks at her, "I'm talking to you!"

"I didn't know you Trader Joe's people picked favorites," Martin offers, wondering just how very red his face is at this point.

"Actually, I didn't know I had favorites, either. But spontaneous comments are generally closer to the truth than any other types of comments, don't you think?"

Martin wants to say, *Well, in that case, I'm in love with you.* But he decides to keep that one to himself. (Besides, it's not really a spontaneous comment—at least, not in the strictest sense of the word.)

There is a sudden song emanating from Susan's purse. "Oh damn," she says, digging for her cell phone. "I'm gonna take this outside. Don't go away."

Martin watches as Susan makes a quick exit to the sidewalk. A part of him wants to walk up to the glass door and press his face against it. He wants to stare at her longingly. But, he knows better than to cater to his inner five-year-old, so he instead reopens the magazine in his hands. To a passerby, he actually looks as if he's taking in the content. He appears so fascinated, in fact, that a passerby might wonder why this man hasn't gone ahead and purchased a subscription...

"I'm back," says Susan, and Martin turns to face her.

"Everything okay?"

"Well, not with my friend Katherine. We were supposed to see that new Mike Nichols film at the triplex, but she had a fender bender on her way from Pasadena."

"Is she okay?"

"Yeah, she's fine, thank God. Just dealing with the information exchange and waiting for the cops to show up."

"So, do you live in this neighborhood?" Martin asks, reminding himself to clean the slate of his knowledge about the chatroom participant and the Atwater restaurant customer.

"No, I'm in Silver Lake. How about you?"

"I live right across the street," Martin admits.

"How cool is that? God, I love this little part of town."

"Me, too," Martin agrees.

"Hey," he adds, after a few seconds of awkward nodding and smiling, "it just occurred to me, I know your name is Susan because you wear it on your chest, but I always forget my nametag when I come to Joe's."

Susan laughs. "Most people do. So, what does your nametag say?"

"Martin," and because it's a reflex, he extends his hand.

"Nice to meet you, Martin," Susan says, smiling broadly and tilting her head as they shake hands.

VIII

The Mama Mia waitress takes their menus and heads into the little restaurant to get their orders going.

"This is a great place," Susan says. "I never come down this far on this side of the street."

"Yeah, this place is kind of a best-kept secret. You can walk by a thirty minute line at Fred 62 and arrive here to find your table waiting for you."

"Good to know," Susan says, generously sharing her serene smile.

"Alright," she says then, "so pick up where you left off. What are you going to do about this creepy guy?"

"Well, I feel kind of bad that I took down that sign."

"Don't go there. You did the right thing. Junkies are irrational. I was married to a cop once. You wouldn't believe some of the stories I heard."

The waitress delivers their iced teas as Martin reminds himself that he doesn't know about how Susan's marriage ended. He doesn't know about the death of her husband. Yet, because he *does* know, he is at a loss. How should he proceed in a way that will seem natural? Should he follow up on her mentioning being married? Should he ask for a sample story regarding irrational junkies? Or, should he continue talking about Scott?

Because the question was the first that occurred to him, he goes for it. "You were married to a cop?" he asks.

"Yup," says Susan, nodding somewhat sadly as she reaches for a packet of sweetener.

"I'm sorry," says Martin, "is this an off-limits topic?"

"Oh, no," she says, briefly touching his arm in a reassuring manner, "not off-limits. Just, sad."

"How so?"

"He was killed."

"On duty?"

"Yup."

"I'm so sorry."

Susan shrugs. It's the kind of shrug that conveys an admission—an admission to powerlessness regarding the past.

"Let's not make this a downer," Susan says. "So... have you ever been married?"

"Let's not make this a downer," Martin agrees, smiling.

CHAPTER TWENTY-TWO

I

"Brenda!" Martin exclaims enthusiastically, as his assistant enters his office on Monday morning.

"Damn, Martin, you're in a particularly good mood. And you're here early. What gives?"

"I don't know, I just kind of sprung out of bed this morning."

"Good weekend, huh?"

"Really good weekend. And you?"

"Well," Brenda says, smiling in a teasing way and doing a sort of dance from the shoulders up, "yeah...

"Check it out!" she exclaims, extending her left hand, palm side down.

"New manicure?" Martin asks, pretending to ignore the diamond on that special finger.

"Martin!" she scolds.

"Did you get engaged this weekend?"

"I did!" she squeals, clapping her hands and jumping up and down.

"Well, congratulations," Martin says, rising from his desk and meeting Brenda halfway for a warm hug.

He stands back and folds his arms in front of him. He feels brotherly and avuncular at once. "So, tell me about this guy. How long you two been together?"

"Five years," Brenda says.

"That's good. Plenty of time for knowing all you need to know."

"Yeah, Mike is great, and I'm psyched."

"Will you be having a big wedding?"

"I hope so," she replies, her energy slowing noticeably. "We'll see, anyway. We'll see what we can afford."

Martin detects a tone in Brenda's voice. There is something in this fairy tale that isn't altogether positive.

"Anyway," she says, determined to return to an upbeat rhythm, "as if that weren't the best news, I have more!"

"I'm always ready for more good news."

"Guess who has the flu?"

"Not the boss of us all?"

"Yup. Just saw Amber. Vivian has called in sick. Apparently, she sounded really bad."

"Of course she did. Powerlessness is foreign to her. So, where's the party?"

"Here, there, and everywhere. All day long!"

"Alright, then. So let me know if I can help with blowing up balloons!"

Brenda is laughing as she leaves Martin's office.

II

Martin looks up just as he hears the quick little taps on his office door.

"Debora!" he says, "come in!"

"Not catching you at a bad time?" she asks.

"No. In fact, today feels remarkably relaxed. Have a seat."

"Thanks," she says, pulling out one of his guest chairs.

"So," she says next, "you getting used to this swanky corner office?"

"It's got some nice perks," Martin admits. "Can I offer you some swanky corner office coffee?"

"I don't know," Debora replies, her tone refreshingly light, "is it special top management coffee?"

"Apparently, Juan Valdez's staff of senior vice presidents picked the beans themselves."

"Impressive," Debora comments, as Martin stands up and crosses to his coffee maker.

"Will it make me smarter?" she asks.

"Do you really want to be?"

"Good point."

"Cream or sugar?"

"Nope. Black is good."

"Hey," Martin says, indicating the seating area by the north wall. "Let's sit over here. I don't have a big need to be at that desk."

Martin places Debora's coffee on the table and prepares a cup for himself as his colleague crosses the room and sits in one of the two comfortable chairs at either side of the VP couch.

"So I wanted to fill you in," she says.

"'Bout what?"

"The event. Len was so happy to learn that you had brought that up in our meeting. I can't even tell you!"

"Good," Martin says, taking a seat on the couch, at the end closest to Debora. "I'm glad to hear that. So, are you indeed going to be there?"

"We are. Yeah, we've got our table lined up. I wanted to run something by you, though. One of the couples we usually invite can't join us this year, and I was thinking about seeing if Cody and his girlfriend would want to take those seats."

"That's a nice thought," Martin offers, somewhat relieved that Debora did not offer the seats to him.

"Yeah, you know, I really like Cody. He's awkward. He's nervous. And there's a part of me that believes he emerged from the womb just in way over his head, but he seems like a really nice, well-meaning guy. And, I don't know, I guess I feel that extending this invitation to him might, I don't know, might make him feel a little more welcome here on Planet Earth."

Martin laughs sincerely and takes a gulp of coffee. "Good one," he says, placing his mug on the VP coaster that came with the VP coffee table.

"Any response from Phil?" Debora asks.

"No," Martin replies, "and having just heard your overview of Cody, I'm a little curious...

"What do you think his story is?" Martin asks, taking the volume down several notches and thereby suggesting the beginning of a confidential dialogue.

"Hmm..." Debora starts twirling a few strands of her long blond hair—a quirky habit Martin noticed in the meeting that brought them all together last week.

"I know what you mean," says Martin. "Enigmatic is the only word I can come up with."

"Actually—" Deborah stands suddenly. "May I shut the door?"

"Of course! Like I said last week, my door is always open, which is the only position it can be in if someone wants to shut it."

Debora returns from her task, and before she begins speaking again, she sits, and she takes a slow sip of coffee. She then looks at Martin directly and deliberately. He patiently waits for her to decide what to say.

"Martin, I consider myself a pretty intuitive gal."

"I just knew you were going to say that!"

"Ha-ha," Debora says, tilting her head and smiling at her boss-among-equals. "But seriously? I don't trust that guy for a minute."

"Yeah?"

"I don't know if you're aware of this, but he and Vivian do a lot of hanging around together."

"Really?"

"Oh yeah. They must go out to lunch at least once a week, and considering how hierarchical Vivian is, that's kind of odd to me."

"How do you know this?" Martin asks.

"Martin, didn't you know? Brad is the all-knowing, all-hearing, all-seeing."

"Really? Brad?" Martin asks incredulously, never having imagined Debora's assistant—the queen of all queens—to be interested in anything other than the next parade in West Hollywood.

"Oh God, yes! I'm telling you, he has the scoop on everyone and everything. The simple mention of Phil's name around him elicits a hiss. And it's a long hiss, Martin. Longer even than the one he uses to respond to Vivian's name."

"Interesting," says Martin.

III

That night, Martin heads to the office elevator banks at 5:30. He's looking forward to getting home. When the *going down* light illuminates, he enters the elevator—not yet too crowded, in spite of the rush-hour timing.

The elevator stops at the eighth floor, and when Martin sees Phil, waiting in the corridor, he nods to him. Phil does not nod back. He also does not board the elevator. He just stands there, looking straight ahead, his steely eyes giving away no secrets.

IV

After cleaning up his dinner dishes (as well as Dude's), Martin turns off the kitchen light and heads to the living room. Susan's card is right there by the phone. Giving Martin her card was Susan's way of saying "call me." And now, with more than forty-eight hours having passed since their impromptu late-lunch date, Martin feels comfortable about pursuing that permission.

He takes the handset out of its resting spot, plops down onto the couch and punches in the number that is refreshingly within his area code.

Two rings pass, and he realizes she might be at Joe's. After four rings, he is convinced of this likelihood. Regardless, her outgoing message is almost as good as a conversation: *Hi Caller. Susan here. But, you probably knew that. Anyway, I look forward to speaking with you! So, define "you" and give me any other details I probably should know!*

Beep.

"Susan!" Martin begins, "Martin here. You know, your favorite customer? God, I hope you're not at work now, meeting a new favorite! Just wanted to give you a buzz, tell you I really enjoyed our lunch on Saturday, and I hope we'll get to do that again. My number is 523-2323. I know, it's like you said the other day—with a number like that, I could sell mattresses! And sometimes, I gotta admit, the idea is appealing. Anyway, I'm rambling. Call when you get a chance. Hope you're well. Bye."

Martin shakes himself out after hitting the *Off* button on his phone. A part of him can't believe that he actually exchanged numbers with Sus323.

He's just about to head into the bonus room and check his email when the phone rings. The noise—and the possible person causing it—make him jump. He picks up the handset and hits the *Talk* button.

"Hello?"

"Martin?"

"Yes?" he replies, not immediately able to place the voice, "Who's this?"

"Martin, it's Barry."

"Barry? How are you?" *besides drunk,* Martin wants to add, from the sound of it.

"Martin, I hope you are doing okay."

"I am, Barry. And I hope you're doing okay. Do you still have family there?"

"No-no-no. Not here. Nearby though it's okay."

"Are *you* okay?"

"Martin, you need to know."

"What?"

"Just be careful, okay?"

"What are you talking about?"

"I just care about you. That's all."

"Is there something specific you can tell me?"

"No I can't. I have to go now. Goodbye."

"Mao?"

"Something like that, Dude. Something like that."

CHAPTER TWENTY-THREE

I

Waiting for his towncar after deboarding the red-eye to La-Guardia, Martin is struck by the change. The air feels altogether different. The energy around him is a yin compared to the yang at LAX. It's been ten years since he visited New York City, and he wonders what to expect from the island that was ground zero on a Tuesday that changed history.

The driver knows the destination—the Radisson at 32nd Street and Broadway. "Koreatown," the driver says.

Martin isn't interested in ethnic specifications, and he would like to tell this to the towncar driver, whose own last name is distinctly immigrant—at least seven of the fourteen consonants therein are relatively high-scorers when one is playing Scrabble. Martin doesn't want to hear any references to what might be a nationalistic prejudice because, for him, that contradicts New York. As he's always seen it—remembering particularly a trip he and Lisa took together back when their marriage was new, fresh, and actually quite stimulating—New York is the original melting pot. It's the ultimate mix of races, languages, attitudes, and income streams, all packed together quite efficiently in little silver tubes that hurry from one stop to the next within a labyrinth of transportation conveniently located just beneath the city itself.

Lisa (and subways) on his mind apparently, Martin remembers an evening in their first L.A. apartment. Lisa was working downtown at the time, and their spacious two-bedroom was in a part of the flats known as Beverly Hills adjacent. They were relaxing in their living room, dinner in the oven, and Lisa—now on her second cocktail—was becoming increasingly animated. "Oh my God," she had said. "I overheard the funniest exchange today!"

"What'd you hear?" Martin had asked, smiling at his bride of five years. (Smiling, because he believed in "for richer, for poorer" and because he thought the "'til death do us part" concept was actually for real.)

"I was standing at the corner of Hill and Sixth, and I overheard this teenage girl stop a businessman. 'Excuse me,' she says, 'um, where is the metro-rail?' And he says: 'Underground!'"

Martin watched as Lisa then guffawed uproariously, took a big sip from her cocktail, and shook her head. "Underground? Get it? Boy, these Angelenos don't even know *what* to make of their new transit system!"

Martin got it. He just didn't laugh as loudly as Lisa did.

Martin's towncar is above ground. No; strike that—it is above *water*. They are crossing the 59th Street bridge. They are heading into Manhattan. Martin looks out the window. Even in the East River, he sees a hurried pace. An energy that is uniquely New York. But it's a good energy. It's an energy he needs. He leans back and smiles as he closes his eyes.

II

The concierge—a woman named Raisa—is extremely apologetic that his room is not yet ready. But, since it's nine o'clock in the morning, Martin lets her know that he didn't expect it to be. Raisa nevertheless assures him that she'll put a rush on the prep work, and she suggests he come back at eleven or so. In the meantime, she offers to check his bag. Martin agrees to that transaction, and once he has received a tag for his all-encompassing carry-on hanger, he heads out to the busy Manhattan morning. He has a craving for one of those greasy New York City breakfasts, preferably at a place that has filled its front window with neon signs proclaiming the World's Greatest Coffee and other international superlatives.

He heads north on Broadway, and immediately he is caught up in the pedestrian traffic. It boggles his mind that there can be so many people heading in the same direction at the same time. Of course, the same dynamic is true on the 405, the 10, the 101, and the 134, but where L.A. freeways are concerned, the concept of a common itinerary is relentlessly irritating and potentially deadly. In New York, the movement on the sidewalks is a more positive phenomenon; it's invigorating.

Back before he began going with Lisa, and just after Rachel had moved to the apartment she still rents in Chelsea, Martin would do a long weekend in Manhattan at least once a year. Even though he was settling into Chicago and coming to appreciate its urban qualities, the New York experience always seemed more vibrant. They had not yet begun to clean up the city, and the rawness was undeniable. Now, as Martin gets closer to Times Square and takes in the large, moving, digital signs of "improvement," he wonders if there's a part of the island that is still raw. Rachel has kept him posted over the years, and her perspective, while influenced by her tendency to default downward, seems to be true. Yes, it's beautiful and clean, but a part of its natural fortitude seems to be missing. At least, it's missing from this central tourist attraction where—only twenty years ago—hookers and hawkers set the tone.

III

When the telephone beside the bed rings, Martin shakes awake. He doesn't even remember falling asleep, and for a split second, he's not sure where he is. "Oh right," he says, looking around the small room with its unexciting airshaft view, "the Radisson. The Big Apple. A business trip."

Grabbing the receiver after the second ring, he practically pulls the entire telephone off the table—the cord is a twisted mess.

"Hello?" he says foggily.

"Marty! I love it. Did you pick that hotel on purpose?"

"Hi Rachel, no, my assistant picked it. Why?"

"It's the Radisson Martinique!"

"Oh yeah? Gee, I wonder if its siblings call it the Radisson Marty..."

"Ha," Rachel says. "So, what's the plan?"

"You tell me. Tonight is wide open."

"Well, I'll be home by six. Why don't you meet me here, and then we can go out to eat. You like sushi?"

"Not really," Martin replies, entertaining a quick, uninvited flashback of that tentacle meal he had (or didn't) in Atwater.

"Neither does Jack."

"Then why did you ask?"

"Because he can't join us tonight," Rachel explains. "Anyway, we'll decide about cuisine after you get here. Lots to choose from. You remember where I live?"

"Yup. Twenty-first and Seventh."

"Two buildings west of Seventh. North side. Fourth floor front."

"Still a walk-up?" Martin asks.

"Unless they put an elevator in today."

"Damn, Rache, you must have the strongest calves in town."

"I think the lady who lives above me has stronger ones."

Martin smiles. It touches him that his sister can joke around and still sound sad.

"Anyway," he says, "I'll head down around six. I should probably hop in the shower right now. I'm feeling a little disoriented."

IV

"Yeah," says Rachel, seeming mesmerized as she twirls a bit of pasta on her fork, "I'm sorry he flaked on us, too. But, that's sort of been the pattern lately. I think he's doing that thing that guys do."

"What do we do?" Martin asks, before taking another bite of his lamb shank.

"Maybe not all guys, but many, in my experience at least, don't want to be the one who breaks up. So, instead, they just act like total jerks until the girl initiates the break-up."

"Is that why you chose a restaurant called *Il Bastardo*?"

Rachel smiles. "I like the seafood here.

"So tell me more about this woman you stalked," Rachel says, grabbing a hot roll from the refilled bread basket that the busboy just delivered.

"I didn't stalk her really," Martin states.

"You don't call that stalking? Please! Just because you're a good guy doesn't mean you're incapable of doing bad things. It doesn't matter, anyway. It sounds like you did it in a thoughtful way, with just the right amount of guilt and self-consciousness."

"Thanks for acknowledging my virtues."

"Anyway, tell me about her. Susan, right?"

"Right. Susan Vargas."

"She's Hispanic?"

"No. Her husband was. He was a cop. Killed on duty."

"Wow. That's heavy. How long ago?"

"I think she said twelve years. She hasn't shared that with me directly, though. That's part of the conversation I overheard."

"Has she brought it up at all?"

"Yeah, when we had lunch on Saturday. But she didn't go into details."

"So what has she told you directly?"

"Not a whole lot, actually. I mean, we've just had that one spontaneous date. And several exchanged phone messages. I am, though, planning to call her later tonight, so if you'd like me to patch you in..."

"Very funny, Marty.

"And you said she works at Trader Joe's?" Rachel asks.

"Yes, just for a month or so, though. Before that, she was an attorney."

"You're kidding," Rachel responds, in a rare moment of inflecting.

"Not only that, a damn good one apparently. She made partner a few years ago. She went to Harvard Law."

"Harvard?! Damn, how'd she get a job at a grocery store? I mean, wouldn't her being majorly overqualified kind of put a damper on the prospect?"

"It might have, but she's been shopping there for more than twenty years. They know her and they like her, and you know, Joe's is a friendly place!"

"Joe's is a madhouse. You know there's one here now."

"Oh yeah? Where?"

"Union Square. I don't even bother trying. Standing on line to buy groceries is just a bit more than I can take. I really think they should let people make appointments."

"Right, and in L.A., they should assign parking spaces."

"Anyway," Rachel says, as the busboy clears their plates, "I guess if there's a Union Square Trader Joe's cashier with *my* name on him, I'm not likely ever to meet him."

"Are you going to stick with Jack then?"

"I don't know. I think I need to break it off. I think it's time, and I know he'll never do it."

"I'm sorry, Rache. I'm sorry that men are the way they are."

"You can't kill 'em. You can't put 'em in the blender. Oh well."

V

"I'm glad you called," Susan says, "and I gotta admit, I was about to give up on you. Figured you'd be asleep by now."

Martin looks at his watch. It's midnight in his current time zone. "I crashed out this afternoon, so I'm screwed in terms of getting even six hours before tomorrow."

"When do you meet with the so-called 'team?'"

"Nine-thirty," Martin replies, his monotone palpable.

"Well, that's fairly reasonable."

"Just formalities. After Chicago, I have no expectations."

"And the flight was okay?" Susan asks.

"Sure, I—"

The hotel phone rings, interrupting Martin.

"That's bizarre," he says to Susan. "A call on the room phone. Hold on a sec—"

Martin places his cell on the bed and grabs the receiver of the old-fashioned beige console. "Hello?"

"Martin! It's Myra. I'm so glad I caught you! There's been an emergency—"

"Hold on," Martin says.

He picks up his cell. "Susan, it's Myra calling. Some emergency at home. Can I call you back in a bit?"

"Yes! Please!"

"Myra!" Martin says, returning to the hotel phone. "What's going on?"

"Oh, Martin, it's Dude! He's in the hospital. And I need for you to take down their number and call them with your credit card information."

"What happened?"

"He fell from your living room window. He either pushed out the screen or it just came out on its own. Thank God Brittany found him when she came home from work this evening. He was around the corner, beat up and trembling under some shrubbery. It must have happened sometime this afternoon. I saw him around noon when I went in to give him a late breakfast."

"Jeez. So where is he?"

"There's an all-night animal hospital over on Eagle Rock. Brittany drove us over, bless her heart. Anyway, the damage is pretty bad, but I don't think he's going to die."

"God. Thanks, Myra. Uh-yeah, give me that number."

VI

After sharing with Susan the details that he learned from the vet, Martin realizes how beat up Dude must be. Major damage in his pelvic area, a paralyzed tail. One surgery so far, and they'll call Martin on his cell if they need to do more.

"I'm so sorry, Martin," Susan offers, her tone sounding genuinely concerned, but still managing to soothe. "Don't worry, though. That place on Eagle Rock is great. I've been there more than a few times with my old geezers. And, remember, cats are incredibly resilient. It's probably gonna hurt your wallet more than anything."

"I don't care so much about the money," Martin responds. "I just want the little guy to make it home. God, and I'm so pissed at myself! That screen in the living room has been loose for weeks. I should have secured it. There was probably some pigeon taunting Dude from the other side."

"Don't blame yourself, Martin. These things happen."

"I just hope he makes it."

"He will, Martin. He will. I'll stop by there tomorrow before my shift and give him a visit. Hey, when do you fly back? Friday?"

"Yeah. I think the flight gets in sometime in the afternoon."

"Good. I have the day off, so how 'bout I come meet you at LAX, and we can drive from there to the vet's."

"That's okay, Susan. Really, that's very nice, but—"

"I'm sorry," she says, her smile apparent, "did I indicate you had a choice in the matter?"

"Susan—"

"Dig up your e-ticket and give me the four-one-one. Then, we're hanging up. You need to try to get some sleep."

CHAPTER TWENTY-FOUR

I

Martin is relieved when Alex, the firm's Regional Vice President based at the headquarters in Lower Manhattan, informs the new Senior VP of a mid-day emergency.

"Martin, I'm terribly sorry," Alex says in his elegant style. "I have to cancel our lunch due to some issue that has come up. I've just learned that I'll be spending the lunch hour on a transnational conference call."

"That's okay, Alex, and not to worry. I think my sister's office is nearby, so I'll just give her a call."

"Good, then. So I'll see you back here at two?"

"It's a plan. Good luck with the call."

"Thanks, Martin."

II

Exiting the building on Church Street, Martin doesn't feel the least bit guilty regarding his blatant lie. Rachel's office is nowhere near "nearby;" it's somewhere on the upper west side. But Martin didn't want Alex to feel responsible for his new team member's lunchtime happiness. And Martin also didn't want to let on that, by virtue of his sudden unavailability, Alex had actually facilitated his new team member's lunchtime happiness.

Martin doesn't know this part of Manhattan very well, but he is comfortable with his instincts. He'll just wander. He might even forego having a full lunch. The bagels during the morning's meeting were plentiful, and he ate more than usual because he was so damned bored.

After a few blocks, it is quite obvious to Martin where he is, and the place that has come to be called Ground Zero has an interesting vibe. Martin doesn't necessarily slow his pace, but he does take it in: it's an odd combination of construction, carnival, and cemetery. He hears the sounds of heavy machinery working toward a common goal, and in front of that is commerce—entrepreneurs selling memorabilia. Politics exist as well. Or at least, political perspective. There are more than a few individuals using bullhorns to share their opinion of what really happened on that fateful day. Sadness is also apparent, and it should be. Martin sees folks reading names and messages. They're crying and hugging one another.

Battery Park is a welcome site after passing the tourist attraction that was inspired by murder, and as he sits on an available bench, as close as he can get to the river's edge, Martin realizes that he's thinking about Lisa. He also realizes that something changed in her after September 11th. It's as if she knew something intuitively. Long before the conspiracy theorists' opinions became loud and clear. Long before the public availability of the documentary, *Loose Change*, Lisa had expressed her own beliefs.

"It's like the O.J. trial," she said one evening, probably in early October of 2001.

"What are you talking about?"

"Remember the guy? The guy with the skunk hair?"

"I don't know," replied Martin, shaking his head and wondering if the bourbon in Lisa's glass has anything to do with her perceptions.

"The guy with the skunk hair," Lisa reiterated. "He was O.J.'s friend. I think he was with him when they did that run on the freeway. You know, the white bronco bullshit? I don't remember his name. But, anyway, you remember the footage of when the verdict came down?"

"Maybe," Martin replied tentatively.

"Sure you do!" Lisa exclaimed, her emotion fully caught up in the moment. "I mean, who can forget it! Anyway, the skunk-hair guy was standing behind O.J., and when he was deemed 'not guilty,' that guy's face said it all. That guy's face—the guy with the skunk hair—his face said it all. It said, 'the jury got it wrong.'"

"So what's that got to do with the terrorist attacks?"

"It's like that footage they've shown a million times!" Lisa explained. "You know—that footage with Bush reading to those school children."

Martin remembers staring at her then, totally confused by her train of thought and wishing she were not getting up to refill her glass.

"What about that footage?" Martin had asked quietly, his heart hoping that the Lisa he'd married would reappear one of these days.

"Okay," she said, returning to the kitchen table, "you know how it shows someone leaning in and whispering something into Bush's ear?"

"Right."

"And his response is kinda weird. I mean, he doesn't look shocked. He doesn't look sad. He just looks like he's thinking. He's thinking, 'okay, so it's done then.'"

"Lisa," Martin had said, "I don't see how you get all this stuff from that one moment. I don't get it."

"Martin," she replied, her tone more assured than con-spiratorial, "I'm a marketing person. I know from marketing. And right now, this administration is marketing some serious bullshit."

Someone has joined Martin on the Battery Park bench, but because it is New York, that person has given Martin a sufficient amount of personal space. Which is to say, the newcomer is at the other end of the bench.

Martin doesn't look over and smile, but rather closes his eyes. And once they're closed, he realizes that whether or not Lisa was correct, the damage had been done. What happened on September 11th compromised whatever faith she had in the powers-that-be. What happened that day robbed her of an innocence. A few years later, when she became enthusiastic about their starting a family, there was a desperation to her mission. Martin realizes now that Lisa probably did not want a baby. She just wanted something to take her mind off her bitterness. By the time Obama won, and it seemed that the pendulum might finally swing back, it was too late. Too late to repair the damage that their marriage had become.

Martin hopes that Lisa is now on the mend. He hopes, even, that her new man is good and kind. He hopes her new man will take care of her. Sitting on the bench in Battery Park, staring into the Hudson River, Martin realizes that he has crossed a bridge in his thinking.

CHAPTER TWENTY-FIVE

I

If someone had told Martin, four weeks or so ago, that his favorite crew member from Trader Joe's would be meeting him at LAX after a post-promotion business trip to New York, he would have looked at them funny. *Really* funny. But here she is, her smile warm and her arms outstretched, ready to give a comforting hug to her new friend whose cat is in the hospital.

"Welcome home, Martin," Susan says, as they embrace.

"Good flight?" she asks then, standing back to look at him directly.

"Pretty smooth," he responds. "And I was on the Grand Canyon side this time!"

"Smart seating! Isn't it awesome from the air?"

"Yeah," Martin replies, as they follow the signage that will get them out of this hub of travel. "Reminds me that I haven't seen it up close."

"You haven't? Oh my God, you have *got* to put that on your short list!"

II

They're passing the oil-related contraptions that are in the small valley off Stocker, and Susan is cackling in the manner of one who has been there/done that.

"Aren't corporations just so idiotically fucked?" she asks.

"I love a non-rhetorical question," Martin replies, happily riding shotgun in Susan's robin's egg blue VW convertible. "And the answer, of course, is 'yes.'"

"I mean, please, and not that you're not worth it, but how much did your firm spend to send you to New York for a few stupid meetings that had no real purpose?"

"They're idiots. I agree."

Martin smiles and looks at the scenery on his right. He is surprised by how comfortable he feels. It feels... right.

III

When they enter the Eagle Rock Emergency Pet Clinic, it is immediately apparent that Susan is a friend of the family.

"Hey, Susan!" comes a warm salutation from the woman behind the front desk's sliding glass windows.

"Hey, Doris. Damn, you're putting in some hours this week."

"Seems that way, doesn't it? So, is this Dude's Dad?"

"Yup. This is Martin."

Doris opens the window further and extends her hand. "Good to meet you," she says to Martin. "We spoke on the phone the other evening."

"Oh, so you're Dude's Doc?"

"I'm one of them," she replies, smiling.

"How's he doing?" Martin asks.

"Meet me at the door and you can see for yourself."

Doris leaves the admissions cubicle, and a few seconds later, the door that is perpendicular to that cubicle opens.

"Welcome to my lair," the vet says, her relaxed kindness a form of person-to-person valium.

"Your baby is going to be okay," Doris assures him, as the three walk down a small corridor, "but he sure did get banged up. We're going to keep him for a few more days. The most recent surgery—there have been three so far—went well. We just need to monitor his functioning. He's still having trouble passing his bowels, and we're not convinced he's urinating as frequently as he should."

Martin makes a mental note to consider something later... to consider the vocabulary that was bandied about during his second date with Susan.

"Dude!" Martin exclaims, when he sees his little boy, looking as if he had just smoked a joint.

Doris opens the cage so that Martin can stroke his baby.

"Dude," he says again, hoping that the tears don't actually fall from his eyes. "You know, this landing-on-your-feet thing shouldn't actually be tested from such heights."

As Martin pets his groggy, drugged cat, he feels the slightest purr, and he sees the slightest smile. He wishes Dude had the strength right now to roll over for a tummy rub, because Martin knows that's what the cat wants more than anything. But, that'll happen in a few weeks, or maybe even in a few days. Right now, Dude is alive. There's a cast on his back right leg, a gash in his left hip, and he's living on an IV drip. But: Dude is alive.

IV

"It's amazing," Martin says, looking up at the flowering trees as he and Susan inch their way west through the Friday night traffic on Los Feliz Boulevard. "Every year, the jacarandas come out of nowhere. When I left for New York, I hadn't yet seen a bloom. Now, the annual event has begun."

"I love them, too," Susan says, keeping her eye on the brake lights just ahead of her. "But don't *ever* park your car under one."

"Really?"

"Seriously. Your A.C. will be spitting periwinkle for days."

"I'm glad you mentioned that. I'll do my best to avoid them, but where I live, I probably won't have a lot of choice."

"Then invest in a car cover," Susan suggests.

"Hmm... Good idea."

They're at the light at Griffith Park Boulevard. Martin looks at his watch. It's nearly seven already. A part of him wants to invite Susan to dinner, but he also feels too jet-lagged, and too emotionally transported by the visit with Dude, to make any overtures.

"You ever been to Home?" Susan asks, as she accelerates through the green light.

"Is that the restaurant on Hillhurst?"

"Yeah, great vibe. Really comforting. You know, like 'home,' I guess."

"I've walked by it, but no, I've never eaten there. Uh, why? You wanna go?"

"I don't know about you, Martin, but I'm over-the-top starving."

"Let's do it!"

V

"It was beyond hard," Susan is saying, as she dips a waffle fry in the small pool of ketchup that she seems to want to control, space-wise. "I mean, I think for the first year, I pretty much cried every day. I mean, I know that cops' wives need to be ready for that sort of thing, but nothing—oh God, nothing!—can prepare you. It's a dropping feeling. And then this weird blackness."

"How long had you been married?" Martin asks quietly.

"Eight years," she replies. "I was thirty-six when he died. We had just started talking about having kids. I'm kinda glad we hadn't got that far, you know? I'm actually grateful I don't have kids. I don't know, maybe that sounds strange or selfish, but I just know I couldn't have done that alone."

Martin looks across the table at his new friend. She is still shaking her head subtly. She is still trying to control her ketchup pool. She is sweet and kind and a little sad. Martin is endeared by all those qualities.

"So!" Susan says, collecting some energy from deep within her soul and directing a decidedly mood-changing smile in Martin's direction. "I told you mine. What about yours?"

"I'm on the verge of signing divorce papers," Martin offers. "We're just dealing with logistics. No chance of reconciliation. For that matter, she's already lined up her next husband."

"Does that hurt?"

"No," Martin replies, smiling almost impishly when he realizes his nod is genuine. "I actually had an interesting revelation about Lisa when I was in New York, and I feel like I'm on the other side of hurt. I wish her well, and I mean that sincerely."

VI

"You sure you want to walk?" Susan asks, after unlocking her car so that Martin can retrieve his hanging carry-on bag.

"Yeah, it's just a block away, and you're pointed toward home. You've done enough driving today, and I appreciate it. Really."

Susan stands and faces Martin, who holds his hanging bag over his shoulder and who is clearly tired from the trip and the visit to the vet.

"Martin," she begins, her tone matter-of-fact and her smile softening that tone. "I think you're a good man, and I am very glad you shop at Trader Joe's."

Martin smiles and hopes that the nearby streetlight is not emphasizing his blush.

"So," he says, "thanks for all your help today. I think we should have a real date sometime soon. What do you think?"

"I'd like that," Susan replies.

She then puts her hand on his neck and gives him the softest, sweetest kiss on the cheek.

"Goodnight, Martin," she says.

CHAPTER TWENTY-SIX

I

Approaching his office on Monday morning, Martin does a double-take. It's Alice, back from her leave. It's Alice, which means Brenda has been relegated back to the eighth floor.

"Alice!" Martin says, with professionally toned-down quasi-enthusiasm, "I'm glad to see you're back at the firm."

"Hello, Martin," Alice says quietly, looking up at him from the desk that has been her station for two decades. "And thank you for the welcome."

As Martin enters his office, he digests the sad tone of his new assistant's voice. She's had some "R & R," as it were, but she clearly has not recovered. He figures he'll just leave her alone today. Let her gradually establish the energy of her return.

Because he is at his special Senior VP coffee station, pouring his first mug of the day, his back is toward the door when Vivian knocks quickly and then enters.

Martin has barely registered the knock when he hears her voice state his name.

"Martin."

This will not be a good visit, he can tell.

"Vivian!" he exclaims, turning and smiling, hanging on, with sheer will, to the relaxed weekend he had, the time with Susan that preceded it, and his generally improving life outside this income-generating hell.

167

She's carrying her Van Gogh mug, so he doesn't need to offer a cup. But, since he's standing on the relaxed side of the corner office, he decides to proceed from there.

"Have a seat!" he says, taking for himself an individual chair, so that she will be forced to use the couch (the subordinate position within the landscape of VP corner offices).

Vivian sits in the individual chair across the long VP coffee table. She clearly is not in the mood to play anything but equal. She clearly also has a bug up her ass.

"Are you feeling better?" Martin asks. "I hear you had a terrible flu."

"I am better, and I'm not here to talk about that."

"So, what's your agenda, Viv?"

(Martin so does not care at this point.)

"Martin," Vivian says, her lips pursed, her short, dark helmet of hair seeming to be tighter than usual, "we had a discussion about corporate philanthropy here at Haley-Mitchell-Phelps. And, as I shared with you, the firm's agenda is established."

"Right," says Martin, "the United Way, RIF, and MADD. I remember."

He steals a sip of the upper management caffeine while she formulates her next statement.

"Right," she says. "Exactly. So: what I want to know is why you are placing your staff in the uncomfortable position of feeling that their jobs are on the line if they don't support Hollywood runaways."

"I didn't do that, Vivian," Martin responds, evenly. "I just shared some information at a meeting. And, by the way, Debora was thrilled. Her husband's on the board of the organization, so she was already signed up. She also did a really sweet thing, I thought. She offered Cody and his girlfriend a seat at their table."

"And Phil?" Vivian asks, the tilt of her head referencing a probable knot at the top of her neck.

"I don't know Phil, Vivian. He's an enigma to me. Maybe if you have questions for him, you should ask him directly. Look: I got work to do."

Martin stands and carries his coffee mug to his desk. He leans into his computer and moves the mouse. Then, he looks up to confront Vivian eye-to-eye. She has risen from the chair and seems to be debating her next move. She is standing near the door, but has not yet decided to pass through it.

"Anything else?" Martin asks his colleague.

When she attempts to glare at him, there is a vulnerability in her eyes.

"We'll talk later," she says.

"Whatever," Martin mutters to himself, as he logs on to check the email that came in during his trip to New York.

"Good for you," Martin hears, not thirty seconds later. He looks up to see the smiling face of Alice.

"Good for me?" he asks his new and inherited assistant.

"That woman's a bitch!" Alice says, depositing a folder in Martin's in-box before leaving the room.

Watching Alice make her exit, Martin is more perplexed than he has been in a while. In a previous economy, Alice would have retired by now. But, here she is, doing the venerable job of an assistant, willing always to learn the latest on the technological frontier, even though when she first learned everything, carbon paper was a staple. Alice is probably just slightly a generation older than Martin, and for this reason, he has anticipated some odd discomfort between them. Now, though, he revisits that expectation. Their co-working began less than fifteen minutes ago and already... she's congratulated him, and she's uttered the word "bitch."

This partnership might work.

II

Debora has a funny habit of chewing with one hand cupped in the air, about an inch away from her mouth. It makes for belabored lunch conversation, but it's also her way of being considerate. In this moment, she nods as she chews because she clearly can't wait to reach that between-bites place that will allow her to comment.

Finally, the opportunity occurs. "Maybe she's upset because everyone she ever tried to love became a Hollywood runaway."

Martin smiles. "I don't know," he says, "I think there's something more to it. I don't think it's just a personality issue. I mean, the bond with Phil thing. That's kind of odd."

Debora leans in and raises her eyebrows, "Maybe they're having an affair."

"Vivian and Phil? I really can't picture that."

"Or maybe you don't want to," Debora comments, her hamburger primed in front of her mouth, predicting another delay in the dialogue.

"God, I almost forgot!" Martin says suddenly. "I got the strangest call from Barry."

Just above her protective hand, Debora's eyes widen. Martin knows he should keep talking.

"I guess it was a week ago. He called me at home. And, God, it's so sad, he definitely sounded drunk."

Martin reads Debora's eyes and the tilt of her head. They're saying *how could you tell?*

"He was slurring a bit. I heard some clinking."

Now Debora looks perplexed.

"Ice."

Debora nods.

"It was weird, though. He told me to be careful. But he wouldn't elaborate, and he definitely wasn't in a chatting frame of mind. I felt like Woodward getting a scoop from Deep Throat. But it was an empty scoop."

"You know," Debora says, returning the remains of her burger to her plate and covering it all with the white napkin of surrender. "I had a good relationship with Barry. And I know you did, too. Maybe we should take him out to dinner. You know, make it seem casual; no agenda. Maybe we can get some information. We could at least whine about Vivian. He might enjoy that."

"Let me think about it."

III

Sitting at his computer that night, Martin realizes how much he looks forward to Dude's return. Per his telephone conversation earlier in the day with Doctor Doris, it is likely the reunion will occur by the middle of the week, possibly even tomorrow. And there will be a lot of post-op tasks. Martin's not too worried about that, though. He's got neighbors who can help. And then there's Susan.

An email from Zac comes in just as Martin is deleting the bogus missives. **Plans!** is the subject matter of his nephew's communication.

```
uncle marty! just got an email from my dad.
he did his usual internet bargaining and got
a really cheap roundtrip for me. hope its
okay that its kinda soon. flying in on sunday,
may 31. flying back two weeks later (june 14).
please confirm that we're cool with all that.
thanks, Z.
```

Martin is cool with all that, though it is quite soon. It is difficult, at the moment, for Martin to imagine having a houseguest for two weeks.

He has just begun his brief reply when he hears his doorbell. Not expecting anyone, he also doesn't feel surprised to hear the sound that indicates a visitor. His sense of having a home is definitely settling in.

"Brittany!" he says, smiling at the neighbor who has once again changed the color and style of her hair.

She gives him a big bear hug.

"Welcome back, Martin! God, I am so sorry about Dude! Is he going to be okay?"

"Thanks, come in. Yeah, he'll be fine. I'll probably be able to bring him home in the next couple of days. Can I get you anything?"

"You got soda?"

"Sure. Diet Coke?"

"I prefer Mountain Dew, but yeah, D.C. is fine."

Martin chuckles to himself as he opens the refrigerator door. He wonders how often someone just happens to have some Mountain Dew in stock.

"Aw!" says Brittany, sadly staring at the cat plate on the floor. "Dude's dishes."

"Let's go in the living room," Martin suggests, leading the way.

"And, hey, I need to thank you," Martin says, over his shoulder. "I hear you found him that evening."

"Yeah, poor thing," she responds, plopping down onto the couch. "He was really sad when I saw him. Who knows how long he had been there."

"Well, Myra thinks it happened in the afternoon, so he probably hadn't been injured that long."

"Yeah," Brittany picks at the couch for a moment and then takes a swig of soda.

"So did you have a good weekend?" Martin asks, as he sits in the cushioned chair to Brittany's right.

"I did actually," she replies, an impish look on her face. "Guess where I went?"

"Where?"

"Vegas!"

"Wow! Cool! So did you look for Lonzo?"

"No, but guess what happened?"

"You got married?"

She rolls her eyes.

"You saw Elvis?" Martin asks next.

"I saw a shitload of Elvises. That place is crawling with them."

"Okay," Martin says, smiling at the kid who once made a home of Hollywood Boulevard, "I give up. What happened to you in Vegas."

"I won twelve thousand dollars!"

"No way! What, at the tables?"

"Oh God, no. I don't play cards when I'm there. Those people are way too serious for me. I like the machines. Especially when they make a lot of noise."

"I'm guessing the machine you picked did make a lot of noise. That's great!"

"Yeah, it was cool. Of course, I'll be taxed on about half of it, but that's okay. Hell, just coming away from that place ahead is winning!"

Brittany takes another swig from the can of Diet Coke and then points to Martin's TV table.

"Myra told me about your television. What a sad soul that Scott is, huh?"

"You're kind to view him that way," Martin offers.

"So you getting a new one?"

"I thought I would, but now with the Dude expense, I may have to wait a bit."

"The vet bill's gonna be pretty high, I bet," Brittany says.

"A couple thousand, probably."

"Isn't there a pet insurance you can get?" she asks.

"Sure, and there's apartment insurance, too. Problem is, we never think about getting that stuff until after an event."

"Maybe you should just take yourself to Vegas."

"I'm not much of a risk-taker," Martin says.

"I'm not so sure about that," Brittany comments, somewhat assuredly.

Martin is struck by the knowing smile on Brittany's face. He acknowledges—to himself, anyway—that this "kid" probably has some amazing skills in the brain department. She's certainly lived a lot.

"Scuse me," Martin says, when the phone rings. He crosses to his landline and picks up the handset. "Hello?"

"Hi Martin," comes the soothing voice, calling from Silver Lake.

"Susan! Thanks for returning my call. Uh, I have a guest here—my neighbor Brittany..."

Brittany stands up, mouths *it's okay*, and begins to head for the door.

"And apparently," Martin says, smiling at Brittany while speaking into the phone, "you've scared her off!"

"I can call back," offers Susan.

"It's okay," Martin says, waving in reply to Brittany's playful blowing of a kiss, "we were just catching up."

"Anyway," Martin says next, relaxing into the couch. "How was your weekend?"

"Didn't really have one. I worked both days. The later shift."

"My condolences."

"So what's the latest on Dude?" Susan asks.

"I spoke with Doctor Doris today. Dude should be coming home in a few days."

"That's good to hear. When I got your message, I got a little worried."

"Nope," Martin replies. "No worries. A very wise woman once told me that cats are incredibly resilient."

Susan's smile is audible.

"Anyway," Martin continues, "I wasn't calling about Dude. I was calling about an event, wondering if you might join me."

"What is it? And when?"

"It's an agency that serves runaway youth here in Hollywood. In fact, my neighbor Brittany—the one who was just here—is going to be honored. She's an alum. She's also the one who found Dude last week."

"I'd support her for either reason. When is it?"

"The twentieth," Martin says. "A week from Wednesday."

"Sign me up. I don't have my work schedule in front of me, but I can always trade with someone if necessary. Where is it? One of the Bev Hills hotels?"

"I think so. I need to check the invitation. Anyway, I've already purchased two tickets, so we're good to go. I'm glad you can join me!"

"I look forward to it, but in the meantime..."

Martin is intrigued. It sounds like Susan might want to see him before the twentieth.

"Yes?" he asks her.

"Let me know when Dude's ready to come home, will ya?"

"Absolutely."

"Oh, damn," Susan says, "that's a call coming in. I need to take that. Anyway, Martin, let me know about Dude and I'll clear my calendar for the event. Goodnight!"

"Goodnight, Susan," Martin replies, not sure if she heard it and also not concerned.

CHAPTER TWENTY-SEVEN

I

"Martin!" Debora calls, emerging from her Prius just as he hits the alarm on his remote and causes his BMW to chirp. He stands in the middle of the lot, and smiles as she approaches.

"Morning," he says.

"Did you think any more about the Barry idea I mentioned yesterday at lunch?"

"Actually, no. Nothing personal, but I promptly forgot about it."

Debora tilts her head and smiles. "Good for you," she says. "Proves you have a life."

"I think I'm starting to acquire one."

"Well," Debora says, her heels sounding particularly loud as they cross toward the elevators, "I've got another item for you to ruminate."

"Shoot."

"And let's stop for a minute," she says, emphasizing the suggestion by placing her hand on his shoulder.

Martin turns and faces her directly. His curiosity is apparent in his face.

"Len had a board meeting last night. With the runaway place. Their CFO has just given notice."

"Okay," says Martin, not sure where Debora's going with this bit of information.

"I'd consider it myself, but with Len on the board, I don't think that would be kosher. Besides, he's given me the heads up on a financial job that might be opening at Children's Hospital."

"What are you getting at?"

"I don't know about you, Martin, but I am *over* this place."

"You're planning to leave?"

"A S A P, and I don't know, it's funny, Len always tells me that I get very bossy when I want to make a change. I assume that because I want to do something different, everybody else should, too. But, Martin, think about it. Vivian is not going anywhere, and she's totally got it in for you. You want to come to work every day with that on your plate? Besides, until they get a Regional Vice President—and who the hell knows if they will—she's going to view herself as top banana."

"Debora, I just got a promotion, I—"

"Look, Martin, I know we're not two colleagues with a lot of history, and with you being 'my boss'"—(a statement compelling Debora to use air quotes)—"I am completely out of line in speaking with you this candidly, but come on, wouldn't you rather do the numbers-crunching game for a *good* cause?"

Martin smiles at Debora and prompts their continued walk to the elevator. "We'll see," is all he can say.

II

When they arrive at the first floor's elevator banks that will take them up to work, Martin is surprised by his own warm reaction to seeing his former assistant. Brenda enters his embrace as naturally as he initiates it.

"So you're back on eight!" Martin says.

"Yup," says Brenda, clinging—in a strangely tight manner—to the scarf she has draped over her shoulders. It's an unusual fashion statement, and there's something about Brenda that seems distracted.

"Is there anything for you to do yet?" Martin asks.

178

"I'm kinda helping Vicky these days," Brenda replies dully, as they enter the elevator together. "Phil's got a big project apparently.

"Oh shit!" Brenda says then, after dropping her cell phone.

When she reaches down to pick it up, Martin notices odd bruises at the top of her arm. Two purple dots, each the size of a dime.

Standing and again clinging to the large scarf that she wears like a shawl, Brenda stares at her phone. "I hope it isn't broken," she says, her voice faltering.

III

Martin has had his office door closed most of the morning. He is feeling a little overwhelmed. It isn't his workload that overwhelms him—not by a longshot. It's everything that happened between the time he activated his car alarm and emerged, ten minutes later, on the ninth floor.

Maybe Debora has a point, and maybe—without knowing it or meaning to—she drove home that point when she used air quotes to punctuate "my boss." He doesn't believe that she was being disrespectful. Debora is inherently respectful. She's a classy woman who clearly thinks things through. She also takes pride in her intuition. She let Martin know that morning that she's looking to move on, and she presented a good case for doing so. The firm is bullshit. The firm is misery. The firm is about creating work—and profit—by doing something for people (and specifically, their money) that they believe they cannot do for themselves.

Martin also is worried about Brenda. Those bruises. The moment he saw them, he envisioned a pinch. The moment he saw them, he remembered the tone that followed her initial excitement when she announced her engagement to her boyfriend of five years. What was his name? Doesn't matter. Martin has a bad feeling, though. And he worries about Brenda. They did a lot of bonding during their couple of weeks together on the ninth floor. He came to feel protective of her.

And what was her comment about Phil having a big project? As Phil's boss (Martin envisions air quotes in this moment, and he envisions them being rendered by Vivian), Martin knows that Phil does not, in fact, have a big project currently. Maybe it's something he's doing for someone else. Maybe this project has something to do with the weekly lunches that he and Vivian have. Martin wonders if she takes him to the Smokehouse. Might as well, with all the smoke she blows...

Martin goes online and finds the website of the runaway organization. It comes up immediately, and its graphics are impressive. There's even cool music that somehow is in complete sync with the changing photographs. The menu on the side has a JOBS link, and he clicks on it. Sure enough, the CFO job is there—posted just yesterday, apparently. Martin clicks on the announcement to reach the details.

```
Position: Chief Financial Officer (CFO)
Preferable Start Date: Monday, June 15th
Salary: Commensurate with experience
Benefits: Generous

HRHY is pleased to announce that it is cur-
rently accepting resumés for a top manage-
ment position. The Chief Financial Officer,
who reports to the Executive Director and
serves on the five-person executive team, is
responsible for overseeing all aspects of the
organization's financial operations. Supervis-
ing a staff of two, the CFO will bring to
this position knowledge of budgets, accounts
receivable, accounts payable, general ledger,
etc. The CFO will be the primary contact to
financial liaisons representing funders and
banks. Staffing the Finance Committee of the
Board of Directors, the CFO will also ensure
that the agency's annual audit is scheduled
and completed efficiently.

Interested individuals are encouraged to sub-
mit their C.V.'s and three business references
electronically to:  ldelgado@hrhy.org.
```

Martin stares at the screen. He realizes he needs three business references, and he needs them fast.

IV

"This was delivered while you were out," Alice says to Martin, smiling as he approaches and handing him a large manila envelope.

"Yeah?" he says, accepting the package. "I wasn't expecting any—"

He cuts himself off when he sees the return address. It's from Lisa's divorce lawyer.

"Thanks, Alice," Martin says, his voice the equivalent of a poker face.

Martin's glad he had kept his door closed all morning. Closing it now will not seem unusual. And once he's done that, he begins tearing open the package.

He grabs a bottle of water from his mini-fridge and sits on his VP couch. He peruses the details. It's all pretty basic for the first page or so. *Irreconcilable Differences,* of course. He wonders how high in the ninetieth percentile column that reasoning scores.

A few pages in, he does a double-take. No alimony? This is different from where things were going a few months back. A few months back, Lisa was making noise about alimony. She was making noise about getting some compensation "for all the shit" she had had to put up with. A few months back, Lisa was trying to convince the judicial system that the individual in this dissolution who had put up with all the shit was her.

"Weird," says Martin, as he makes a beeline for his desk and the computer that is its centerpiece.

He logs onto his personal email account, and he immediately finds the couple of bold messages from Lisa—the ones he chose not to open. He opens them now. On April 9th, Lisa wrote:

```
Hi Martin,

Sorry to be bothering you there in cyberspace.
Just wanted to let you know that I've re-
thought the whole alimony idea. It's okay. I
don't need for you to write me a check every
```

```
month. I was just feeling hurt and disap-
pointed, you know?

Anyway, I'll be talking with my lawyer in the
morning, so we'll revise the specifics.

I really do hope you're well.

Thanks for being my husband for so many years.

XO, Lisa
```

XO, Martin thinks to himself. "Ex-oh," he says aloud. "She's about to be my ex. Oh?"

He opens the subsequent email, which came just over two weeks later.

```
Hi again, Martin,

I guess I don't blame you for not returning my
calls or emails. Nothing new to report, re-
ally. Just wanted to touch base. According to
Malcolm, the papers are in the works, so we
should be "official" fairly soon.

I think of you often, and I wish good
thoughts.

XXO, Lisa
```

"Ex-ex," Martin says, chuckling to himself. "That's two divorces and no alimony. I may have made an L.A. record."

V

The quick buzz on his office phone's console jolts Martin out of an afternoon reverie.

"Yes, Alice?" he asks, depressing the old-fashioned boss/secretary button.

"A Doctor Doris is on line one," Alice states, her tone an indication of her having been at that meeting way back when—that meeting where the existing phone system's intercom feature was introduced as the wave of the future.

"Thanks, Alice," Martin says, congenially.

He then presses the button for line one. "Doctor Doris!"

"Dude's Dad!" she replies.

"Speaking," he says with a casual smile. "So how's my boy?"

"Your boy is still a little lethargic, but we think that home is the best place for him right now."

"Really?" Martin responds, feeling more relieved than he could have imagined. "So I can pick him up this evening?"

"Yes," says Doctor Doris. "And, of course, we're 24/7, so 'whenever' is technically fine, but if you could get here before eight, which is when I leave, I would really prefer that. There are a lot of details to review. You're going to need to do some 'ministering,' and—forgive me, I'm being prejudiced here—but the other folks on duty don't always give all the details that I think they should."

"Doctor Doris," Martin says, "I will absolutely make every effort to get there before eight. Thank you! Thank you for being such a nice vet. I appreciate it."

"Hope to see you later, Mr. Sheffield."

Just as soon as Martin hangs up with Doctor Doris, he immediately calls Susan. It's three-thirty now, and after four rings, Martin guesses she's still at Joe's.

"Hello?" comes her response. Her voice breathless. Her "hello" curious.

"Susan! God! You must have just walked in the door!"

"Who's calling please?"

"It's... Martin."

"Martin! Oh my God! Sorry to sound so officious. I *did* just get home from a weird eight to three shift, and today was a fucking madhouse of customers with serious attitude problems.

"It was so fucking weird," Susan continues, obviously needing to vent, "I swear, at one point, I turned to the manager on duty and *begged* him to give out prozac at the tasting station back by the eggs. I swear! We had nothing but freaks today. And they were *all* angry."

"So are you missing your job at the law firm?"

Susan laughs. "Oh no! Not in a lifetime.

"Oh, shit!" she says then.

"Susan?"

"Sorry, I just spilled some Smartwater on my chair. Fuck."

Martin is enjoying this exchange thoroughly. He loves it that the sweet woman he first met by eavesdropping on her cordial chat room offerings drops the "f-bomb" every chance she gets. Probably something she picked up at Harvard Law...

"Anyway, Susan?"

"Yes, Martin, I'm so sorry."

"Dude's coming home!"

"That's great!" Susan exclaims, her voice trilling and melting at the same time. "Tonight, you mean?"

"Yeah. I just talked to Doctor Doris. She hopes that I can get there before eight, which is when she leaves."

"Oh, Martin. I'm so glad. Your little boy pulled through."

"He did!"

"So, can I help you?"

"How do you mean?" Martin asks.

"Get him home. I have a hunch it's a two-person job."

VI

It's just after seven, and Doctor Doris is explaining the aftercare.

"You'll need to swab this wound twice daily," she explains, using a Q-tip to demonstrate the process of spreading an antibiotic throughout and within the one-inch deep hole in Dude's right hip.

Martin watches carefully. He can't remember ever having this sense of responsibility.

"I also recommend that you palpate his bladder area regularly. Here," Doctor Doris says, reaching for Martin's hand. "Let me show you."

Martin allows his hand to be placed on Dude's fur, in the vicinity—apparently—of his bladder.

"Do you feel that?" Doctor Doris asks.

"I'm not sure what I'm supposed to be feeling."

"At the moment, it's relatively full. So, hopefully, he'll be urinating within the next couple of hours. Anyway, I want you to—if you can—log what you're feeling now, and just be sure that it goes down from there."

"Want me to check, too?" Susan offers.

Martin gives her a look that conveys his being at a total loss.

Susan puts her hand on Dude, just past where his leg joins the rest of his body. "Okay," she says to her friend, Doris, "so what I'm feeling right now is what—? Three-quarters of a tank?"

Doctor Doris laughs.

"Exactly," the good veterinarian says.

VII

For the first five minutes or so, they ride in silence. Martin at the wheel of his BMW; Susan shotgun and Dude on her lap.

They're now on Fletcher, just about to make the right onto Glendale/Rowena.

"Sorry I'm so quiet, Martin," Susan offers.

"No apology necessary," he replies. "I'm a little preoccupied myself."

"Dude's gonna be okay," she comments reassuringly, stroking the cat's chin and chest, and causing Dude to lift up a forearm—his sign of begging for something close to a tummy rub.

Martin notices as Susan accommodates Dude's need. He also notices as the light turns red at Silver Lake Boulevard.

"Oh, my," Susan says.

"What?" Martin asks quietly, bringing the car to a stop at the intersection.

"Good news" she announces, smiling tentatively and not raising her tone of voice. "He pee'd!"

VIII

Martin appreciates that while he and Susan have not—technically speaking—been on a real date, this third rendezvous has led them to his apartment, and she has taken off her pants. He didn't watch that particular action, of course. She took them off privately, in the bathroom. And while "slipping into something more comfortable" could justifiably be checked off on a list of potential reasons as to why Susan changed clothes, the typical meaning of that phrase—when a man and a woman are alone— rarely conjures up an image of a pair of jeans partially soaked through in cat pee.

Susan's jeans, which she rinsed through in the tub, are now hanging from Martin's shower curtain rod, and she has donned the sweats that he was relieved he had washed recently. Martin, too, has changed out of his previous costume, and they are both sitting on the carpeted living room floor, watching Dude.

"Do you think we should feel his bladder area now," Susan asks, "since we know it's empty?"

"I suppose," Martin says. "I'm still not quite sure what I'm feeling."

Technically speaking, on their not-a-third-date, Susan and Martin do not hold hands. But, sitting on the carpeted living room floor, dressed in matching sweats, their hands touch for more than a few seconds. And Martin knows exactly what he's feeling.

CHAPTER TWENTY-EIGHT

I

Walking briskly on Ventura Boulevard, during his lunch hour on Thursday, Martin realizes that he has established a new routine. Whereas before, he used to hole-up in his office, eating a sandwich or a salad he had grabbed quickly from the building's lobby-level deli, he is now spending his lunch hour walking. And, beginning today, he made the wise decision to remove not only his jacket, but also his tie, before he left the building.

He also has begun taking his lunch hour later in the day. He likes returning to the office at two-thirty. It means he's just got three to three-and-a-half hours to go. And, if he gets to three-thirty or so and still feels frustrated, he injects a little mantra: *If I got through "The English Patient,"* he says to himself, *I can get through this. If I got through...*

Martin never could understand how completely moved Lisa had been by that movie. As far as he was concerned, it was a story about spoiled rich people. For Lisa, though, it was a four-Kleenex experience. Martin smiles as he recalls the different moods they were entertaining as they left the theatre. He was thinking about nearly three hours of his life that he would never get back. She was still in some place—some ethereal place to which the movie had taken her.

Martin hopes that Lisa's new husband will like the movies that Lisa likes. It will make things more peaceful for both of them.

Having pressed the crosswalk button, Martin is waiting to make his way back to the north side of Ventura. Gazing around, he notices the pita place on the corner across the Boulevard. He sees a couple, sitting at one of the outside tables. It's Brenda, Martin is sure. It's Brenda and a man. Her fiancé? Must be. They seem to be deeply involved in a conversation.

As the light begins blinking (telling him not only to walk but to walk within so many seconds), and as he crosses the street, Martin decides to make a point of not noticing them. Sunglasses come in handy at times like these.

II

"My goodness, Martin," Vivian says, coming up behind him at the elevator banks that will take them to the ninth floor, "you're looking awfully casual this afternoon."

"I, uh, don't like dressing up for a lunchtime walk, Vivian," Martin replies, entering the elevator ahead of her.

She is smiling, but her severely-plucked brows are raised *over* the top of her eyeglass frames as she follows him into the upwardly-mobile cubicle.

"I just wonder how that would look if you ran into a client," Vivian states, with a telling lack of inflection.

Martin presses the 9 button and doesn't make eye contact. "Maybe it would make me look approachable," he says quietly.

Standing with his hands clasped behind him and his attention directed to the elevator's indicator lights above the now-closed doors, Martin continues. "I realize we might not be going for 'approachable' at Haley-Mitchell-Phelps, but what the hell, Viv—" He looks at her now: "Isn't there something to be said anymore for shock value?"

Vivian's expression is one Martin has never witnessed before. Vivian is at a loss.

III

Back in his office with the door closed, Martin thinks about what he saw when he passed the pita place. That guy... that guy talking to Brenda must have been her fiancé. And Martin draws this conclusion not because the guy was treating her with tenderness and not because they were engaging in some public display of affection. Rather, because he was scolding her. He was chewing her out. And she was begging for his understanding and forgiveness.

Martin calls Brenda's extension. He knows he'll get her voicemail, as it is unlikely that she's returned yet. But he wants to leave a message while the idea is fresh. Accordingly, after the beep: "Brenda, it's Martin! I miss you! So... how 'bout I take you out to lunch. Are you available tomorrow? I know Fridays are often pre-planned, lunchwise, but if you're available, let's go out!"

IV

At a quarter 'til five, Martin's intercom buzzes. It is the ever-efficient Alice, announcing a call on line one from Dennis McPhee.

"Thanks, Alice!" Martin says.

"Dennis!" Martin exclaims into the receiver, greeting his former mentor in the Midwest, "isn't it happy hour downstairs? What are you doing still in the office?"

"I'm not in the office, actually. I'm at LaGuardia. Waiting for a flight back to Chicago. What's up?"

"Well, Dennis," Martin says, smiling, "after twelve years at Haley-Mitchell-Phelps, I'm actually looking at other possibilities, so I'm alerting my potential references."

"You're a brave soul," Dennis responds, his tone having gone from easy to ominous.

"How do you mean?"

"In this market?"

"I'm actually looking to get out of the market, Dennis. I'm looking at a CFO position at a nonprofit organization."

"What, did you win the lottery or something?"

"I know I'll take a pay cut," Martin admits, not caring. "Anyway, can I count on you to sing my praises?"

"Of course you can, Martin. Oh—hold on, I think that's an announcement about my flight."

Martin waits for ten seconds or so before Dennis returns.

"Look," Dennis says, "thanks for the heads-up. If I get a call, I'll pitch you, okay? I gotta run."

"Thanks, Dennis."

Martin hangs up and looks at the telephone. Because he doesn't believe for a minute that Dennis needed to wrap up the conversation so quickly, Martin is struck by the dynamic that caused the dialogue to end: Dennis is not interested in hearing about what Martin wants to do next. Dennis is not interested in hearing about why Martin is considering leaving "the market." Dennis *is* the market. It is all he knows, and it is probably all he will ever know. Whatever exists outside of that market actually doesn't exist. Or at least, it doesn't exist for Dennis.

V

Martin has no choice but to park under a jacaranda tree. The good news is that it's a very short walk home. As he approaches Vermont Avenue, he sees Brittany and Jason sauntering down to the building.

Martin is waiting for the light, but he doesn't want to miss them.

"Brittany! Jason!" he calls out, waving his right arm broadly.

While Martin surprises himself with his willingness to blurt out their names, the energy behind that spontaneous moment does not seem to distract any passers-by. As for Brittany and Jason, they both turn and smile, and Brittany—being Brittany—waves and jumps around as they wait for Martin to cross the street.

VI

"Oh, Dude!" Brittany exclaims, as she enters Martin's living room and sees the recuperating cat on the floor.

She immediately drops down to his level, and within a few seconds, she is lying on the floor facing him.

"How ya doin', Dude?" Brittany is asking the cat whose bladder may or may not be at a quarter tank.

"Oh, Martin," she says then, rolling away in such a way that she stops just long enough to seem to be asking for a tummy rub, "how lucky is this cat to have you!"

Brittany suddenly pops up off the floor, gymnast style.

"That cat," Martin responds, "is also lucky to have you. Don't forget that.

"Hey," Martin says, heading to the kitchen. "Can I get you guys anything? Soda?"

"Whatever ya got!" says Jason.

"Well," says Martin, returning with a can of soda balanced on his palm, "I got Mountain Dew for Mizz Brittany—"

"OMG, Martin!" she exclaims, grabbing the can.

"Hey," Martin says, "it's important to have what your friends drink. Jason?"

"I love it," says Jason, smiling, as Brittany pops the top. "Martin, you probably don't have what I want to drink, but—hell—a Mountain Dew?"

"I've got Diet Coke," Martin offers, shrugging.

"You're getting warmer," Jason responds, his tone wry. "Sure. I'll take a Diet Coke."

VII

Martin appreciates the time that Jason is taking to formulate his response. Martin also notices how Brittany watches her friend. Her respect for him is evident.

"I wish there *were* something you could do," Jason says finally. "Because, just from what you've told us, your hunch is probably correct. And even though I don't know Brenda, I hate the thought of any woman entering into a marriage with a man who is abusive."

Jason turns in that moment and looks at Brittany. She's returned to a prone position on the floor. She is no longer facing Martin and Jason. She is only facing Dude. And she is petting him very gently. Without words, she has told her human friends

191

to go ahead with their conversation. Without words, she has indicated that she would rather not participate.

"I realize I can't come out and ask her," Martin says, "but is there something I can do to—I don't know—approach the subject?"

"It's tricky," Jason replies. "You said you're having lunch with her tomorrow?"

"Yeah. She was actually really cheerful when she returned my call this afternoon."

"Good. That's good. And I think your best bet? When you have lunch? Keep it as cheerful as possible. If you want to 'get at' something, ask her about the wedding plans. See where that leads you."

Martin then follows Jason's gaze. He's looking at Brittany. And Jason's face is filled with caring and love.

The first few times he saw them together, Martin wondered if Brittany and Jason were "an item." He no longer entertains that question. Rather, he sees them as two people who look out for each other in the best possible way. And for each of them, the other is a gift.

CHAPTER TWENTY-NINE

I

Having just grabbed his jacket off the coat hook on the back of his office door, Martin has a near head-on with Vivian.

"Jeez, Viv!" he says, noticing the bit of coffee sloshing in her Van Gogh mug.

"I need to talk to you, Martin," Vivian says, her tone stern.

"Sorry, I've got a lunch appointment."

"Call them and tell them you'll be fifteen minutes late."

"No can do, Vivian," Martin says, smiling as he stands still and extends an arm that is meant to direct her back from whence she came.

Vivian reluctantly backsteps into Alice's work area, providing Martin with just enough space to pull shut his office door.

"I should be back by two o'clock," he tells Vivian. "If you want to meet then, we can... I think, anyway. Um, Alice?"

Alice, who is grinning broadly, looks up from her computer screen, "Yes, boss?"

"Am I available at two?"

"Let me check. Uh—"

Alice saves and closes the document that she is working on. She begins to go into the Accessories menu, but she stops. She then quietly swivels in her chair. "Vivian?" she says meekly, her shoulders conveying a sense of servitude as she otherwise confronts the bitch with the Van Gogh mug, "you know, I came into this business just around the time of the typewriter's automatic return feature. I have a little trouble manipulating my software when someone is looking over my shoulder."

"Oh, Alice," Vivian responds, patting the shoulder of the inherited assistant who is post-retirement age and would no doubt be living in San Diego now if only the economy had not gone sour, "I am so sorry."

Vivian, smiling tightly, steps to the other side of Alice's desk. As she stands there, cradling her mug, she tilts her head in a way that is indisputably condescending. Martin continues to stand just outside his door. He can see Alice's screen, but because he is standing at a sufficient distance, he cannot be accused of looking over her shoulder.

"Damn! Boss!" Alice says, after clicking a few buttons. She is now looking at the opening spread on her computer's next game of FreeCell Solitaire.

"Martin," she says, still staring at the screen and shaking her head from side to side, "you've got back-to-back phone meetings all afternoon!"

Alice closes the screen and turns to her boss. "You sure you have time for this lunch appointment?"

"Duty calls!" Martin responds.

"Viv," he says, as he begins to head away from their little impromptu confab, "I'm finding these days that email is the best first step. Send me a message, okay?"

II

"So things are okay with Alice?" Brenda asks, dabbing into her salad in a noncommittal fashion.

"Alice is surprising," Martin offers. "She's a lot more hip than I would have predicted, that's for sure."

"Hip!" Brenda says, smiling at her former boss. "I would never expect you to use that word!"

Martin shrugs as he looks into the eyes of his former assistant. He can't tell if the sadness there is real or if he is imagining it.

He shrugs again and takes another bite of his turkey sandwich.

"So!" he says, returning the sandwich half to its proper place and reaching for his iced tea, "how are the wedding plans going?"

Brenda looks down suddenly.

"Brenda?"

A saline film covers her eyes when she looks up.

"I'm so sorry," Martin says, quietly. "Did something happen?"

Brenda puts her fork down, and she places her hands in her lap. "I love Mike so much," she tells the table's edge. "I do. But," she looks at Martin then, a tear slowly rolling out of her left eye, "I don't know. I just don't know."

Martin is quietly amazed by what is happening right now. And he is really glad he had that discussion with Jason. He will not ask a specific question. He'll just go with the flow of the conversation.

"Well, you know, Brenda," he says, "I just got out of a long marriage myself."

"Did you know going in?"

"What do you mean?"

"Did you know it wouldn't work?"

"Oh, God, no," Martin responds, "I thought it would last forever. I mean, that's what those vows are all about, right? *But:* looking back? There were plenty of signs. Plenty of indicators that we would not always be able to communicate on an equal level—that we would not always be able to work things out."

"Like what?"

"I don't want to get into that," Martin states firmly, picking up his sandwich again. As he takes a bite and chews, he understands more clearly Jason's advice. This stuff between two people is personal. Really, really personal.

Brenda stabs at her salad—a sesame chicken concoction that is destined for a doggie bag. "I'm just kinda dreading telling my parents," she says.

"Why?" Martin asks.

"They love Mike!"

"You don't need to marry the man your parents love, Brenda. I mean, if you do, then—I don't know, move to some third world country, adopt a mom and dad, and let them make arrangements with another mom and dad."

When Brenda laughs—loudly and genuinely—Martin is relieved. Because, just as that statement emerged from his lips, he immediately regretted having made it.

III

Walking the couple of blocks back toward the office building, Martin and Brenda pass a flower vendor. Martin stops, asks how much, and buys two yellow roses.

As they step away from the transaction, Martin hands one of the roses to Brenda.

"For you," he says, smiling.

"Oh, Martin," Brenda replies, accepting the gift in a hand already occupied by a rectangular Styrofoam container that holds seven-eighths of her lunchtime salad. "That's so sweet."

She then catches his sidelong glance in a conspiratorial way. "So?" she asks. "Who's the other one for?"

"The other one is for Alice," Martin replies.

"That's sweet," Brenda says. "Hey, by the way, I've been meaning to tell you. You look really good. You've lost some weight, huh?"

"Twenty pounds," Martin reports.

"Good for you," Brenda says, as they near the entrance to their building. "Can I ask you a personal question?"

"Weight Watchers," Martin replies, as if that would answer any pending inquiries. "I didn't join or anything. Just got all the inside scoring info from my older sister."

Off Brenda's scolding smile, Martin says, "What? That wasn't your question?"

"No," Brenda replies. "It's a bit more personal than that."

"Ask away. Answering is another matter."

"Do you have a girlfriend?"

Martin smiles and shakes his head just a bit.

"What?" Brenda says, glancing up at her former boss. "And look at you getting all red!"

"Look at you!" Brenda says again, putting her free hand on his arm and thereby enforcing their full stop fifteen or so feet in front of the office building's main entrance.

"Martin," she says, her smile revealing more girl than she revealed during their lunch, "it's a simple question.

"What?" she asks then, much more quietly. "Are you gay?"

Martin laughs. "I'm not gay, Brenda. I'm just amused."

"Okay," Brenda says, laughing (sort of) with him, "so you're amused. But you haven't told me... Girlfriend?"

"I don't know."

"Martin! You either do or you don't have a girlfriend!"

"Brenda, my dear," Martin says, taking her arm as if he were Paul Heinreid and she Bette Davis, "I've come to learn that there are a lot of advantages to being my age.

"And," Martin adds, as they get within a foot of the interminably spinning revolving door, "not knowing whether or not I have a girlfriend could be one of them."

CHAPTER THIRTY

I

Dude doesn't rebel as Martin swabs the antibiotic into the inch-deep hole in the cat's right hip. The routines, Martin realizes, are getting easier.

Putting the Q-tip aside, he checks Dude's bladder area. And then, sitting there on the floor of the living room, Martin starts to laugh. He still has no earthly idea what he's feeling for. Not a clue. But... he goes through the motions.

When the phone rings, Martin leaps to the opportunity to answer some other call.

"Martin!" the caller states, enthusiastically.

He's not able immediately to place the voice.

"Yes?" he says, "who's calling?"

"Martin, it's Debora. Debora from work. Sorry to be calling you at home, and I know you didn't give me your number..."

"Debora, it's okay, actually, but who did give you my number?"

"Brad," she says, tentatively. "You know? My uber-assistant?"

"Right," says Martin, chuckling as he makes his way into the kitchen to refill his coffee mug. "I've become increasingly appreciative of the resourcefulness of office assistants.

"So," Martin says, "that's cool that he gave you my number. Did he tell you why you would be calling me on a Saturday morning?"

"Ha-ha," Debora replies.

Martin is smiling as he returns to the living room with a full cup of coffee and a fine night ahead.

"It's about the event this coming Wednesday," Debora says.

"What about it? And, hey, what happened with Cody? Are he and his girlfriend joining you?"

"Yes," Debora replies, "and I thought that would complete our table, but two of our usual couple friends have bowed out, so we're looking at four seats to fill."

Martin is sitting on the floor now. Maybe he does this to feel closer to Dude. Maybe he does this to feel as fit as Brittany. It doesn't matter. He's sitting on the floor. And, at the moment, he has a follow-up question for Debora.

"Four seats?" he asks, taking a swig of his coffee. "Is that usual?"

"It's not. But I think the nonprofit screwed up. On the other hand, you know what? I don't blame them in a way. I don't blame them for not seeing it coming. The timing, though, really sucks. Wednesday night is the *American Idol* final. I mean, who wants to be away from their living room—or the Nokia Theatre—on that particular night? You know what I mean?"

"I don't watch that show," Martin states, realizing that he somehow managed a several-week holiday from any mention of this bizarre national obsession.

"That might be smart of you," Debora replies. "Regardless, do you know what I want to say to these people?"

(Martin envisions Debora twirling her hair.)

"TiVo!" she exclaims. "You don't have to pass up this opportunity to support the Hollywood Runaway and Homeless Youth Network. Just put that damn show on TiVo!

"I mean, Martin," Debora continues, "these two couples who have canceled... I mean, I *know* they have TiVo."

Martin, who would need a TV even to have TiVo, doesn't know what to say. For that matter, he doesn't know what Debora wants from him. It suddenly occurs to him that the not-knowing might be his ticket to moving this conversation toward some sort of conclusion.

"So, Debora," Martin says, "what can I do for you?"

"Well," Debora says, "I'm looking to fill four seats."

"Mmm," says Martin, thinking. "I had lunch with Brenda yesterday. Maybe if you extended one to her."

"Doesn't she have a boyfriend?"

"Not sure. Offer her one or two. See what happens."

"Okay," Debora says. "And what about you?"

"What about me?"

"How many tickets did you purchase?"

"Two. I'll be bringing my friend, Susan."

"Would you two like to join us, then?" Debora asks.

Martin doesn't need to spend a lot of time considering this proposition. Given the likelihood that Debora and Len's table will be in a prime location, and given the opportunity it will provide for Martin to chat with at least one HRHY board member, it's a no-brainer.

"That'd be great, Debora. Thank you."

"By the way," he says, "did I tell you I looked into that CFO job?"

"You did?" Debora responds, her energy down a notch.

"I checked out the online description and studied the organization's website a bit."

"So are you going to go for it?"

"I think so. I've been making some calls to get my references together, and hopefully, I'll have a chance this weekend to bring my resumé up to date. It's weird. I haven't played the job search game in twelve years. Longer, actually. H-M-P recruited me."

After a short pause, Martin feels a strange wave of discomfort.

"Are you there?" he asks.

"Oh, yeah, sure. Sorry. Something just distracted me. Anyway, thanks for helping me work out this table thing."

"Not a problem," Martin replies. "Let me know what Brenda says."

"I will. I'll ask her on Monday."

"Cool. Have a good rest of your weekend."

"I will. You, too, Martin. 'Bye."

"See ya."

After he hangs up, Martin begins to second-guess his disclosure. He wonders if he should have told Debora about his plans to apply for that job. He shakes away his concern, and reminds himself that it was Debora's idea. His phone rings again. As he retrieves the handset, he suspects a caller with a script – the alleged final notice on his car's nonexistent warranty...

"Yes?"

"Martin, it's Debora again."

"What's up? Did another couple pull out?"

"No. I just wanted to explain something. I know I sounded kind of weird there at the end of our conversation."

"You sounded distracted," Martin states.

"Right. I, uh—the thing is, I was starting to think about going for that job myself. I don't know. I had a talk with Len about it, and he didn't think my being his wife would be an issue. But, you know, I also have that lead on a likely opening at Children's Hospital, and hell, if I start looking seriously, there will be lots of possibilities."

"Debora, it's an open market. If you want to go for the job, go for the job."

"No, Martin. I think I'll pass. Besides, I was going to list you as a reference. I can't very well list my competitor as a reference, can I?"

"That might send a strange signal," Martin responds, smiling.

"Anyway," Debora says, "sorry to bother you again. I just wanted to explain myself."

"I appreciate it."

II

Martin is sifting through his more casual button-down shirts when the doorbell rings.

"Damn," he says, heading out of the bedroom, "It's like Grand Central Station in here."

In the building's hallway, Brittany is bouncing and clapping. "Yay!" she says, "You're home!"

Martin grins at the ever-cheerful former runaway. "So, what's up?" he asks.

"I have a surprise for you," she replies, smiling broadly. "I just gotta go downstairs and then I'll be right back."

"And I'll be right here," Martin says, watching Brittany skip down the hall toward the elevator.

Closing his door, Martin wonders if maybe he should try one of those Mountain Dews. If it could give him the spring that seems always to be in Brittany's step, it might be worth the calories...

He decides to do some dishes while waiting for her return.

III

"That was fast," Martin says, after opening the door.

In response, Brittany takes one leap to the left, revealing a large box with a big bow on it. "Ta-Da!" she trills.

"What's this?"

"Best Buy was having a sale. I bought you a new television."

"Brittany! My God!"

"And if you refuse to accept it, I'll never speak to you again."

She gets behind the box and begins to push it into Martin's apartment. "Don't forget!" she says to her stunned neighbor. "I won all that money in Vegas. And I've got a good chunk of change in my savings account, too, so—"

"I'm touched and I don't know what else to say."

Brittany gets on her tiptoes and kisses Martin on the cheek. "I think you deserve nice surprises," she says. "I think everybody does.

"Want me to help you set it up?" she asks then.

"Actually, I, uh, was just thinking while I was doing some dishes. I could use your help with something else. I need a woman's opinion."

Brittany cocks her head and raises her eyebrows.

"I have a date tonight," Martin explains.

"Yay!" Brittany responds, clapping her hands.

"I was just perusing my shirt collection. Um, you mind helping me figure out what to wear?"

IV

Taking Brittany's advice, Martin has plugged in the iron and pulled down the ironing board that, fortunately, is a feature within one of his kitchen's classic cabinets.

"Edendale's a great place," Brittany comments, opening Martin's fridge and grabbing a Mountain Dew. "You mind?"

"Of course not. Those are for you."

He places his dark green cotton shirt on the ironing board. "So you been there? The Edendale?"

"A few times," she replies, hoisting herself up to sit on the countertop. "I used to date the bartender, actually."

"Oh?"

"And! I'd rather talk about root canal!"

Martin laughs as he moves the iron over the back of his shirt. "Bad ending, huh?"

"He was a weasel. A fucking weasel. I mean, why can't guys just break up when they want to?"

"You and my sister should write a book."

"Your sister and I should do your ironing," Brittany says, dismounting from her perch.

"Here," she says, using her hip to gently nudge him out of the way. "This'll go a lot faster if I do it."

"We men are hopeless, aren't we?"

Brittany laughs quietly as she begins ironing. "So when it came time to end your marriage, was it you or her?"

"I thought we were going to talk about root canal."

Brittany smiles. "So tell me about your date tonight," she says, rearranging Martin's shirt so as to press one of the sleeves.

"Why do I feel like I'm in some avant-garde play right now?"

"Probably because you live east of Western. So? Your date?"

"Her name's Susan. You'll meet her Wednesday night. She's coming with me to the event."

"Oh, God," Brittany says, her tone ominous as she puts down the iron and reaches for the Mountain Dew. "Don't remind me."

"What? Aren't you excited about being honored?"

"Being honored is fine," she replies. "Giving a speech makes me want to break out in hives."

"Is it a big crowd?"

"I think they generally fill the room. I don't know. Maybe six or seven hundred?

"Of course," she adds, gently sliding the iron between the buttons on the front of Martin's shirt, "with the *AI* event that night, there could be a lot of no-shows."

"*AI?*" Martin asks, not making the connection.

"*American Idol,* silly! What? No speaky English?"

Martin assumes an apologetic look. "I'm the guy who's never watched it."

"You're kidding!" Brittany says. "What's been holding you back?"

"I don't like that whole reality show genre." Martin explains.

"It's not a reality show. It's a talent show. And it's beautiful. I swear, I'm such a sap. By the final six or seven weeks, I can't get through an episode without crying. I mean, God, Martin, it's about dreams. It's about risk-taking. It's about taking a lot of shit, putting it on the line, competing with people who have become your newest friends, wanting to win and not wanting anyone else to lose. It's amazing. It's people younger than me being so incredibly fucking brave."

"So maybe making a speech on Wednesday night doesn't seem so scary, after all?" Martin suggests.

"I thought we were going to talk about root canal," Brittany replies. She then grabs the hanger from the countertop, hangs Martin's shirt on it, and turns off the iron.

V

"Hey!" says Susan, smiling as she opens the door. "Come on in! I just need to throw some cat food down for the old geezers."

"Thanks," Martin says, entering the home that Susan once shared with her husband, the fallen cop.

"Follow me into the kitchen," she says. "I want to introduce you to Bubba and Fran."

Martin feels self-conscious as he walks through the beautiful dining room. The silver pieces that line the shelves of the antique dry sink are probably more valuable than the entire contents of his one-bedroom apartment on Vermont.

The brightly-lit kitchen is state-of-the-art in terms of appliances, and the room is remarkably clean. Martin is grateful for the collage of photographs on the refrigerator door. Without them, he might feel as if he had just stepped into an Ikea catalog.

"So where are these alleged geezers?" Martin asks, grounding himself through the hands-in-pocket stance that he knows is a sign of insecurity.

Susan responds by holding up a can of cat food. "You'll see them..." she says, lifting the pop-top loop and pulling it, "...now!"

Sure enough, a large black and white cat lumbers into the kitchen.

"Bubba?" Martin asks.

"Good guess!" Susan responds, bending over to fork half the can's contents onto one of two small plates.

She then taps the fork on the second plate, and Martin guesses—again, correctly—that this is her way of calling the other old geezer.

Sure enough, not two seconds later, a diminutive grey cat—whose angular features reveal the likelihood of Siamese forebears—comes trotting in.

"And this is Fran," Susan says lovingly, as she forks the remaining food onto Fran's plate.

"Do they get along?"

"Martin!" Susan replies, her tone teasing. "They're cats! If they got along, they'd have to turn in their badges!"

VI

Waiting for Susan to return from the ladies' room, Martin surveys the restaurant. Lots of couples; most of them young. He's glad he's not one of those young people, possibly on one of those dates that is full of questions. He's glad he has a marriage behind him and that the marriage did not produce any children.

He's glad he is relatively free. Being free—combined with being older—gives him a remarkably settled feeling.

"You look bemused," Susan comments, returning to her chair across from him.

"I'm still digesting that delicious steak."

"I'm glad you're a meat-eater."

"I don't think I've ever heard that from a woman before," Martin comments, probably looking even more bemused than he did a second ago.

"I tried to date a guy once," Susan explains, leaning into the table as if she would prefer no one else hear what she is about to say. "Not only was he a vegan, but he was utterly judgmental about everybody else's eating preferences. We had a few meals, and then he promptly announced that unless I was willing to change my habits, he would have to move on."

"To greener pastures?"

"Yeah," says Susan, laughing at the visual. "Exactly. He's probably lying on a bed of arugula now with some woman who lives on an I.V. filled with pomegranate juice.

"So, do you cook?" Susan asks then.

"No," Martin replies, "I'm kind of a textbook bachelor when it comes to eating at home. For me, it's all about avoiding those pesky steam burns!"

"Ah yes," says Susan, nodding, "the consistent warning on frozen dinner packaging. The law firm I used to work for once *litigated* a case about steam burns, can you believe it?"

"Nothing in the legal field would shock me," Martin responds. "I truly believe that there are people who get up in the morning with a strong desire to sue somebody, and then they just go about their day litigiously."

Susan laughs. "Well put, my friend."

VII

Driving home from Susan's, Martin has rolled down both front windows, and he is enjoying the smell of the pre-dawn air. When they had reached her house and she had invited him in for brandy or some decaf, he didn't expect that they would sit on her living room couch for five hours. By two o'clock, they had finished the pot of decaf and had moved on to Smartwater. By four, there were five empty Smartwater bottles on the floor between them, and they had covered a lot of ground.

Susan had told Martin about the scene at her law firm downtown and about the incidents that led her to opt for an easier life. She had watched a colleague essentially move into the firm, working twenty hours a day in preparation for a case. When the case was concluded and the colleague had won—scoring a huge amount of cash for the firm—it was clear that the winning had taken its toll. One day, the colleague did not show up. Later that afternoon, Susan and her fellow partners learned that he had suffered a stroke. Apparently, he had been unsuccessful in avoiding steam burns.

Martin had shared with Susan his current plans to leave H-M-P. He told her about Vivian and her officious demeanor. He confessed that he was starting to act adolescent at work. He even shared the story about Alice, looking at the Solitaire spread and claiming her boss had an afternoon full of appointments. He told her about his weird phone call from Barry.

"What do you think that was about?" Susan had asked.

Martin did not have an answer, but the question stays with him. The possible explanations—none of which seem good—crowd his mind. Even the cool air outside can't make them go away.

Waiting for the light to change at Commonwealth, Martin switches gears in his mind. Fran, Susan's "lap cat," spent many of those living room hours sitting on Martin.

"She's the hostess with the mostest!" Susan had said.

Susan also had shared with Martin how she adopted both Bubba and Fran within two weeks of her husband's death. "I don't know," she had said, "I was so pissed at him. I just hated him for getting killed. And since Rafael was allergic, I figured a good way to punish him would be to get two kittens."

CHAPTER THIRTY-ONE

I

The event's pre-dinner mingling area in the famously pink hotel on Sunset in Beverly Hills is crowded and abuzz. Martin keeps thinking that he has spied Brittany, but the group this nonprofit organization attracts includes more than a few young women with royal blue streaks in their hair.

Susan has had her arm linked through Martin's since the valet took off with his car, and Martin loves the feeling. He loves the feeling of being the escort to a woman who, in truth, is giving him a remarkable amount of strength simply by existing.

"Would you like a drink?" Martin asks Susan.

She moves her head back and forth, as if the deciding game is challenging her. "You know? Yeah, a glass of wine might be nice."

They head toward one of the three bar stations, but their itinerary is quickly interrupted.

"Martin!" comes the familiar voice of Debora. With spontaneous synchronicity, the escort stance that Martin and Susan have been holding since they emerged from his car is broken. They both turn to answer the call.

"Oh my God!" Susan exclaims, upstaging any introductions that Martin and Debora might make. "Len Rosenthal!"

Martin and Debora exchange shrugs as Susan and Len hug.

"This is wild," Susan says, smiling broadly after she has pulled away from the hug. She looks at Martin then, "You work with—?"

"Debora. This is Debora Stevens. And," Martin extends his hand, "good to meet you, Len. You obviously know my friend Susan."

"Unbelievable," Len replies, shaking his head and smiling.

Len then turns to his wife. "Susan was the second attorney on that malpractice case that nearly killed my career five years ago. And to this day," he adds, now looking at Susan, "I know that you were really the lead attorney."

"You won that case?" exclaims Debora. "Well, then, I want to hug you, too!"

"Okay," Susan says, laughing as she accepts Debora's hug. Then, with a hand gesture that shoos away the politics behind her memories of the case, Susan effectively dismisses any lingering hard feelings she may have had against her co-litigant. "I'm just so damned glad we won," she says to Len. "That woman who filed against you makes the 'Octomom' look like Mother of the Year."

Martin is enjoying witnessing Susan's comfort. He admires her capacity to move forward in her life so fluidly. At the same time, he's taking in the age difference between his colleague and her husband. Having not met Len previously, Martin is a bit surprised to see that he is probably a good twenty years older than his wife. Martin pegs Debora to be in her late thirties. Len looks to be in his late fifties.

Hmm, Martin thinks. *No wonder she twirls her hair.*

II

The table Len bought is only about four rows back from the stage, and Martin is pleased with his placement among the twelve who are benefiting from their host's generous purchase. While Brenda is not among them (Martin had learned from Debora on Monday that his former assistant passed on the opportunity), it seems Debora was able to fill the place settings.

At Martin's right is Susan, and to her right is a colleague of Len's—the premiere oncologist of Children's Hospital. To Martin's left is a woman who introduces herself enthusiastically.

"I'm Gwendolyn Friedman," she says, "and I serve on the board of HRHY. You?"

"Martin Sheffield," he responds, extending his hand. "Good to meet you. I respect the work of HRHY. In fact, one of your honorees has become a good friend of mine."

"Oh really?" Gwendolyn asks. "Which one? You know, as a board member, I am always looking for closer contacts with those deep pockets out there!"

"In that case," Martin replies, "I'm going to disappoint you. My friend has deep pockets in her heart, but she's not one of the incredibly wealthy honorees. At least, not by financial standards. My friend is Brittany Burton. The alum-of-the-year."

Gwendolyn processes her responses quickly. No longer needing the ching-ching side of her brain, she's accessing that part of her soul that serves on the board because she believes in the cause.

"Good for you," she says. "Good for you."

Martin is glad that the delivery of salads is occurring at just this point. He's glad, because he doesn't want to continue on this particular dialogue path with Gwendolyn. *Good for me?* he thinks to himself, as he accepts from Susan the tureen of salad dressing that is working its way around the table. *Good for me? Like, what? I'm doing Brittany a favor by being her friend? Guess again, board lady!*

III

"You having fun?" Martin asks Susan, as he participates in the post-dinner coffee session by passing the silver cube of sweeteners to her.

"It's an event," she shrugs. "I've been to a lot of these, and as they go, this one's a little better than average."

She leans in, "I just wish they'd get started with the program, you know?"

"Yeah," Martin agrees. "I'm feeling nervous for Brittany."

IV

Although Conan was billed as the Emcee (and although he did a great job of comedically setting up the night's program), the Chairman of the Board—a man with the unfortunate name of Clem Altschul—is doing the duties of introducing each of the honorees. As the applause for the Corporate Philanthropist of the Year slowly dies down, Clem once again speaks into the microphone.

"Thank you, supporters. And thank you, Miguel. You know, I gotta tell you folks, Miguel really sold himself short in his comments just now. The fact of the matter is, the Consolidated District has donated more than five hundred thousand dollars to HRHY in the past decade.

"Remarkable," Clem says, nodding his head as he accepts the expected applause.

Clem then holds out an arm; an arm that tells people to "pipe down." With this crowd, so many of whom go to dinners like this too many times a year, it's easy to affect the concept of piping down.

"Finally," Clem says, "we are very pleased to bestow an honor on a young lady who *proves* the effectiveness of, and the reason for, Hollywood Runaway and Homeless Youth. Please join me in welcoming our alumna of the year, Miss Brittany Burton."

Clapping along with his fellow audience members, Martin wants to do more. He wants to stand up. He wants to give Brittany the ovation she deserves. He knows better, though, and so he simply sits there, clapping enthusiastically. And as he watches his wonderful friend walk out on stage, it strikes him that he's never seen Brittany walk so quietly. He's never seen her *not* bounce.

There's a slight look of fear when she takes the podium. But, then, immediately, there's that impish smile. She looks around the room, possibly allowing potential listeners to make their judgments. And then, having given all of them a sufficient amount of time, she smiles broadly, she spreads out her arms, and she says, leaning into the microphone: "Here I am, folks. Your American Idol!"

The crowd roars, and most everyone rises to their feet. Laughing and clapping simultaneously, Susan and Martin are among the guests standing.

Susan leans into Martin. "Fucking brilliant," she says.

V

"... I don't know what I would have done without Hollywood Runaway," Brittany is saying—about ninety seconds into her somewhat prepared speech. "You know, people have these prejudices. Everybody does. We all do. I do. Um, and where runaways are concerned, I think people just don't really get it. They think that kids run because they don't want to be responsible. Or they think that kids run because they wanna have some kind of glamorous life. Or they just hate their parents' rules. That is so not true, and that's what I want to tell you. When I left Nebraska twelve years ago, I wasn't chasing some dream. I was running. From a nightmare. I don't even know if my mom is alive anymore. I don't know, but back then, she was pretty much beaten up all the time. My dad had rules, you see. And I guess mom was always breaking them. I wanted to protect her, but I also needed to take care of myself, and when he started hitting me, I was outta there. I had to get outta there."

The room is remarkably silent. And, quick study that she is, Brittany's exhalations are no longer being picked up by the microphone and amplified throughout the room.

"Hollywood runaways are not bad kids," Brittany is sharing. "Hollywood runaways are kids who are desperate for guidance and help. And I learned, early on, working with HRHY, that they get it. The people at the agency get it. It's not where you've been. It's where you're going."

The sudden applause in the room strikes Martin. Granted, he joins it—ultimately—but he would not have initiated it. It's nervous applause. It's the applause of people who want to believe that they understand the situation. It's the applause of people who would probably be totally screwed if they ever were in the position of desperation that Brittany has described.

"Thank you," says Brittany, acknowledging the applause. "Thank you. And on the subject of thanks, I want to give a nod to a few people. I was *so* happy to see Cheryl here tonight. Cheryl Clark is one of the first people I met in Hollywood who helped me to 'get it.' Cheryl was my case manager, and she met with me, like, I don't know, three times a week. She was the person who kept reminding me. It wasn't my fault. It wasn't me. There is nothing wrong with *me*.

"Cheryl is the one who set me up with classes, with housing, with employment possibilities. Always reminding me to keep looking ahead.

"And another person I gotta thank," Brittany states, reviving her impish smile, "is my buddy Jason. Jason is a staff member of HRHY, but when I knew him, when I met him, he was just another kid on the Boulevard. The difference, of course, was that he wasn't homeless. The difference was that—" Brittany begins to giggle now "—he didn't stink like the rest of us!

"Jason was so nice to let me use his family's shower. And you know what? I'm just thinking right now... I'm just remembering. I was in that shower once when a pretty strong earthquake hit. It wasn't the Northridge quake or anything, but it was pretty intense. You know, like a five point something. I remember coming out of the shower, wrapped in a towel, and—"

Brittany seems to be stumped for a minute. The audience is spellbound.

"—the thing about earthquakes is that they last a really short length of time. But when they're just starting, you can't get ahead to the minute or two away when the shaking will stop. It's hard to look ahead, you know? Personal problems are like that, too. And, sure, they last a whole lot longer than a minute or two—most of them—but they don't have to swallow you up."

Brittany looks down for a few seconds. Then, she shakes her head subtly, looks back up and smiles. "Anyway, I, uh, have one more acknowledgement I'd like to make. I have a new friend. A terrific friend. His name is Martin and he's my neighbor. He's here tonight. He's here to support me and to support the agency. I remember when I met him the first time, I didn't think we'd become friends. You know, he's older. But we are friends, and that feels good. He's the same age as my dad would be now. Is... now. Anyway, thank you, Martin. Thank you for being such a good friend.

"Thanks to everybody. Goodnight."

CHAPTER THIRTY-TWO

I

"Here you are, Martin," Alice says, placing a sheet of paper in front of him. "Anything else I can do to prep for the meeting?"

"No," Martin replies, scanning the short agenda.

"And this looks good," he says, handing the sheet back to her. "Please make five copies of that and also five copies of the updated accounts spreadsheet."

"Five?" Alice asks.

"Yes. Oh! I'm sorry! Did I forget to invite you to the meeting?"

"You'd like me in on it?"

"Yes," he responds. Then, smiling mischievously, he adds, "unless there's some solitaire tournament that creates a conflict."

"Not a problem," Alice says, returning his smile. "And you sure you want to meet in here and not the small conference room?"

"Yeah, here is fine."

II

"Hey," says Debora, poking her head into Martin's office and finding him in the seating area, having claimed one of the individual chairs.

"God, is it ten already?"

"I thought I'd drop in early. Is that okay?"

"Sure. Come in. Coffee?"

"No, thanks. I just chugged about four cups downstairs. Wasn't that a great event last night?"

217

"It was," Martin agrees, still touched by Brittany's comments, "but I feel bad I didn't get a chance to meet Cody's girlfriend. I mean, I couldn't exactly chat with them across that large table, and they bolted out right after the program ended."

"They had to get home," Debora shares. "Oh my God, though, she is such a sweetie, and she and Cody are so cute together. She's from Iowa, can you believe it? Did you know there are people in L.A. from *Iowa*?"

"She did have kind of a heartland look to her."

"*And* she's a kindergarten teacher," Debora states, as if to seal the deal.

"They have kindergartens in L.A.?" Martin asks.

"Hmm..." he adds then, appearing introspective. "It's kind of nice to know that people still want to teach kindergarten."

"I agree," Debora says. "Anyway, great event! And I'm so glad we were able to put that table together."

"Yes," Martin comments, his tone conveying some distraction. "Yes. And speaking of which, I don't think we should speak of which during the meeting."

"Right. Mr. Phil might be wired."

Martin rolls his eyes at the concept. He knows that Debora is joking, but the implication isn't far from the truth. Phil continues to give the impression that he's working for another team.

III

Alice was smart to bring the two guest chairs over from their usual position at Martin's desk. The group is able to spread out, and the sense of sitting in a circle has a collegial feel to it.

Martin has just responded to a question from Cody, who has a client who seems especially fussy of late. Debora relates a similar experience that occurred with someone on her docket about a year ago. "I was able to keep the client ultimately," Debora is sharing, "but the process required a lot of hand-holding."

When the door to Martin's office opens, Debora stops speaking. The only one who doesn't look in the direction of the door is Phil. He sits in the individual chair facing Martin's, and he stares at his team leader coldly.

"Hi, guys!" says Vivian, her tone absurdly friendly as she enters the room. "Mind if I join you?"

Do we have any choice? Martin wants to say, but he squelches that impulse quickly, responding instead with an evenly delivered, "Have a seat."

IV

"So," Vivian is saying now, her little speech having begun a full five minutes ago, "that's the news from headquarters. Any calls from the press are to be directed to William in H.R. He, in turn, will relay details to and from New York."

"Why is New York worried about this?" Martin asks. "I mean, do they have any clues as to why these questions are coming up?"

"It's the press, Martin," Vivian responds, her tone close to angry. "They like to *create* issues."

"That's not a convincing response," Martin says, the coldness of his tone causing Debora, Cody, and Alice to lower their gazes rather self-consciously.

"Look," Vivian says. "We're financial advisors, not magicians. And sometimes a client forgets their own responsibility in the matter. They also forget that they need to *own* their risks. The especially forgetful ones who also happen to have friends in the media can inspire an investigation. But they're wasting their time. And we all know that."

Vivian looks at her watch and stands. "I've gotta run, folks. Just follow the procedures, refer anyone to William, and don't give this subject more talk-time than it already has received. It's a non-issue, and the mature way to handle such a thing is to let it die. Okay?"

V

"Debora," Martin says, as Cody and Phil head for the door and Alice returns the guest chairs to Martin's desk area, "can you hang back for a minute?"

"Sure."

Alice quickly gathers her file folder and leaves the room, pulling the door closed behind her.

Debora, who has just helped herself to a mug of coffee, returns to her seat on the couch. "Jeez," she says, "what was that really about?"

"In my opinion? That was really about get the hell out of here as soon as possible."

"Did you submit your resumé to HRHY?"

"Yeah, I emailed a copy on Monday."

"I'll call Len. Maybe he can expedite the process."

"What about you?" Martin asks.

"I haven't submitted anything anywhere. The position at Children's remains an indefinite likelihood, if that makes sense. But, I'm not comfortable with this. Maybe we should see if we can get together with Barry."

"That's right. I forgot about that. I'll call him today. Maybe he'll be able to do lunch this weekend. It might be a better time to catch him, assuming the self-medicating begins in the evening."

"That's true, but we also might get more out of him if he's had a few."

"I'd rather not," Martin states. "It's just not something I like to watch."

"What about Cody?" Debora asks.

"How do you mean?"

"I don't know," she responds, some serious hair twirling keeping her left hand busy, "I feel kind of protective of him. I just would hate to see him get caught up in something. He seems like such an innocent guy, you know?"

"Maybe Barry can give us some advice on that score. But, you know, there are a lot of nice, innocent people here. We can't protect everybody."

"Yeah, I see your point. How about your friend, Susan?" Debora asks.

"What about her?"

"She might have some insights. She's probably seen everything at the law firm where she works."

"She's not there anymore, but, yeah, that's a good idea. I'll, uh, share the latest when I talk to her."

"So," Debora says, adapting a smile that is a refreshing change from the mood Vivian brought to Martin's office, "is Susan a love interest or just a friend?"

"What is it about you girls?"

"What do you mean?"

"I think that the stereotype about us guys being weasels is matched by you gals wanting to pinpoint the exact meaning of every pairing," Martin explains, his tone light. "Brenda quizzed me last week."

"So?" Debora says in response, twirling her hair in a more amused and teasing way, "I'm still waiting for the answer."

Across the room, Martin's intercom buzzes.

"Susan on line one," Alice announces, telephonically.

"Shall I put her on speaker?" Martin asks Debora, as he heads for his desk. "You could ask her yourself."

"No," Debora responds, standing up and heading for the door. "I'll just leave you two lovebirds alone."

"Susan!" Martin says enthusiastically, after pushing the appropriate button on his executive phone.

"Hey, Martin, I hope it's okay that I called you at work."

"Of course! Everything okay?"

"Sure. Just enjoying a long morning. I don't have to go into Joe's until one, so I'm still in my robe."

Martin pictures a white terry cloth number. Something out of the L.L. Bean catalog.

"I'd like to be in a robe right now," he comments.

"You mean that corner office didn't come with one?" Susan asks.

"Are you kidding? If it had come with any apparel, it would have been a conservative selection of neckties."

"I can picture them. Anyway, I just wanted to let you know again how much fun I had last night. That speech that Brittany delivered really made the evening for me. What a lovely young lady. I hope I'll have more chances to be in her remarkable presence."

"I hope you will, too," Martin agrees. "Hey! Here's a spontaneous thought..."

"The best kind!"

"I don't know if she and Jason will be available, but shall I see if they're free Saturday night? We could get together at my place. Get some Thai delivery or something. You know, hang out like we're all their age."

"I would love that!" Susan responds. "And that's perfect. I'm off at five on Saturday."

"Well, put that in your book, and I'll confirm with them."

"Cool. And, you know, even if they can't make it, we could still get together."

"Absolutely," says Martin.

"Alright, then, we're on. I'll let you go now, and I will see you Saturday night!"

"Excellent! Have fun at work."

"I almost always do. Bye, Martin."

"Bye."

Martin looks wistfully at the phone after he has hung up. A love interest or just a friend? Martin realizes that it doesn't matter. Susan is lovely, interesting, and friendly. Knowing her—and now knowing her well enough to receive an unexpected phone call in the middle of an otherwise disturbing morning—is more than he might have hoped for when he first started making those strategic trips to Trader Joe's. He chuckles when he thinks of the bizarre beginning. It all started in a menopause chatroom.

Martin wonders if there will ever be a time when he can confess to Susan his knowledge of her Sus323 handle. Martin wonders, for that matter, if Susan still conducts dialogues at that site. His own need to visit it ended weeks ago, just after he came home with a doggie bag full of tentacles.

VI

Returning from his lunchtime walk at two-thirty, Martin is pleased to listen to a voicemail from a Luisa Delgado at Hollywood Runaway. He immediately calls her back.

"Oh, hi, Mr. Sheffield," Luisa says. "Thank you so much for returning my call so promptly."

"I was pleased to receive it," Martin offers.

"I've been reviewing resumés, and we want to start setting up interviews. But, just so we aren't wasting your time or ours, I wanted to share with you the salary range. I'm not sure if you are aware of the likelihood that this could probably be a pretty drastic cut in pay for you."

"I'm okay with a cut—depending, I guess, on the definition of 'drastic'," Martin replies. "What's the range?"

"Well, the position caps at ninety thousand, and we're looking to bring someone in at sixty thousand. You know, we are struggling like the rest of the world with economic challenges, so we have to cut corners as much as possible. I'm quite sure that the board is going to want to stick with the sixty thousand-dollar figure."

Although this news makes Martin stir in his chair a bit (is that his wallet getting a case of the hiccups?), he knows that he cannot let financial fear stop him. "I'd like an interview, Ms. Delgado," he states with cheerful confidence.

"Good!" she replies. "I'm glad that's a workable figure for you. So... the interview process will start with your meeting our E.D."

"E.D.?" Martin asks.

"I'm sorry. I forget that people who haven't been in non-profit don't hear that right. I'm not meaning to sound like some Viagra ad! I'm referring to our Executive Director. Her name is Gail Tryce."

"No problem regarding the confusion," Martin shares. "It's like with me in the finance biz. When someone mentions buying a new C.D., I don't usually think of music."

"Well, that's probably a really good reason to be thinking about a career change, Mr. Sheffield. Anyway, I'll look at some calendars here and call you back tomorrow. Maybe we can set something up for next week?"

"Just let me know when and I'll be there."

"Excellent. You'll hear from me again very soon."

After hanging up with Ms. Delgado, it occurs to Martin that he should check his accrued vacation time. No reason not to take a week off when Zac is in town. And if he happens to get a job that begins on June fifteenth, the very day following Zac's flight back east, so be it. At the moment, he feels no remorse about sticking it to Haley-Mitchell-Phelps.

VII

"Yes, boss?" Alice says, entering Martin's office.

Martin smiles at his assistant, and because he knows that her calling him "boss" does not come from a place of subservience, he doesn't ask her to defer from that greeting.

"Yeah, I'm confused. I just checked my accrued vacation time, and it looks like I've got five days available. And I want to take them actually quite soon. I've got a nephew coming in from the east coast. Staying with me for two weeks. But who do I ask?"

Alice smiles. "I'll take care of it. Which week you looking at?"

"The week of June eighth, I guess. I mean, I hate the idea of not being available to Zac the first week he's here, but—"

"Have you got sick time?"

"Yeah, but—"

"That's good. So you can take a few days off that week, too."

Martin tilts his head at Alice. Her sense of insider knowledge is rather impressive.

"I got friends in personnel," Alice says, "and at the moment, you don't technically have a boss in this region. So? We'll just make it happen. I'll have those five days approved by tomorrow."

"You rock, Alice!"

"I'm as *old* as the rock, Martin. If I can't pull this off, then what good am I?"

Martin smiles as he watches Alice leave his office. He then pulls up the calendar on his computer. With any luck, he has only one more full week at the ostensibly venerable house of H-M-P.

CHAPTER THIRTY-THREE

I

Martin is the first to arrive at Houston's on Arroyo Parkway in Pasadena. And, once he enters the place, he is a little surprised that Barry chose it. The restaurant is busy, loud, and family-friendly—an ambiance that is inherently distracting.

He looks at his watch—five minutes early. He gives his name to the hostess and steps outside. As he paces the length of the walkway that borders the parking lot, he tries not to focus on the lunch ahead. He'd rather think about the night ahead. Brittany and Jason were excited by the plan to gather at Martin's for a "night in," and when Martin saw Myra on Friday evening, he extended the invitation to her as well. And of course, it'll be great to see Susan—his friend who might be a love interest.

Martin is so engrossed in his anticipation regarding the evening that when Barry taps him on the shoulder, he seems stunned initially.

"Didn't mean to surprise you," Barry says, his smile quite sincere. "This was the plan, wasn't it?"

"Barry!" Martin says, extending his hand. "Good to see you."

"So we're waiting for Debora?"

"Yeah, but we can probably check inside. Maybe with two of us here, we can get a table."

II

"I am *so* sorry," Debora says, as she breathlessly approaches the table. "Barry! Hello!"

Barry stands to embrace Debora, and Martin remains seated. Regarding her delay, Martin is sorrier even than Debora is. Because of her lateness, their former boss has managed to plow through one-and-a-half bloody marys.

"Really, guys, sorry," Debora says, taking a seat. "We had a plumbing mishap at the house that put me about ten minutes behind schedule, and then I ran into some horrible traffic. I should have had your cell numbers with me, but that would have been too smart, I guess. Anyway, Barry! How are you?"

"I'm coping," he says, nodding in a rather furtive way, trying perhaps to convince himself of the truth in his answer.

"You look good," Debora says, her smile tense, her statement a lie.

Martin realizes that Debora has hardly seen Barry since he took his early and unplanned retirement. It is no wonder that she immediately grabs a menu and preoccupies herself by studying its contents.

III

In response to Debora's question, Barry puts down the few bites that remain of his fifteen-dollar cheeseburger. Between the meal's protein and the coffee he ordered following his second bloody mary, Barry is becoming more focused. And Martin is beginning to pay attention to their former boss's insinuations.

"I spoke with Alan the other day," Barry says.

"Right!" Debora exclaims. "Alan! Why in the world haven't they replaced him? You know, Barry, Vivian seems to think she's the Regional Director these days."

"Well," Barry says, "that's understandable. You've got two Senior VPs in the L.A. office. Vivian and Martin. But, of course, Vivian is the *senior* Senior VP, so she naturally feels likes she's in charge. She also wants to *be* in charge. That's her personality."

"But what about Alan?" Martin wants to know.

"He is so happy at his current job. You know, he took a bit of a pay cut."

"Where's he working?" Martin asks.

"Cal Tech. He loves it. It's still the numbers-crunching game, of course, but he likes the work they do."

Barry raises his hand, as the waitress walks by.

Martin dreads Barry's potential order from the bar and is relieved when his former boss simply asks for the check.

"Sorry, kids," Barry says. "I've got to cut this short. My granddaughter is in a dance recital this afternoon."

"Aw, Barry," Debora responds, "that's so sweet. How old is she?"

"Five, I think. Maybe six."

Barry grabs the check as soon as the waitress delivers it, and he hands it back to her with his credit card. He then looks at Martin and Debora. "It's good to have family. It really is. And the younger the better."

As Barry takes another sip from his coffee, Martin decides to go for it. "Barry," he says. "What's your prediction for the future of Haley-Mitchell-Phelps?"

"Haley-Mitchell-Phelps?" Barry echoes.

The waitress delivers the credit card print-out to Barry, and as he enters the tip, does the math, and signs off, he says, "I think the future of H-M-P is something neither one of you should have to experience."

IV

It's been three minutes since Barry left Houston's, and Martin and Debora are each sipping a bloody mary.

"Shit, Martin," Debora is saying, "this is beyond ominous."

"I know. Thank God I've got that interview on Monday."

"Oh, you got it? Oh my God, that's great!"

"What about you?" Martin asks.

"Jesus. A part of me just wants to give notice on Monday." She embraces her own shoulders, as if she has a chill. Then, she suddenly shakes her head. "What am I saying? You're my boss!"

"So, are you giving notice?"

"I'm thinking about it. God, I don't want to not work, but—" Debora takes a large swig of her bloody mary, and because she uses the straw, her posture closely resembles that of a co-ed at a soda fountain in the 'Fifties.

"I mean, it's weird for me," Debora says, sitting back. "Len and I are very comfortable!"

Then why are you twirling your hair? Martin wants to ask.

"I mean," Debora continues, "a lot of wives in my position spend their days shopping the boutiques on Ventura Boulevard or doing charity events. I mean, I don't *have* to work!"

"But you would prefer to," Martin suggests.

"Well, yeah."

As Martin waves to the waitress, asking for the check that will reflect their two drinks, a part of him wants to tell Debora about Susan's career change. He wants to tell Debora about the Harvard Law graduate who is now happily working at Trader Joe's. But Martin isn't sure that Debora can hear this bit of wisdom properly. Debora is a little too tense. Debora also would probably have difficulty working a cash register. The task would probably be particularly difficult for her because she so often would have one hand tied up in her hair.

V

"Hey there," Martin says, opening his front door and happy to see Susan's beautiful smile.

"Hi, Martin," she responds, giving him a quick kiss on the cheek.

"Looks like you did a little shopping after your shift," he says then, indicating the TJ's canvas tote she is carrying.

"Yeah, I thought I'd pick up some supplies for us. Give it that frat party feel."

"Cool," says Martin, leading the way into the kitchen. "I never was very good at preparing for a frat party. Tell me what to do."

"Well, it's pretty easy," says Susan, as she begins to empty the bag. "I don't think any amount of breathing is going to change the bouquet of this Two-Buck Chuck, so we can just wait on that. These yummy chicken sticks can go in the freezer 'til we're ready to pop them—" She interrupts herself as she does a quick scan of the kitchen. "No microwave?"

"I'm re-assembling my life at a slow pace."

"Well, if you want to go slow, then you definitely don't need a microwave. No prob," she says, opening the freezer. "Oven works just as well. Probably better, in fact."

"And," she continues, somewhat dramatically, as she extracts another item from the bag, "this savory soy ginger dressing is the perfect dipping sauce for those subtle curry sticks."

Martin smiles. "Oh my. So, is your store currently holding auditions for a spokesmodel?"

"I spent half the afternoon working the tasting station. Can you tell?"

"What were you serving?" Martin asks.

"Mac and cheese."

"Damn! You should have called. I would have come over for a taste. So is it fun working that station?"

As Susan removes the final items from her tote—a package of assorted cheese slices and a box of crackers—her facial expression changes. She seems to be remembering something. Something that will answer his question with a story.

"I had a really interesting visitor there today," she begins. "A woman I've seen at the store maybe once or twice before. Eccentric from head to toe. She's probably in her mid- to late-sixties, and she speaks in kind of a refined, almost royal way."

Susan smiles then, probably replaying the woman's voice in her head. "Anyway," she continues, "Madame Eccentic arrived just as the last of the mac and cheese samples had been taken, so the wait was going to be for a few minutes. And, you know, usually when that happens, people continue their shopping and then come back around. But, she decided to pour herself a little cup of coffee and just hang there. She talked about the weather. She talked about some of the items in her cart. She told me about her car. And then, she looked at me in the most piercing way, and she said, 'Young lady, you are about to help reunite a mother and daughter.'"

"Hmm," is Martin's response, not altogether taken aback. (It's Trader Joe's on Hyperion, after all.) "So what did you say to that?"

"I don't remember. I'm not sure I said anything. The timer on the microwave went off then, and there were a lot of people standing around like Pavlov's dog—waiting for their free tastes.

"It was weird, though," Susan adds, somewhat distantly. "It made me think about Brittany. That comment she made during her speech has stuck with me. Haunted me...

"Isn't it so sad?" she says to Martin then. "Can you imagine not knowing if your mother is alive? And the thing is, if her mother *is* still alive, that question is real for both of them."

Susan shakes her head in an attempt to climb out of these depressing thoughts. "It's just that I had such a close relationship with my own mother. It's so hard to imagine—"

"Hello, Saturday nighters!" comes the upbeat voice of Brittany, who lets herself in and proceeds to bounce into the kitchen.

Despite the proximity of the front door to the kitchen, Martin doesn't worry that Brittany overheard anything Susan was saying. After all, Brittany is not one to break stride. She's not one to slow her Tigger-like carriage long enough to listen to comments that are occurring in another room.

"Brittany!" Martin says, giving his friend a hug. "You remember Susan from the other night?"

"Hi Susan!" Brittany says cheerfully. Then, pulling a six-pack of Mountain Dew out of a plastic bag, "Look, Martin, I brought my own!"

"You didn't have to do that," Martin responds.

Susan smiles and laughs. "Mountain Dew!?" she exclaims. "They still make that?"

"They will as long as I'm around," Brittany replies, pulling one of the cans from the six-pack and opening the fridge to store the rest.

"Where's Jason?" Martin asks.

Brittany gets a pinched look on her face. "He had to go to the agency."

"Why? I thought he had the night off?"

"He did, and so technically, he didn't *have* to go, but one of the kids he's particularly close to was having an episode, and he might be the only person who can get him through it."

"What kind of an episode?" Martin asks, as he grabs the plate of cheese and crackers that Susan has prepared and leads his guests into the living room.

"I'm not even sure. Might be drug-related, might be some other sort of chemical imbalance. I don't know," Brittany shrugs, minimalizing the drama.

She then shifts focus and mood as she plops on the floor and cuddles Dude.

"Dude!" she squeals. "Super Dude! How's the ol' back end area?"

"He's looking better than the last time I saw him," Susan comments. "A little less groggy."

"Yeah, he seems to be coming along." Martin responds, just about to sit when the doorbell rings. Heading for the front hall, he adds, "I'm still not sure about the bladder thing."

"It's okay," Susan says. "If there were a problem, you'd know."

Martin opens the door, and Myra—dressed in an assortment of patterns and colors—makes a dramatic entrance. As she takes a few steps into Martin's front hallway, she has a very worried look on her face. "I just saw that damned junkie," she whispers, somewhat breathless. "He actually asked me to hold the elevator for him, and I did the exact opposite. I couldn't push that close-the-door button fast enough! I did not want to ride in that cage with him."

"Hmm," says Martin, accepting the small brown bag Myra hands him, "I wonder why he was heading up."

Myra follows Martin into the kitchen, where he opens the bag to discover a small bottle of peach schnapps.

"Interesting choice," he says to his guest.

"It's got a fun kick. Where is your glassware?"

As Martin reaches to open the cupboard above him, he realizes he hasn't accommodated all his guests. Handing Myra a glass, he calls into the living room, "Susan! Would you like a glass of that wine you brought?"

"Only if you'll join me," is her response.

"Good," Myra says, filling a small juice glass with a few ounces of her fruity beverage, "more schnapps for me!"

Martin rifles through his drawers in search of the all-purpose implement that includes a corkscrew. Although his visits to Myra's apartment have revealed that she's not the neatest tenant in the building, he still feels self-conscious about his drawers. They always seem to lack a theme.

"So," Martin says to Myra, "aside from this evening's run-in with your down-the-hall neighbor, have you seen him much lately?"

"No, but the other evening, the music coming out of his place was ungodly loud! And it was very disturbing music. Jolting, you know?"

Having found the corkscrew implement, Martin is fighting his way through the cork. He clearly does not have a routine in this department, and Myra picks up on his struggle.

"Oh, give me that!" she says, first placing her glass of schnapps on the counter. "You're probably used to those two-arm numbers that take all the work out of the process."

Myra makes a few swift moves. "There you go," she says, pulling the cork quietly out of its slumber.

"Now," she says, "do you need help finding the wineglasses?"

"I don't have any," Martin says, pulling instead two somewhat matching tumblers from his cupboard.

"I'm re-assembling my life at a slow pace," he explains.

"No you're not! You're just waiting for some woman to come along and re-assemble it for you! Pshaw! Bachelors!"

As he fills the two tumblers with an inch or so of wine, Martin smiles at her comment. Even Myra wants to talk about relationships!

VI

When Martin and Myra enter the living room, Susan does a double-take. "Oh my God!" she says, somewhat quietly. "I was just telling Martin about our chat this afternoon."

"Trader Joe's!" Myra says, extending her hand. "But now, of course, you've taken off your name tag, so you'll have to re-introduce yourself."

"Susan."

"Myra. Good to see you again. And, by the way, that was some great mac and cheese."

"Hey, Myra!" Brittany says from the floor.

"Hello, my dear. And hello, Dude."

Brittany helps Dude wave to Myra.

"Yup," Myra says, settling into the most worn end of the used couch Martin bought off craigslist, "you made some fine mac and cheese. In fact, I bought two boxes. But, don't worry, gang. I didn't scarf them down when I got home."

She turns to Martin, "Did you say we're ordering Thai?"

"Thai or whatever anybody wants. I have a slew of menus!"

Martin shrugs then, unfamiliar with the role of host and wondering if he should put on some music.

As Myra begins to quiz Susan about all-things-Trader-Joe's, and as Brittany divides her attention between that conversation and her ability to make Dude look like he's in some sort of feline heaven, Martin, too, divides his attention. He thinks about the difference a year can make.

Last year at around this time, he and Lisa had a wedding to attend. And while it was certainly not the first wedding they attended as a couple—not by a long shot—it was the first time they had been invited to a wedding that had all the trappings of a *Club Med* experience. The couple—Janice and Matt—had decided to make an event of their nuptials. A weekend event.

Complete with canoeing, volleyball, moonlight dancing, and even a limbo competition. Lisa was jazzed about the entire concept, and she couldn't accept her husband's reticence.

"Think of it as a mini-vacation!" she had told Martin. "I mean, what fun! Partying with friends all weekend... A change of scene... What a great getaway!"

At the time, Martin was too deeply entrenched in his wrong marriage to home in on those aspects of Lisa's rationale that reflected her incapacity to understand him. But, thinking about it now, he realizes the absurdity of her attempt to convince him. Yes, it would be a "mini-vacation," if the definition of vacation is being somewhere other than home. And, if that is, in fact, the definition, then "change of scene" and "getaway" are redundant. As for "partying," Martin never really used that word in the verb form. And while he valued the concept of "friends," it was presumptuous of Lisa to place that label on an unknown contingent of people.

Perhaps, Martin realizes now, when someone frequently uses "party" as a verb, then "friends" just happen.

As for "fun?" It was tedious. When they arrived at the resort, they were given a three-page schedule of events, and within an hour of checking in, they were expected to report to the lake, where mimosas and canoes awaited them. Martin started to wonder if they had made a mistake in not sewing name tags into their clothes...

As for the lakeside activities, Martin had no interest in either the mimosas or the canoes, and his lack of sportsmanship brought a scolding from Lisa when they returned to their bungalow, ostensibly to dress for volleyball.

"Why can't you just have fun?" Lisa had screamed. "God, you're such a downer sometimes!"

"Lisa, look. This just isn't my thing. I told you that when we got the invitation."

"But we're a couple, Martin!"

"Right," Martin had said, his energy challenged, "and I need a couple of hours by myself. I'm gonna pass on the volleyball."

"But how will that look?"

"Maybe it'll look like I don't want to play volleyball..."

"Where are you, Martin?" Susan asks, her kind and curious tone snapping him back into the moment.

"Sorry, guys," Martin says to the odd assortment of friends with whom he's having fun not really partying. "I went somewhere else for a minute."

"I do that a lot," Brittany states, popping up from the floor and bouncing toward the kitchen, another Mountain Dew in her near-future.

"Okay if I put those chicken sticks in the oven?" Susan asks, rising from her chair.

"Go for it!" Martin replies.

"You want more wine?"

"I'm good," he responds, looking at the tumbler that is no less full than it was when he went into his memory trance.

VII

"That was Jason," Martin shares, returning from the bonus room, "he says not to count on him tonight."

"Everything okay?" Susan asks.

"He said things were settling down, but he wanted to stick around."

"I like that Jason," Myra states, grunting without apology as she stands. "And I love my schnapps. Mind if I get more?"

"It's yours to get, Myra," Martin replies, smiling broadly at the wacky woman who's showing just a slight imbalance as she heads out to his kitchen.

"Should we order?" he asks Susan and Brittany.

"God!" Brittany says, holding her stomach and rolling a bit on the floor, "I don't think so. I'm so full from the crackers and cheese and those chicken sticks."

"Susan?"

"I'm kinda full, too, but maybe we should check in with Myra after she gets back from the kitchen."

"Maybe she could bring up the mac and cheese," Brittany suggests.

VIII

After the mac and cheese box is split three ways (though having suggested it, Brittany ultimately deferred), the party breaks up. Myra and Brittany bid their goodnights, leaving Martin and Susan to enjoy the quiet of cleaning up.

"That was fun," Susan says.

"Yeah?"

"Yeah. You know, I like real people. I mean, I like the kind of people you meet just because. You know... as opposed to the people you meet because your career or your optimum lifestyle tells you that you *should* meet them."

Martin nods as he places another orphan tumbler in the sink.

"So, you had a few opportunities to speak with Brittany tonight," he says. "Will Myra's prediction at the tasting station come true?"

"Funny you should ask."

"Oh?"

"God," Susan says, pouring herself another inch of the Two-Buck Chuck and leaning against the counter. "It really is so sad. I asked her why she hadn't been in touch with her mother, and she told me she tried once, about six years ago."

"And?"

"The line was disconnected."

"She hasn't tried since?"

"No," Susan replies. "She said she knew that there would be ways to track her down, but at that point, she was afraid. There was a strong part of her that didn't want to know."

"Sad."

"Right. *But.* Or maybe I should say '*and,*' the additional news is that she gave me all the information."

"What do you mean?" Martin asks.

"Well, I told her that my old firm can find anything or anyone. So, she gave me the names of her mom and her dad, and she asked me for only one thing."

"What's that?"

"Not to tell her if I proceed," Susan explains.

"But what if you get good news?"

"Then, she'll want to hear it."

"Oh, I see," Martin says. "And if you get bad news, then she'll never know you got it."

"That's the unspoken plan," says Susan.

CHAPTER THIRTY-FOUR

I

At nine-thirty on Monday morning, Gail Tryce comes around from behind her mess of a desk and extends a warm, confident hand to Martin.

"Welcome to Hollywood Runaway," she says, looking up at him with the kind of big watery eyes one wants to dive into.

"I apologize for the mess," she continues, speaking with the kind of sultry voice that calms any person in the room. She indicates with her hand that he should help himself to one of her two guest chairs.

"And," she says, as she settles into the other chair, "I'm very sorry I couldn't reserve the conference room for us. The Board Development Committee is having a meeting this morning."

"Oh?"

"Yes. It's kind of impromptu. Two of our regular foundation funders didn't renew this year, so the Committee is freaking out. And I gotta tell you," she adds, reaching for the file folder that probably contains all the 4-1-1 of Martin, "I can't complain. In the nonprofit world, it's a gift to have a Board that is paying such close attention to the funding needs."

Gail Tryce opens the folder, and as she refreshes her memory by perusing the pages of Martin's resumé, Martin looks around the room. While the floor space is lacking, and there is certainly no room for a couch or some top-of-the-line Senior VP coffee and fridge area, the walls make up the difference. Gail's walls are covered with beautiful art pieces, most of which appear to be originals, signed by the artist, and many of which include a telling note of love and thanks.

"Don't you love that piece?" Gail asks.

Martin has been staring at a watercolor. Its abstract composition reveals people in a huddle, showing various signs of happiness. Above them, a roof opens up to a skyful of stars. A line on the bottom, written in ink, says, "I ran away and I came home."

"It's beautiful," Martin says, turning to Gail and hoping that the saline film on his eyes does not give in to gravity's temptations.

Gail smiles at him for a moment, the wanna-be tears something she's probably seen many times before. "So, Mr. Sheffield? Looking for a change?"

II

"So, how'd the interview go?" Susan asks, when Martin calls her back from his office that afternoon.

"I don't know," Martin replies. "At first, I thought I was blowing it."

"How so?"

"I don't know. I've just never had such a non-corporate interview."

"But do you think it went okay?"

"Yeah, I do. We ended up talking for more than an hour, and she told me she was anxious to move fast. She said that she hoped I'd be able to meet with a few board members before the week is over."

"Damn, Martin. That sounds really promising!"

"It does. I know that. But I don't want to get my hopes up. You know, I'm just ready to bolt this place right now. It's hard."

"I totally understand that bolt-right-now mentality."

"So," Martin says, wondering if his maybe-a-girlfriend is lounging about in a beautiful white terry robe, "what are you up to today?"

"I called the firm," Susan reports. "You know, regarding Brittany."

"And?"

"I got some numbers, and I called the numbers, and check this out: her dad is in prison."

"That sounds right. What else?"

"And her mom has a number. I didn't call her, of course, but I learned that she's still living there, outside of Lincoln. She's in a trailer park. On welfare. And, most importantly, she's alive."

"So what's next?" Martin asks.

"I'd like to share this information with Brittany. But I think it would be most comfortable to do that at your place. Can you check when you get home tonight? If she's available, I could come over."

"Sounds good," Martin says.

III

Brittany's bounce loses some energy as she enters the living room and sees Susan.

"Hey" she says to the woman who may or may not be Martin's girlfriend.

"Hey," Susan says back.

Brittany slowly lowers herself to the floor, so she can stroke Dude. From a lying position, she looks up at Susan.

"I guess you got some news for me, huh?" Brittany asks.

"I do," Susan says. "Two pieces of news. The first is that your father is in prison."

Brittney nods.

"And the second piece of news is that your mom is alive."

Brittney pulls Dude into a ball on the floor.

Susan holds out a little post-it, which adheres to and dangles from her pinky.

"I have her phone number," Susan says, quietly.

IV

Brittany took Martin up on his offer to let her use his phone, and after sitting in the bonus room with the door shut for nearly an hour, she emerges.

243

Martin is sitting on the couch. Susan is sitting in the cushioned chair at his right.

"So?" Martin asks, as Brittany slowly crosses the room and places the handset back in its cradle.

She turns to look at them both.

"How ya doin', Brittany?" Martin asks.

She holds her hands at her sides and her head down as she walks over to where Martin is sitting. With none of the usual Brittany fanfare, she sits beside him.

"You okay?" Martin asks.

It's a question that opens the floodgates.

"Oh, Martin," she says, crying as she curls against him in that same way she curls against Dude. "I don't know what to do! My mom is having a really bad time."

"How so, sweetie?" Susan asks, gently and quietly. "What's happening with her?"

Brittany sits up, rubs her face and gives herself a moment to stop crying. She then slinks down to the floor and takes her station beside Dude. After petting the cat for several seconds, she looks up at Martin and Susan. "She's just really poor, you know? She lives in a trailer, and she's on welfare, and she hasn't had a job in about four years. And you know, she's not all that old. She just turned fifty. Her life should be better than it is."

Martin and Susan wait in silence, each knowing that Brittany will share more as the seconds elapse.

"I just feel bad," Brittany says, reaching over to lure Dude into a roll-over.

"I mean, I don't regret getting out of there," she continues, her focus on the cat, her tone quiet. "I had to, and I know it was the right decision.

"But, you know," she says, returning her gaze to Martin and Susan, "I've got this great life here. Nice apartment. Good friends. I just wish my mom had a life like mine. I feel so bad for her."

Brittany exhales quite loudly. "And she asked me if I would come and see her."

Brittany casts her eyes down, revealing to Martin and Susan that the idea doesn't appeal to her. "I wish I wanted to do that," she says.

"Well, you know," Martin offers after a moment, keeping his tone low in respect for his friend's justifiable emotions. "Planes do fly in both directions."

"Yeah," says Brittany. "I was just thinking about that, too. Can I get a Mountain Dew?"

"Of course," Martin responds.

When Brittany steps out of the room for a moment, Martin looks over at Susan. She is clearly moved, and she also is clearly formulating thoughts.

After a minute or so in the kitchen, Brittany returns to the living room. She seems to have a bit more energy than she has displayed all evening. It may be the caffeine. It may be the sugar. It may be her irrepressible survival skills.

She sits on the floor and attempts a smile.

"Susan," she says, somewhat quietly, "thank you for doing this. I know that it's going to take me some time to process everything, but I'm glad to know. I'm glad that my mom's alive—even though her life sucks.

"And, of course," Brittany adds, still introspective after a long swig of her favorite elixir, "it doesn't actually suck all that much when compared to what she was going through with my dad."

CHAPTER THIRTY-FIVE

I

Driving to the seven-thirty breakfast meeting where he will meet a few board members from Hollywood Runaway, Martin feels a bit nervous. Just two days since his interview with Gail, this is happening much more quickly than he expected. Gail is clearly a go-getter. And fortunately, she doesn't seem to approach her goals with the selfish heartlessness of certain Senior Vice Presidents in the for-profit sector.

Martin makes the left from Sunset onto Doheny, figuring it'll be another three or four minutes before he gets to the Four Seasons Hotel. When Gail informed him of the meeting's venue, she sensed his surprise and quickly explained: "Most problems in Los Angeles are east and south. And most of the money is north and west. The board members are busy individuals, so I like to 'come to them' whenever possible, particularly when I want them to see things from my perspective."

Gail also had provided Martin with a little background information on the Board Chair and the two members of the Personnel Committee who would be attending the meeting. "You might remember Clem Altschul from the event," Gail had said. "He's the Chair, and he made most of the introductions that night. You need to know that he's rather conservative. I suggest you dress accordingly for the meeting. But please know, though," she added with a smile in her voice, "that once you start working here, you're going to find you don't have enough pairs of jeans."

Martin had smiled when he heard that comment. He smiled in spite of knowing the definition of "expectation"...

"Abby is the Chair of the Personnel Committee," Gail had continued. "She's a head-hunter, and she's a textbook extrovert. She's also very funny. Frankly, I always enjoy being in any small meeting that includes Clem and Abby. Because if it weren't for board responsibilities, I don't think that twain would *ever* meet! Anyway, be sure to laugh at her jokes, but don't upstage her. It's important for her to emerge from any meeting having been the wittiest."

"I'll keep my jokes to myself," Martin had said.

"Exactly. Now: Luis is probably the toughest nut to crack. He's been in city government for eons—currently a housing expert working out of the mayor's office. You may recall a time or two when he ran for city council and lost. In my opinion, he's still bitter. But we need that connection to the policymakers downtown, so he's a valuable board member. Anyway, don't let him get to you, because he'll try."

Martin is just finishing his review of the verbal cliff notes when he pulls into the parking lot and awaits a valet.

II

Entering the lobby, Martin immediately recognizes Clem. And he assumes that the man sitting in an overstuffed chair to Clem's left is Luis. Martin wonders if his being five minutes early will score him any brownie points. He also is not surprised that the noted extrovert will be the last to arrive.

Martin approaches the men, and Clem—who is sitting on a couch—happens to look up just as Martin nears them.

"Hello, gentlemen," Martin says, nodding. "I'm Martin Sheffield."

"Mr. Sheffield," Clem responds, standing as he extends his hand. "Good to meet you. Clem Altschul, and this—"

"Luis Santiago," the city hall guy says, taking his turn at a handshake.

III

"Boys, boys, *boys!*" Abby gushes, after rushing across the floor of Gardens, the hotel's award-winning restaurant.

Clem, Luis, and Martin all scoot their chairs back, preparing to stand up.

"Oh, don't stand," she says. "Or do! Or don't! *I* don't care!"

"Clem!" she exclaims, kissing her colleague on the cheek, "you did a fabulous job the other night. Just fabulous.

"Luis, my favorite policy man!" she effuses then, working her away around the table like the second hand on a Rolex. "I didn't even get a chance to speak with you at the event!"

She gives him his own peck on the cheek and then reaches Martin and extends her hand.

"Hello," she says, "you must be Martin. So, so sorry to keep all of you waiting."

"Not to worry, Abby," Clem says, as she takes her chair with Martin's gentlemanly assistance, "we've only been here for about five minutes. But we should order soon. I've got a nine-thirty appointment in Century City."

IV

Small talk having dominated the fifteen or so minutes between various arrivals and the subsequent delivery of their breakfast orders, Martin is feeling relatively comfortable. He realizes that his years of practiced collegial enthusiasm have prepared him well. The only irony exists in the reason he is *at* this interview: he'd rather not have too many of these meetings in the course of a workweek. He'd rather *never* have these meetings.

With plates in front of all parties, there is a slight lapse in the conversation. Then, as Luis picks up his fork, he makes a statement that changes the tone. "Well," he says, "enough of the informalities. Shall we find out about Martin Sheffield?"

Martin quickly catches a glance between Clem and Abby. From the subtleties in their exchange, Martin gathers that they might have opened the discussion in a less abrupt manner. Validating his inference—and perhaps to bridge the gap of the board members' differing interview techniques—Abby immediately jumps in: "I, for one, am dying to know why you are making such a dramatic career change!

"I admire your bravery," she continues, her tone more curious than critical, "particularly at this time in our economy. But I'm also a little thrown off by it. Why the switch to nonprofit?"

"That's a reasonable question," Martin replies.

"Thanks! I've been working on it *all* morning!"

Martin laughs (even though he finds this particular joke to be a little trite). "Good one," he says, reinforcing his laugh.

"I find it suspicious," Luis says immediately. "You are willing to take such a drastic cut in pay? Martin, you realize you'd be making less than a third of what you're making now."

"I do realize that, Luis, and I appreciate that this choice of mine might seem suspicious. However," Martin continues, "I have recently had a change in lifestyle whereby I no longer need the kind of income I am making now."

"Downsizing!" Abby exclaims. "I tell you, it is the hottest thing going these days!"

"I think there's a lot to be said for downsizing," Martin offers, nodding his head. "And, there's a lot to be said for doing meaningful work. I've had the very good fortune, over the past few months, of becoming friends with a staff member of the agency as well as with a young woman who was once served by the agency—Brittany, the alum who received the award the other night."

"Oh, God!" Abby says, holding her cloth napkin up to her chest. "Wasn't that the most beautiful speech? I think she's one of the most eloquent alums we have ever honored!"

"And what staff member do you know?" Clem asks, his attention primarily directed at the steak he is cutting.

"Jason," Martin replies. "One of your outreach workers. He and Brittany are good friends, so I met him through her. She's a neighbor of mine."

"Ah, yes," says Luis. "It's coming back to me now. Are you the father figure who Brittany thanked?"

"Father figure?" Martin asks, genuinely thrown off by the question.

"I recall Brittany thanking a neighbor. Was that you?"

"Yes," says Martin. "I was very touched by that."

"You know," Luis states, looking at his pancakes but clearly directing his comment to Martin, "staff positions in the non-profit sector are not about filling some emotional, familial need. They're about doing serious work."

"That's what I would expect," Martin says.

"Luis," Abby jumps in, looking directly at her colleague in the most persuasive way, "I think we might be getting off-point here."

"Actually, no, Abby," Luis replies, his tone increasingly heated. "I think it is very important that we make sure that we are hiring someone who appreciates good *business*. At this time in the economy, we cannot do anything but pay attention to the business end of things."

"Martin," Clem says, looking up from his current affair with breakfast sirloin, "please give us your impression of the business end of things. What do you bring to the table?"

"More than twenty-five years of professional accounting experience," Martin replies, returning his fork to his plate and looking directly at Clem. "Over the course of my career, I've been offered consistent opportunities to grow professionally."

Martin then directs a glance to Luis. "I've always been re-sponsible for—and have kept apprised of—knowing the rules and regulations that apply to procedures. I'm up to date with all the software and the best presentation technology."

Martin then turns to Abby. "And because I've managed ac-counts, I've also dealt with the people who represent those ac-counts. Which is to say, I guess, that I've had good opportunities to develop my people skills, and I've used those opportunities."

"Love it," says Abby, pulling another curl off her croissant. "Works and plays well with others!"

Suddenly, Luis reaches into his pocket and pulls out his cell phone. Undoubtedly on vibrate, the gadget has caught his attention. "Excuse me," he says, after reading the screen.

As Luis stands up and heads for the nearest door to the lush outdoor area, Clem and Abby raise four eyebrows between them.

"So tell us, Martin," Clem says next. "What is the absolute number one reason we should hire you?"

Martin glances down at the remains of his eggs benedict, and he thinks about the question for a few seconds. He then looks at Clem and at Abby. "I'm a good worker," he says.

"Simple answer," Clem says. "I like that. Hmm... And the reason we shouldn't?"

"Shouldn't... hire me?" Martin asks.

Clem nods.

Martin studies his plate and its small pools of soon-to-be-dried-up yolk. He's not coming up with anything. He feels like he's being tricked. *Hmm...* he thinks. *Reason not to hire me...* After a few too many seconds pass by, he regains eye contact with Clem and Abby.

"You know," Martin says, "it might be easier for me to answer that question after Luis returns."

Clem and Abby both smile.

"Good one," Abby says.

V

Martin is remarkably close to being on time for work, especially considering he began his day with a breakfast meeting on the west side. It is only about twenty after nine when he approaches his little corner of hell and makes eye contact with Alice.

"Morning, boss."

"Morning, Alice. What's cookin'?"

"Vivian, from all signs."

"Really?"

"Yeah, she's been circling like a shark. I guess she didn't think I'd remember to deliver the message she gave me at eight-thirty."

"Yeah, you're so inefficient," Martin says, teasingly. "I've been meaning to talk to you about that. So, any clue what she wants?"

"She wants you for lunch."

"On a plate, or across the table?"

Alice chuckles.

VI

"Thank you," Vivian says, as she collects Martin's menu and returns it, with hers, to the server who has just taken their order.

Martin reaches for his water glass and takes a long sip. He would rather look at the bad wall art than make eye contact with his alleged equal on the food chain.

"Martin," Vivian says then, willing to stare *through* him if that's what it takes to get his attention.

Martin smiles as he meets her gaze. "You rang, my compadre?" he says.

"I'm not in the mood for flippancy."

"Sorry, Viv. What's up? What's the Daily Grill occasion?"

"I heard it through the grapevine today that Debora is likely to leave."

"Really?"

"That doesn't concern you?"

"Vivian," Martin replies, "I'm not sure how to answer that..." (*Could we wait for Luis to return?* Martin thinks.)

"Well," Vivian says, "I know you and she have had many tête-à-têtes in the past few weeks. I would think if she were feeling a little cabin fever, you might know."

"I'm not sure what Debora's plans are," Martin responds, in all honesty. "But I also don't think we should worry. Given the current market, anyone who leaves Haley-Mitchell-Phelps can probably be replaced quite quickly."

"That's not a very humane perspective," says Vivian.

VII

Having left the apartment that morning at a quarter 'til seven, Martin is happy to put his key in the lock twelve hours later. As soon as he enters, it is very clear that Dude missed him terribly. The cat, who has adapted a charming Quasimodo lurch as he's worked his way from here to there in the back-leg cast, meets Martin in the kitchen. And his soft chirp of a meow is somehow more comical than ever.

"I hear you, buddy," Martin says, as he also hears the phone ring. Martin scoops out several forkfuls of cat food and then quickly places the empty can on the counter so as to reach the telephone before the machine takes it.

"Hello!" Martin says anxiously, having just made it on the fourth ring.

"Uncle Marty!"

"Zac! How ya doin?"

"I'm great," Zac replies, his monotone belying the likely truth that he really is feeling quite fine.

"School over?"

"Oh, yeah. Finished up finals last week."

"How'd they go?" Martin asks.

"Not bad, I guess. I don't think I flunked anything."

"So, are you back home?"

"No way," Zac responds. "I decided to crash with some friends in Philly until I head out to see you."

"Wow? Your mom was okay with that?" Martin asks, somewhat surprised.

"Yeah, you know I've been training her for a few years. It's starting to kick in. Besides," Zac adds, " she kinda has her hands full right now with Carol."

"*Carol?*"

"Yeah, she's been getting into some trouble."

"*Carol?*" Martin asks again, remembering when his youngest niece was going through her Amish stage. That couldn't have been more than five years ago.

"What kind of trouble is she getting into?" Martin asks.

"I don't know," Zac replies. "Staying out late. Ditching school some days. Mom isn't too specific otherwise."

"What about Nancy?" Martin inquires, referring to the other teenage girl in the family.

"She seems to be on track. I think she's already lined up a summer job, in fact. You know, she's always had that entrepreneurial spirit.

"So, hey!" Zac says. "Enough about them. Let's talk about me. My flight is this Sunday."

"I know. I can't believe it's so soon."

"You ready?"

"Absolutely," Martin responds. "In fact, I got that second week off."

"You did? Way cool."

"And I was thinking it might be nice to drive up the coast. The Big Sur experience is pretty amazing."

"Okay," Zac says.

Martin doesn't attempt to interpret Zac's lack of overt enthusiasm. If his nephew *didn't* want to do a little road trip, he'd speak up.

"So I'll look into motels up in the Monterey area. You know, just two nights, and then we'll head back down. The landscape is worth the drive, believe me."

"Sounds cool, Uncle Marty. So? You have my flight details?"

"Yeah, I saved the email. You arrive around nine that night, if I recall."

"Yeah, something like that. Anyway, you have my cell number, so if you can't dig up the details, just give me a call."

"Great," Martin says, realizing that he's actually looking forward to his nephew's visit. "So I guess the next time we talk will be when I pick you up at LAX."

"LAX," Zac repeats. "What a name for an airport."

"I know," Martin agrees. "It sort of makes one expect delays, doesn't it?"

"Funny. Okay, Uncle Marty. So, I'll see you Sunday then."

"Yup. Have a safe flight."

"I'm planning on it."

CHAPTER THIRTY-SIX

I

Just about to pull into his parking space on level P3, Martin sees Brenda getting out of her Jetta. He rolls down his window and calls out to her.

"Oh, hey!" she says, a relaxed smile underscoring her easy, but enthusiastic, reply.

"Hang on a sec," Martin says, as he maneuvers his small car into the space that has had his name on it for far too many years.

By the time Martin emerges from the driver's seat, Brenda is standing nearby.

"I haven't seen you in a while," she says. "How's life on nine?"

"Life on nine stinks with intrigue," he replies, as they walk together to the elevator. "How's life on eight?"

"Shit if I know. Any idea when they're going to hire my new boss?"

"Personnel keeps telling me that they're sorting through resumés," Martin says, not altogether sure he believes the news he is repeating.

"You mean you haven't even started interviewing yet?" Brenda asks, incredulously.

Martin wants to tell his former assistant that he's in fact had two interviews this week, and he's feeling hopeful. But he knows she's not inquiring about *his* future.

"Nope," he says instead. "Either there's a bottleneck in H.R. or there's a bottleneck in New York."

"Or there's a bottleneck between Vivian's head and her ass," Brenda offers.

"Come to think of it," Martin states, as they reach the first set of elevators and he hits the up arrow button, "she does look like a bottle, doesn't she?"

"A bottle of prune juice."

"No," Martin chuckles, as they enter the elevator, "she's too thin for that visual. She also has no cleansing qualities, in my opinion.

"So how are you doing otherwise?" Martin asks, after the doors have closed and no third parties have joined their conversation.

Brenda holds up her left hand, where the ring that once was is no longer.

"New manicure?" he asks.

"No man!" she replies. "I cure!"

"Oh boy," she says then. "That was pretty clever. I may have to send that one to *Cosmo!*"

"You broke up?" Martin confirms, ensuring that he delivers the question in a tone that sounds unbiased.

"Yeah," she says, as they exit the first elevator and head to the second. "That weekend after you and I had lunch."

"And you feel okay?"

"Some days are really hard, but overall? I feel grateful. Grateful that I didn't make a huge mistake."

"Good for you," Martin says, patting Brenda on the back as they wait for the ride that will take them to their respective floors.

II

Alice is on the phone and looks up as Martin approaches.

"Oh," she then says into the receiver, "here he is now."

Martin raises his eyebrows inquisitively as he heads for his office.

"A Gail Tryce," Alice reports. "Line one."

"Thanks, Alice," Martin utters, giving away no secrets before he shuts his office door and quickly crosses to his desk.

258

"Gail!" Martin says, having grabbed the phone and pushed the appropriate button from the guests' side of his fully-windowed power corner.

"Good morning, Martin," she replies, her smooth voice seeming even deeper than usual. "Are you surprised to be hearing from me so soon?"

"A little, maybe. So, do you have news, or are you just calling to chat?"

"I like your style, Martin, which is why I pushed so hard for you."

For a second, Martin feels a tightness. He wants an "and," but after that opening statement, he fears a "but."

"And..." Gail says then, a slight lilt in her voice, "as it turns out, I probably didn't need to push that hard. Clem and Abby were very impressed."

"And Luis?"

"He will be impressed. Just give him time."

"Are you offering me the job?"

"No, I was just calling to chat." Gail begins to laugh. "Yes!" she says, "I'm offering you the job!"

Envisioning Gail in that small office of hers, where the base of the few windows are just above an average person's eyeline, Martin smiles.

"I accept," he says.

III

As soon as he had hung up with Gail, Martin crossed to his coffee station, poured himself a mug, and sank into his VP couch. He doesn't know how much time has passed since then. And he can't even put his finger on what he's feeling right now. He wishes he could just blink his eyes and be completely gone from Haley-Mitchell-Phelps. He wishes he could dispense with the formalities of giving notice, of compiling whatever needs to be compiled for his successor ... of saying a few sincere goodbyes. As far as he's concerned, he did all that—at least, in his head—weeks ago.

Draining his coffee mug, Martin realizes that he needs to get going on the first step. Ironically, the step that he dreads the most is the very one he has fantasized about: telling Vivian.

IV

"Come in, Martin!" Vivian says, looking up from a file folder and making an attempt at some sort of warmth

Martin slowly approaches one of her guest chairs as Vivian closes the folder and stands.

"Can I get you some coffee?" she asks, carrying her Van Gogh mug over to her own version of the VP lounge area.

"I'm good," Martin says.

He wishes he could enjoy this more, but just as he doesn't trust working with Vivian, he also doesn't trust telling her that he's done with that chapter of his life.

"So," she says, sauntering back to her desk and opting for the power seat that creates a backdrop of the windowed corner. "What can I do for you?"

"Well," Martin replies. "I've got some news."

"Debora?" she asks, cocking her head and looking at him over her power glasses.

"No. In fact, I haven't seen her all week."

"You know, Martin," Vivian says, putting her mug down and clasping her hands tightly in front of her. "It concerns me a bit that you are so distanced from your staff. I strongly recommend your showing a little more interest and a little more concern. If you don't manage your staff, they may very well end up managing you."

Martin smiles and just looks at her.

She looks back, giving him one of her own smiles. A harsh smile. A smile that is informed by contempt.

"Vivian," Martin begins, "I'm not sure why you're smiling, but I'm smiling because I'm here to give you my notice. I've accepted another position, and I begin work on June fifteenth."

In a nanosecond, Vivian is clearly and indisputably no longer smiling. In fact, Martin has never seen her look so close to spitting nails.

"June fifteenth," she says, unclasping her hands and fanning them out on the desktop.

She then looks at Martin through narrow eyes.

"That doesn't give us much time, now, does it?" she asks (rhetorically).

"I can't do anything about that, Vivian."

"This is not going to look good, Martin. You know this is career suicide."

"It depends on how you define career.

"Look," Martin says, standing and pushing her guest chair back toward her so that it is flush with the desk (as uninviting as it should be), "there's no reason for us to discuss this because there is nothing to discuss. Just let me know what I can do between now and then."

He heads for the door, and then pauses. Turning around—but only slightly—Martin adds, "Oh, and I'll be taking the week of the eighth off. It's already approved, and I've already made plans."

He taps her doorframe twice and makes his way back to his own VP corner.

V

When Martin returns from his celebratory lunch with Debora, Alice smiles at him. He had shared his news with her that morning, as soon as he returned from Vivian's office. Alice was overjoyed to hear about it. "You are doing the right thing," she had said. "You are taking care of yourself, and you're showing some good priorities. Good for you."

Now, Alice follows him into his office.

"What's up, boss?" Martin asks.

"I just want you to know. My contacts in the other corner have shared with me that Vivian has been on the phone with New York. All morning."

"Good for her," Martin says, shrugging.

"All I'm saying is you might want to start packing now."

"That'd be fine with me," Martin replies, circling to the business side of his desk. "Any particular reason you think that?"

"I think this firm has become like some reality show. You know, forming alliances."

"I don't watch reality shows."

"You don't have to, Martin. The commercials pretty much tell you everything you need to know."

"I'll give you that one," Martin responds, nodding.

"Regardless, all I'm saying is, I think you're about to be kicked off the island."

"Wanna come with me?" Martin asks.

Alice smiles as she heads back to her station. "This place can't hurt me," she says. "I'm just a quote-unquote lowly, old-fashioned secretary."

Alice turns before making her exit. "I don't like the firm, but the drama is consistently entertaining."

VI

Martin is checking his email when he is distracted by Brenda's exuberant entrance into his office.

"Oh my God!" she is saying, rushing over to his desk. "I just heard! You're out of here!"

"Word travels fast," Martin says, standing and suggesting, with his arm, that they sit in his "lounge area."

"Can I get you some water or coffee?" Martin asks, as Brenda follows him to the more comfortable quadrant of his office.

"Water is cool."

"You're right," Martin replies. "The refrigerator does that, you know."

Brenda plops down onto the couch and accepts the small bottle of Arrowhead. Martin grabs one for himself and takes a seat on the chair where he is most likely to see anyone enter the room.

For a minute, they both just guzzle water. For a minute, they both just breathe.

"So, when I saw you this morning— ?" Brenda begins to ask.

"I didn't know," Martin says. "I got the phone call and the offer just after I came in."

"So you really haven't interviewed for your replacement downstairs?"

"No. I really haven't. And I have no idea what is going on. Really."

"So, do you think my job is secure?" Brenda asks.

"Who knows? Do you want it to be?"

"What do you mean?"

"I mean," Martin says, "do you love this job? Would you be just fucking heartbroken if you lost it?"

Brenda looks stunned. "Wow," she comments. "I've never heard you drop the 'f-bomb' before. I need to process that for a minute... It makes me realize how important this conversation is.

"It's interesting," she says, a few seconds later, "You know, I've been here for so long."

"How long?"

"God, it'll be eight years in October."

"And do you want to be here for eight more?"

Martin watches Brenda's facial expression. It is different from any she has ever worn while in the office. She's clearly thinking about something outside of Haley-Mitchell-Phelps.

"You know," Brenda says, "when I was in college, I did a lot of waitressing, and I really loved it. I loved the interactions, the movement, the energy. And when I finally got out of college, it just felt like I should get another kind of job. So, you know, I looked around and landed here. And, I remember, about two years in, I was thinking that I missed the restaurant world. That maybe if I got back into it, I could, you know, do something like open my own place. I'm a great cook, by the way. Did you know that?"

"I didn't," Martin says, smiling at his former assistant, who is now practically prone on his VP couch. (The doctor is *in*.)

"Yeah," Brenda says, sitting up suddenly. "I really wanted to do that."

"So what happened?" Martin asks.

"Mike happened."

"Mike?"

Brenda holds up her ringless left hand. The man-i-cure.

"He didn't want me to do it. He thought it was a dumb idea. So... I agreed with him."

"It's not too late!" says Martin.

"But, Martin, I'm about to turn thirty! That is so *old* for restaurant work in this town!"

"I am not even listening to that argument," Martin states.

The two colleagues are each taking a swig of Arrowhead when Vivian enters the room with no fanfare.

"Hello, Brenda," she says first, "please excuse Martin and me."

"Adios, amigo," Brenda says, leaving her water on the table and pretty much running out of the room.

"Vivian? Can I get you something?"

"You can get me your keys, your clicker, and your garage guest pass. I've got someone from security—" Vivian turns then and calls out, "Maurice!" —and Maurice strolls into the room, his smile contradicting Vivian's countenance.

Martin reaches into his pocket and pulls out his wallet. He finds within it the garage guest pass. He hands that to Vivian.

He then pulls his keys out of his front pocket and removes those that belong to the office. He hands both to her.

Then, he holds out his car keys and dangles them in front of her.

"My clicker is understandably in my car," Martin says. "Would you like to go down and get it?"

Vivian turns to Maurice, who, by the looks of his bemused facial expression, is probably working on a film treatment called *Survivor: H-M-P.*

"Maurice," Vivian says, as Martin returns his keys to his pocket, "when Martin is done collecting his personal items, I would like for you to accompany him downstairs and retrieve his clicker."

"Yes, ma'am," Maurice says, offering an officious salute only after her back is turned.

Martin smiles as the woman who is shaped like a tall bottle makes her exit. And it is only after that occurrence that he offers *his* full salute.

"Maurice!" Martin says, "this shouldn't take too long. Would you like some bottled water?"

"That'd be cool."

"Yeah, well, it's the fridge that makes it cool," Martin says.

VII

Martin had always imagined that if he ever had the chance to go to Trader Joe's during "work hours," he'd sail right through. He'd pull into the parking lot and have his choice of spaces. He'd get the best cart or the cleanest basket available and he'd saunter through the aisles with no competition.

So, when he arrives at the store at four-fifteen that Thursday afternoon, he is overwhelmed by the throngs of shoppers. He's also touched. There's a world that exists outside that workday grind. A busy, thriving world.

VIII

Martin feels silly, standing in Susan's line. He's clearly a candidate for one of the express cashiers, but he doesn't mind waiting. He doesn't even mind the strange glances he gets from other shoppers. The strange glances that wonder why he is standing there... Martin, without a cart. Martin, without a basket even.

When his number finally comes up, and Susan turns to greet him, she automatically reaches to the shelf where his basket of goods might be waiting. After a false sweep, she turns and looks at him curiously, and he hands her a bottle of champagne.

Susan retains her crewmember demeanor as she scans the item and as Martin heads for the console where he will swipe his card and punch in his PIN.

When they resume eye contact, both their smiles are over the top.

"You got the job?" Susan asks.

"Yeah," he says, approving the expense of more than thirty dollars.

Then Martin picks up the bottle of champagne. "And *this* is for us."

"I'm off at nine."

"You wanna come over?"

"Yes! Yes!" she replies, nodding. "Yes! I do!"

IX

Martin is laughing as he approaches Vermont. He's laughing because Trader Joe's took a full forty-five minutes of his life. And finding parking, just to be home, took another thirty.

He's laughing because he doesn't really care. If he tabulated all those years at H-M-P... *Oh, don't go there,* he immediately says to himself, as he walks across the street and heads north from Kingswell.

Within thirty seconds, a loud, cheerful voice peels through the air: "Martin-Martin!"

He looks across Vermont and sees Brittany, bouncing to arrive at the crosswalk that will allow them to greet on *their* side of the avenue.

X

"Oh-my-god, oh-my-god, oh-my-god," she says, giving him a bear hug with nervous enthusiasm. "Martin, I did it!"

"What did you do?"

"Bought a plane ticket. My mom will be here Monday."

"Wow!" Martin responds, standing back and so allowing her to release her clinging hug. "That's soon. That's four days from now."

"Yeah," says Brittany, as they approach their building, "I just didn't want to drag it out. I mean it wasn't cheap, but you know I got that Vegas money and—"

"How long is she staying?" Martin asks.

"'Til Sunday," Brittany replies, nodding. "And I'm going to take next week off."

"Good for you, Brittany. Good for you. And you're feeling okay about it?"

"I'm feeling whatever. You know, all I can do is the next thing. That's all any of us can do."

They've arrived at their building, and Martin is prepped with his key. He lets them in, and they head for the elevator.

"So," Brittany says next, nodding at the small Trader Joe's bag, "what'd ya get?"

Martin extracts the bottle of champagne.

"Celebrating?" Brittany asks.

"Yeah. I'm also taking next week off. In fact, as of right now, I'm unemployed."

"No way!" Brittany squeals, as the elevator doors open and they both enter into the small cell. "Did you get fired?"

"Yes," replies Martin, pushing both her button and his. "But only after I gave notice. I got the job at Hollywood Runaway..."

When Brittany leaps to hug Martin, they both worry for a minute that the elevator cables might break.

"I love that so much!" she says, pulling away from the hug, just as the light above the doors indicates arrival at floor three. "You are so right for that place."

The doors open. Brittany begins to step out. "Hey," she says, suddenly turning, and using her hand to prevent the doors from closing. "You're not gonna drink that champagne alone, are you?"

"No," Martin responds. "I'm expecting Susan."

"Yes!" Brittany squeals, clapping her hands and so removing them from the hold on the door.

As Martin is left alone in the upward-bound elevator, he can only imagine the happy dance that is taking his young friend down the hall. And because his mind is looking ahead, Martin doesn't notice the posting on one of the elevator's narrower walls. A memo from David, their building's manager, indicates that, earlier that week, a tenant named Scott was arrested for burglarizing a private home in the neighborhood...

CHAPTER THIRTY-SEVEN

I

When Martin opens his eyes on Friday morning and sees Susan's peaceful, sleeping face, his own sense of peace grows by leaps and bounds. He quietly slips out of bed, puts on his sweats, and heads for the kitchen. Dude, who opted out of sharing the bed with more than one human, meets Martin *en route* and accompanies him into the room where cat food and coffee are the first order of the day.

After scooping half a can of Trader Joe's finest onto Dude's plate, Martin gets the can of Bay Blend out of the fridge. He then decides to shut the kitchen door, in the event that the coffee grinder might wake Susan from an otherwise restful sleep.

When the grinding exercise is complete and Martin has re-opened the kitchen door, he smiles through the remaining coffee prep tasks. And he smiles at the night that just passed. Champagne. Soft music. Some making out in the living room. And then the ultimate move to that land of intimacy.

He suddenly entertains a memory of something he overheard on that late afternoon in the restaurant that serves tentacles. He remembers Susan's implication that her libido had gone AWOL. Martin begs to differ. There wasn't anything about their lovemaking that wasn't sensuous, heated, and perfect. And he thinks she could very well be the best kisser he's ever had the pleasure to kiss.

As the coffee continues to drip into the carafe, Martin wanders to the window and looks out over the post office parking lot, which is filled with electric vehicles. He loves his view. From the observatory to his left to the kitschy House of Pies sign straight ahead; from the real estate in the distance to the retail at the right, he loves what he sees. This is the kind of Los Angeles he was looking for when he moved from Chicago twelve years ago. He doesn't need a corner office. He has a corner apartment.

"Mornin'," he hears then, and he turns to see the woman who is helping to make everything seem so right. She obviously found his robe, and it gives her an especially cuddly look. A part of him, though, wants to walk her back to the bedroom and help her take it off.

II

Martin loves it that he can enjoy a leisurely Mama Mia breakfast at nine-thirty on a Friday morning. He reaches for his coffee and notices a smile on Susan's face. She is directing that smile behind him, and so he is compelled to turn.

"Jason!" he says.

"Hey," says Jason, maneuvering through the maze of tables and chairs. "Mind if I join you two for a quick cup of decaf."

"Decaf?" Susan asks.

"Yeah, I need to get home and get some sleep. But I'm not quite ready."

"You worked last night?" Martin asks.

"Yeah," Jason replies. "From ten until six."

"Whew!" says Susan, reaching for her own hit of caffeine so as to swallow the concept of a graveyard shift.

"And I just had breakfast with Brittany before she headed off to work," Jason says.

"So she filled you in?" Martin asks.

"About her mom? Yeah. In fact, I'm going to drive with her to the airport on Monday."

"That's good to hear," Martin says. "So, what do you think?"

"I think it's great that she got in touch. And I think it's courageous of her to plan this reunion. And it's definitely better they do it here than in Nebraska."

"Any predictions?" Susan asks.

"You mean, about the outcome of the visit?"

Susan nods.

"I wouldn't even try to go there," Jason states. He then interrupts the dialogue and looks up at the waitress. "Decaf please?

"Anyway," he continues, "it's likely to be a roller-coaster of sorts, but the cool thing is that Brittany knows that. She's also got some of the best coping skills I've ever seen in a person. So, no matter what happens, she'll be fine. And that's all I care about."

"She's really lucky to have you, Jason," Susan says, reaching across the table and touching his arm.

"We're both lucky."

III

After walking Susan to her car, which she had to park about halfway between her Silver Lake house and his Los Feliz apartment, Martin and she engage in some public display of affection. And while they don't specify when their next rendezvous will be, Martin sees her off without concern regarding that eventuality. As he saunters home, he knows he is smiling in a telling manner. And he doesn't mind telling others, through his smile, that he just had a really good night. One of the best nights in a very long time.

Back home, he just happens to be within peripheral vision of his answering machine. Surprised to see a blinking light, he presses the button that will reveal the details.

"Hi, Marty," comes the slightly nasal voice of his younger sister. "It's Rache. I know you're at work, so it's kind of silly for me to be calling you right now, but I'm kind of in a silly mood. I'm taking a mental health day. It's noon-thirty and I'm still in my pajamas, can you believe it? Oh my God, I have to tell you, I had the funniest, most pitiful dream last night. I dreamt that Jack and I were on a cross-country trip, and when we got to Saint Louis, I asked him to hold the subway doors so I could run up and look at the arch. Can you believe that? A see-America road trip by subway! Jeez, do you think I've been living in New York too long? Anyway, call me when you get a chance. Love you bro!"

Martin smiles longer even than the sound of the beep. He then goes into the kitchen, where his cell phone should be fully charged. Having those free rollover minutes is especially convenient now.

IV

"Rachel!" he says enthusiastically, after hearing her never enthusiastic "Hello?"

"Marty! Are you home today or did you check your messages from work?"

"I'm home, and work is history."

"What do you mean?" Rachel asks.

"I got a new job!"

"But you just got that promotion and raise—"

"Well, there were strings attached," Martin states.

"How do you mean?"

"I mean, it was a promotion to hell, and everything thereafter proceeded to raise the hairs on the back of my neck."

"Wow. So? Where's your new job? Another financial firm?"

"No, actually," Martin replies. "I'm joining the nonprofit sector."

"No kidding? What agency? What will you be doing?"

"I'm going to be the CFO of an organization called Hollywood Runaway and Homeless Youth."

"Cool! And you're okay with the big drop in income?" Rachel asks.

"I'm totally okay with that. I actually welcome it."

"Good for you, Marty! Good for you. You know, I think you'll like nonprofit. I think we were kinda raised for nonprofit type of work."

"You're probably right," Martin agrees.

"Yeah, you know, I actually never really understood that career path you took. It just didn't seem right somehow."

"In retrospect, I think I agree. But, you know, I got out of college at a weird time. It was all about pale yellow ties back then. It was all about making a boatload of money, or at least being in that world."

"Oh, God, yeah, I remember those yellow ties. They had a shelf life, didn't they?"

Martin smiles at the content of this impromptu conversation.

"Hey," Rachel says then, "I spoke with Reggie earlier. I hear Zac is heading out this weekend."

"He is! He arrives Sunday."

"So whatcha got planned?"

"Well," Martin replies, "it's cool 'cause, now, I've got the whole time off. I don't know what we'll do next week, but I thought the following week, we might head up the coast."

"Sounds nice. You know, I gotta get out there one of these days."

"You've been saying that for years," Martin reminds her.

"I know," Rachel replies, sounding like a scolded child.

"So you talked to Reggie?" Martin asks then. "What's new with her?"

"Well, she's the same. You know, pretty centered, but damn, they seem to be having some major problems with Carol."

"Yeah, Zac made that implication. Any details?"

"Interesting details, actually. Reggie seems to think that our darling little niece is no longer, as Reggie put it, 'in tacto.'"

"Okay," Martin responds. "I'm totally picturing air quotes right now."

"Yeah, but I could only do one because I'm holding the phone. Anyway, yeah, seems our little niecey-poo might be involved in some sexual experimentation."

"Safe sexual experimentation, I hope," Martin comments.

"I hope so, too."

"And Reggie's not flipping out?"

"No," Rachel replies. "I think she's flipping *in*. She seems to be confiding in the older girls a lot, and apparently, Sara has been especially helpful."

"Is Sara still in D.C.?" Martin asks.

"Yeah, oh, didn't you hear?"

"I guess not."

"She's working for the Obama administration," Rachel shares, revealing a hint of enthusiasm. "Department of Education. It's a pretty good job, apparently. She's even been invited to a few White House events."

"Wow," Martin responds, genuinely impressed. "And how's the rest of her life?"

"Good. She's living with a guy. I forget his name—"

Martin interrupts: "And Reggie's okay with that?"

"Well, sure. I mean Sara's twenty-five."

"Oh, damn!" Rachel blurts out suddenly. "I just realized I gotta go. I promised a friend I'd call her before three, and I've got about two minutes to keep that promise."

"Well, I won't let you break it. Look, though, I want you to plan a trip out here. I'm serious. If you're not out here before the end of the calendar year, I will disown you."

Rachel's voice conveys a smile. "I will do that, Marty. Talk to you soon. Have a great time with Zac."

"Bye."

After hanging up the phone, Martin looks across the room and meets the loving gaze of his becasted cat.

It's noon on a Friday in Los Angeles, and Martin has absolutely no plans. He wanders into the kitchen and takes a look out the window. He reads the marquee on the movie theatre across the street. A few possibilities. He decides to lie down for a while. The first screening at the LF3 rarely begins before one-thirty.

CHAPTER THIRTY-EIGHT

I

"Hello, stranger," Susan says smoothly, smiling to Martin as she activates the brake on the handcart that is stacked with small, orange-colored fruits.

"Hi," he replies, not caring if he's blushing. "I see they have you on Cutie-duty."

"Good one," she says, as she begins to stack the small orange fruits on their designated shelves. "So what are you doing at Joe's on a Sunday?"

"Stocking up for Zac's visit."

"Good idea. Hey," she says then, "do you realize we were on the phone for three hours last night?"

"I enjoyed every minute of it."

"I did, too," she agrees, her nod reinforcing her statement.

"So after Zac and I have a chance to settle in, I'll figure out the rest of the week. See when we could all get together."

"Sounds good," says Susan, "and I was thinking, too, depending, I guess, on how things go with Brittany and her mom, it might be nice to get all of you over to my house for dinner one night. Nothing fancy. What do you think?"

"We'll know more by the middle of the week, probably," Martin replies.

"I'm weirdly nervous about their reunion," Susan confides, placing the last box of Cuties on the stack.

"I know. Me, too."

"Well, my friend," Susan says then, tilting her head and smiling broadly. "My Cutie-duty has come to an end, and I need to report back to my task-master.

"See ya later," she adds, kicking the brake on the cart and rolling it back toward the storage area that is known to employees only.

II

"Myra!" Martin exclaims, as he approaches the elevator, carrying two double Trader Joe's bags.

"Hello, Martin," Myra replies, her tone uncharacteristically dull.

"What's wrong?" Martin asks.

"I don't know. Just not feeling myself today."

"How so?" he asks.

"It's hard to explain," she says, tentatively. "Um, Martin? You mind if I follow you upstairs? Maybe right now, I need some company. Are you free?"

"Sure," says Martin, trying extra hard to maintain a light tone, as the elevator doors close and he pushes the 5 button. "You wanna stop at your place and pick up your schnapps?"

"Schnapps before three? I think not!"

Martin is glad to hear a little lilt in her voice. And he hopes he can bring out more of her natural tendency to emote. Witnessing a Myra who is less than engaged and relatively unenthused is almost scary, in a laws-of-the-universe kind of way.

They ride in silence to the fifth floor, and when the doors open there, Myra immediately steps into the hallway.

"Here," she says then, putting her arm out. "Let me take one of those so you can get your keys."

Martin hands her the lighter of the two bags as they head for his door.

"God, I can smell our manager taking a day off," Myra comments, the scent of marijuana lingering in the air.

"Yeah," Martin responds, as he opens the door. "Seems to be his favorite pastime."

"Well," says Myra, following Martin into his kitchen, "I don't suppose I should judge. God knows, when I was his age, I was doing a lot more than pot."

Martin directs a glance in Myra's direction. It says *Really?* in a playful way.

"But it's not interesting," Myra says, responding to his inquisitive expression.

"Can I get you anything?" Martin asks, as he begins to put the groceries away.

"I'll let you know," Myra replies.

"So what's up? I've never witnessed this introspective side of you."

"That's a very good word for it," Myra says. "I guess that's how I'm feeling. I had the strangest dream last night."

"This seems to be my week for hearing about dreams. You want to tell me about it?"

"It wasn't a bad dream. It was just strange. I dreamt that I was with Lonzo. Our former neighbor. Dude's dad. The missing man. We were in Vegas and we were about to get married at one of those drive-through chapels. But he suddenly stopped. He said, 'Wait, Myra! Hold on! We'll come back here, I promise, but right now, I have a feeling.' And then he grabbed my hand and we ran to some casino that was next door to the chapel. He fought through the crowd, me behind him, and he approached a roulette table. He pulled out this wad of cash. My God, it must have been thousands of dollars. And he put it all down on Number One. All of it."

"They put cash on the table in Vegas?" Martin asks. "I thought they used chips."

"A dream, Martin. A *dream*."

"Right."

"And then the dealer spun the wheel," Myra continues. "And the spinning seemed to go on forever. I looked at Lonzo as the wheel was spinning, and he got this wild look in his eyes. It was frightening, actually. It was diabolical. I wanted to run in that moment, but he grabbed my arm. He held it so tight it hurt. And we watched the wheel come to a stop. The ball landed on

Number One. I turned to look at him. I turned to witness what I expected would be euphoria, and he wasn't there. Just then, you, Martin, came through the crowd. You looked so sweet and innocent among those Vegas people. And when you approached the table, the dealer congratulated you and handed you Lonzo's fortune."

"Wow," Martin says, his eyes suddenly tearing up. "But, you know, I already have Lonzo's fortune."

"What do you mean?" Myra asks.

"I've got Dude."

III

"Wow, cool," Zac says, looking through the front windshield and sounding like he's still on East Coast time.

"What's that?" Martin asks, as he cruises north on LaBrea, in that area off Stocker that is distinctly (and repeatedly) identified as having a fifty-five mile per hour speed limit.

"The lights and the mountains."

"Yeah," Martin agrees, "it's a clear night."

Martin smiles as he drives. Among the things that are clear this night is Zac's complete exhaustion. While they were waiting for his duffle at baggage claim, Martin's nephew indicated that he probably had not slept in twenty-four hours. The night before, apparently, was quite a party night in Philly. Apparently, if Zac did sleep, he no longer remembers...

"So is it always this crazy?" Zac asks then.

"How do you mean?" Martin replies, as he takes a quick opportunity to change lanes and get out from in back of a slow-moving pick-up.

"The traffic," Zac says, in a voice that describes eyes wanting to close. "I mean, what time is it?"

"Almost ten-thirty," Martin responds, after conferring with the clock on the dashboard.

"Wow. And it's Sunday."

"How do you mean?" Martin asks.

"This is like Saturday night traffic. It's crazy."

"I don't think L.A. has any sense of time," Martin offers. "It is its own universe. Its own time zone. Its own attitude."

"You like it then."

"I'm liking it a lot now. I don't think I knew L.A. until I moved out of the Valley."

"Olympic," Zac comments, after noticing a street sign up ahead.

"Exactly. Where we make our right."

"That's a pretty self-impressed name for a street."

"It's a pretty impressive street," Martin says, inching his way to the intersection and looking for an opportunity to go right on red.

"So what did you mean about the Valley?" Zac asks, as Martin makes the turn onto Olympic and the road ahead looks like a runway cleared for take-off.

"The Valley?" Martin reiterates. "I don't know. It's on the other side of those hills you were noticing. Those hills you called mountains. And there's nothing wrong with it. I mean, the Valley is a good place to exist quietly. It feels safe. But? This side of the hills? To me, this is the city. This is the place to really feel alive."

Martin looks over at Zac, and his nephew has suddenly dropped into a deep sleep that will probably result in a rather bad neck cramp.

IV

"So this is it!" Martin says, Zac's duffle bag over his shoulder and his nephew following him into the humble one-bedroom.

"Mao."

"And this is Dude."

"Dude!" Zac says, looking down at the friendly feline. "Wow, he's pretty rad in that cast."

"That reminds me," Martin says. "I think this is the week it comes off."

"Dude!" Zac says again, lowering himself to the floor, where he sits cross-legged and enjoys bonding with his other-species cousin.

Martin leaves them to their greetings and takes Zac's duffle back to the bedroom. When he returns, Zac is once again asleep, this time prone and in the relative comfort of Martin's front entryway.

"Dude," Martin says, tapping his nephew on the shoulder.

"Dude," he repeats.

Zac shakes himself into consciousness. "That's the name of your cat, dude."

"That's everybody's name, Zac. Look," Martin says then, grabbing his nephew's arm and helping him stand, "I'm gonna let you sleep in my bed tonight, because you seriously need it. I'll sleep on the couch."

"Are you sure?"

"Yep. Come on back."

"Good. 'Cause I'm so tired, I could probably sleep anywhere."

"I've noticed."

"You know what, though?" Zac says, his eyes at much more than half-mast. "I have totally gotta find my toothbrush because my mouth is rank."

"Yeah," Martin says. "I've noticed."

CHAPTER THIRTY-NINE

I

"Damn, this is so cool, Uncle Marty."

They are sitting under the Fred 62 awning, on the side street, and Martin made sure to take the chair facing away from Vermont. He figured his nephew, well-rested after fourteen hours of sleep, would appreciate the view of the major thoroughfare.

Zac takes another bite from his burger, and then returns it to his plate. "I can't believe this," he says, "I fully expected I'd be looking at surfers the whole time I was out here."

"There is that option," Martin offers. "In fact, we will definitely have to do the Venice boardwalk this week. It's a must-see."

"You just point me wherever, Uncle Marty," Zac responds, enthusiastically. "So. Fred 62. What's that about? I mean, the name."

"Well, according to lore, the two guys who opened this place are both named Fred, and they were both born in 'Sixty-two."

"Old guys," Zac comments.

"Hey," Martin says.

"Sorry," Zac offers, pulling some fries out of the small, grease-stained brown paper bag in which they were delivered.

"And how weird is that, by the way?" Zac says.

"What?" Martin asks.

"Fred. Who names their kid Fred? Do you think that was some kind of fallout from the Flintstones' popularity?"

Martin smiles at his nephew's comment. "I don't know," he says. "You know, they used to make Flintstones vitamins, back in the early Sixties. Maybe two women thought they were taking birth control, and now, their ignorance is making money hand-over-fist here on swanky Vermont Avenue."

"I like that," Zac responds, nodding. "Good theory, Uncle Marty."

II

After their lunch, Martin and Zac walk over to Hillhurst so that Martin can fork over a bit too much money for a cat carrier from For Pets Only.

Returning to the apartment, Zac turns down the opportunity to accompany his uncle on the cast-removing vet trip. But, he does offer to help get Dude into the contraption, and they both learn, rather quickly, that the sheer presence of the carrier proved a sufficient tip-off. They find Dude under the bed, in a location on the floor that is equidistant from either side. He is barely within reach of either Martin or Zac—each of whom is prone on the floor; each of whom has claimed a side of the bed. And Dude uses his claws, accompanied by hissing, to let the guys know that this battle might go on for a while.

Once Martin and Zac realize they are losing the game, they decide to play it differently. They wander out into the living room, put the TV on, and begin making small talk. About twenty minutes later, Dude emerges, dragging his cast with him. And when he is well into the living room, Zac leaps up and closes the bedroom door.

Dude senses the excitement, and he particularly senses his being the centerpiece of that energy. He quickly hobbles into the kitchen, where he effectively paints himself into a corner. By the time Zac shoves him into the carrier, Martin doesn't care how the cat is feeling. He just wants to get on the road and return before rush-hour traffic turns his afternoon plan into a major excursion.

III

"Dude's dad!" Doctor Doris says, opening the door to the inner sanctum of all things vet, "Come on in!"

"Thanks," Martin says, carrying the case (and Dude within it), as they make their way down the short hall.

"Here we go," Doctor Doris says then, giving Martin (and Dude) a welcome into the examining room.

"Just put the case on the table," she says.

"So, how's our boy doing?" the kind vet asks, as she opens the door to the carrier and puts it on a slant that will force Dude to emerge.

"He was fine until I brought that case home," Martin replies.

"I know," Doctor Doris says, as Martin puts the now-empty case on the floor. "Aren't they the royalest of beasts?

"I mean," she continues, as she looks at the healing gash in Dude's right hip, "they are just not happy with anything short of a staff. And please, should they really have to come to me? I mean, truly, this cat and all others fully expect doctors to make house calls. You know—bring it to them! And God forbid we should interrupt their precious eighteen hours of sleep a day."

Martin laughs at the monologue. He wishes that more Doctor Dorises existed in the arena of human medical care.

"He's looking good, Martin," she says, after giving Dude a thorough once-over. "You done good."

"Thank you," Martin replies. "It was a little dicey at first, but I figured out the routine. So? Is the cast coming off?"

"Are you not watching?"

Suddenly, the cast is history, and Dude stands.

"Oh my God!" Martin says. "When did that happen?"

"Looks pretty good," Doctor Doris comments, observing Dude as he takes a walk across the examining table. "I think we're all healed here."

"Wow," says Martin.

"Okay, so now," the vet says, "you wanna see the best part?"

"What's that?" Martin asks.

"Check this out."

Doctor Doris retrieves the cat carrier and places it on the table. Dude walks right into it.

"Your baby knows where he wants to be," the kind doctor says. "And right now? He wants to be home."

IV

Martin arrives home with Dude, and upon entering, he is surprised to hear two voices in his living room.

"Martin!" Brittany exclaims, jumping up from the chair as he enters the room and places the carrier on the floor.

"And Dude!" she says next, plopping to the floor and manipulating the double-release latch so as to free the cat from the carrier.

Dude quickly emerges.

"No cast!" Brittany squeals, clapping.

"No cast," Martin agrees.

"So," he says then. "How are you? Didn't your mom come in today?"

"She's asleep," says Brittany. "I came up here wanting to see you and, well, I've been hanging with Zac! You're out of Mountain Dew, by the way."

"My apologies. I'll restock tomorrow. So, what's going on with your mom? How is it so far?"

"It's weird. I mean, that's pretty much to be expected. But, you know, I wanted to ask you. Um, like, if I need to call you, can I do that? I mean, any time of day?"

"Of course!" Martin replies. "Of course you can."

"That's good to hear. I'm not sure I'll need to, but I just have this feeling there will be some difficult moments when I might need to hear the voice of someone in my present, you know?

"Anyway," she says, quickly rising to her feet, "I should probably head back down there. Bye, Zac!"

"See ya, Brittany. Good talking to you!"

After Martin walks Brittany to the door, he returns to the living room, where Zac is in veg-out mode, staring at the television.

"You watching something?" Martin asks.

"Not really," Zac responds, grabbing the remote, quickly finding the *Power* button, and turning the television off. "Wanna put some music on?"

Martin crosses to his sound system and pushes the button that will lead him to radio options. He scrolls down from KPCC's talk to the jazz at 88.1. He then turns to his nephew. "Can I get you anything?"

"Do you have beer?"

"Uh... no. We could probably walk somewhere and get some, if you want."

"Nah," Zac says. "It's okay."

For a few minutes, the radio is the only thing producing noise in Martin's living room. He's fine with that, actually. In fact, he appreciates that Zac doesn't feel a need to talk incessantly. But Martin also wonders if there's more he could be doing as a host.

As if to answer that curiosity, Zac speaks up. "You know, Uncle Marty, it's cool that we're just hanging. In fact, if you want to do something by yourself or whatever, that's okay with me. I'm still kinda jet-lagged, I think. Or maybe just wiped out from that week of partying in Philly. I'm cool just sitting here."

"If you're sure," Martin responds, standing. "I should probably check my email."

"Go for it."

"You want a Diet Coke? I'm getting one for myself."

"Thanks. I might grab one later."

V

Martin relaxes into his computer chair and just sits there with his eyes closed for a few minutes. He likes being alone, even if it is in the relatively small confines of his bonus room. He's also glad Zac said what he did just then. Two weeks is a long visit. Knowing they don't have to be joined at the hip the whole time will probably make it a lot easier for both of them. Martin also reminds himself of the full rationale behind the visit. Zac isn't in Los Angeles simply because he wanted to spend time with his favorite uncle. Zac is in Los Angeles also because he wanted to delay—for as long as possible—the inevitability of an endless summer with his family and its disproportionately high percentage of female hormones.

Martin reaches down and pushes the button on his hard drive. It'll take a few minutes for the machine to load all that needs to be loaded. As he watches the icons appear, he notices the time indicator on the bottom right of the screen. Somehow it seems to be much later than six o'clock. Were this a Monday one week ago, he'd just be heading home from work. He'd be crawling on the freeway, his necktie and suit jacket tossed on the passenger seat. Were this a Monday five weeks ago, he might be planning a trip to Trader Joe's, in the hopes of seeing a certain crewmember and waiting for as long as necessary to let her ring him up. Were this a Monday ten weeks ago, cat food would not be among the items in his cart.

The hourglass icon seems to have disappeared, so Martin makes the moves to get to his email inbox. Ten of ten messages begin to appear boldly. After deleting the Viagra ads and a few forwards from Aunt Betty, four messages remain. Curiously, three are from H-M-P folks (Debora, Brenda, and Alice). The other one is from Lisa. He decides to open them in the order received.

Debora sent hers at ten-fifteen that morning. The subject is **update**.

Dear Martin,

I hope you are enjoying the 4th day of the rest of your life. I miss knowing that you're a floor above, but I'm working at getting out of here altogether. The Children's Hospital job was posted last Friday, so I've submitted my resume. Don't know if Len's tenure there will help or hurt me. We'll see.

As for this place, it's feeling even creepier. I'm actually writing this from my personal account on my laptop because I don't for a minute feel safe about talking about anything internal on the company email. Vivian immediately named Phil "Interim Senior VP" and on Friday, we had a staff meeting (V, P, C, and me) that lasted for two interminable hours. It was really horrible, and I'm worried about Cody. He seems to only have one option when it comes to higher-ups, and that is to kiss ass. So, he was especially deferential but also extremely nervous. I wish I could take him aside and give him some kind of big sister talking-to, you know?

And the relationship between Vivian and Phil – particularly as it played out during the meeting – just makes me want to throw up. They're like two people who should be behind a closed door fucking their brains out. They glance at each other in secretive ways. They allude to inside jokes. It's just disgusting.

Are you free for lunch this week? I remember you mentioned a nephew visiting soon, but I forget the timing. I'd love to see you, maybe at the end of the week? I could meet you somewhere. Let me know.

All best,
Debora

Martin hits the *Reply* key and begins typing.

Hi Debora,

Your news re the office is not surprising. Interim Senior VP? Whatever. You're smart to email me from your laptop.

My nephew is here now. Arrived last night and will be here for two weeks. But we're not going to be doing everything together 24/7, and he might in fact like it if I get out of his hair for a while later this week. Thursday or Friday? You pick. We could meet at Mo's.

BTW, any great ideas for entertaining my houseguest? Zac is 20. He's really sweet and low-maintenance. But I feel kind of negligent in the activity-planning department.

I hope you get a call soon re the hospital job.

Let me know about lunch.

See ya soon,
Martin

Martin reviews his message before sending it. He looks forward to hearing back. For that matter, it'll be good to see Debora later in the week. She was becoming a friend, and she should remain one.

His in-box back in front of him, Martin sees that Brenda is next in line. She sent her email at eleven-thirty. The subject is **Thank you!**

```
hi martin, i'm writing from the old office
building just counting the minutes as another
day creeps by. so you got booted on thursday?
(i didn't just hear that today by the way - it
was pretty much the buzz on friday) i hope
you made the most of it! anyways i wanted to
say thanks because you've been a big help to
me. the mike thing and then the whole idea of
not staying here forever. i talked with my
parents over the weekend about the restaurant
idea and they were nice about it. dad even had
some ideas. i'll keep you posted. let me know
if you ever want to get together for lunch.
thanks again, Brenda
```

Martin reads Brenda's message about three times before hitting the *Reply* button. He's touched that he was able to help her. He's also concerned. She wrote this message at work, and she sent it from her computer there. Hopefully, she is not high up enough on the food chain to be monitored closely.

```
Hi Brenda,

Good to hear from you. By now, you are home,
so that's good, right?

I could probably do lunch next week. I have a
nephew in town, and he and I are driving up
the coast next Tuesday (returning Thursday).
My new job in Hollywood starts the following
Monday. So... lunch on Monday or Friday of next
week? Let me know if either of those works.

Hang in there!
Martin
```

Martin hits *Send* and moves on to the next in line. Lisa, writing at one-eighteen. The subject is **The House**.

```
Dear Martin,

Well, it's all final. I hope you are enjoying
your life and that a new love enters into it
soon, if that hasn't happened already. Glen
and I are heading to Vegas this weekend for a
quickie wedding. We're actually looking for-
ward to exchanging vows in the middle of sin
city. Why not, right?

I'm writing about the house. Glen and I have
decided to live at his place in Sherman Oaks.
In fact, he's spent the last six months or
so doing some major renovations there, and
it's really comfortable. So… I'm wondering
about our place on La Maida, and I'm wondering
specifically if you want to move back there. We
could work out a deal. Why don't you call me
on my cell when you want to talk about it –
the number is 818-828-8804.

xo, Lisa
```

"Interesting," Martin says out loud. "Interesting."

He sits back in his chair and absorbs the quiet shock he is feeling. He isn't shocked because Lisa is getting married in Vegas. That plan actually goes with her party-girl character. He also isn't shocked that she and her new husband will be living in his place in Sherman Oaks. She's always been comfortable in the Valley, and Sherman Oaks is probably considered a step up from Valley Village. Martin isn't even shocked that Lisa has made this generous offer of the house. Lisa always had a generous spirit. (It just tended to get diluted by other spirits.) The thing that shocks Martin is this: he has no interest in returning to the house on La Maida. Its beautiful landscaping, its strong architectural details, its solid foundation, and its sense of ownership are all wonderful features, but it's… over the hill.

Martin gets up to retrieve his telephone from the living room, and when he enters that space, he is not altogether surprised to see Zac stretched out on the couch and clearly in deep

REM. And Dude, whose mobility has greatly improved since about four hours ago, is stretched out on the back of the couch, about eighteen inches above Zac. They are yin and yang in some state of peaceful semi-consciousness; two post-adolescent lads, sleeping off their most recent adventures.

VI

She picks up after the second ring (though, at her end—and from her cell phone—it's not likely a "ring").

"Lisa," Martin says, keeping his tone even.

"Martin?"

"Yeah. What? Did you forget the sound of my voice?" he asks, his tone congenial.

"It's just so weird to hear it," she confesses. "How are you?"

"I'm doing well."

"How's the job?" she asks.

"The firm is the same as ever," Martin replies, not wanting to go into the job change discussion.

"And you're happy with your life in general?"

"I am, actually, " Martin replies.

"Love interest?"

"Something might be starting, but I don't want to talk about it."

"That's okay, Martin. I won't pry. So... you must have received my email."

"I did."

"Good," says Lisa. "So here's what I'm thinking. You know, the mortgage payment is very reasonable at this point. Just over two thousand a month. And the taxes aren't too bad. So, I was thinking if you would take over those payments, then we could just, you know, keep the house in my name and someday, if we feel like selling it, then maybe you could get a cut of the sale."

Martin smiles as he takes in her statements. Lisa's soliloquy was rather typical. Laced with presumption and logic. Sure to win over the person at the other end.

"So?" she asks, after waiting a good ten seconds. "What do you think?"

"I think I don't want to move," Martin replies.

"Really?" Her tone is friendly, but also incredulous.

"It's funny, you know," Martin begins. "After I read your email—and I just opened it about twenty minutes ago—I immediately thought about a conversation I had late last week. I was having breakfast with some friends, and my friend Jason was describing these two palm trees in front of his building—and his building's partner—over on Normandie."

"His building's *partner*?" Lisa says.

"Well, they're two buildings that face each other. They have different landlords, but they share a courtyard and sort of look alike. Both built in the late forties. Two-story, ten-unit apartment buildings. Anyway, Jason was telling us that there's a really tall palm tree in front of his building, which is the northernmost building. And then there's a really tall palm tree in front of the other building. And the palm tree in front of his building is home to a flock of green parrots."

"Green parrots?"

"Yeah," Martin says. "Apparently there are a lot of them in L.A. They escaped—or were released—from some place in Pasadena years ago. Some place that caught on fire. And they've been procreating ever since."

"Wow. So there's a tree full of green parrots in front of his building."

"Right," Martin says. "And then there's the other palm tree—the one just south. And it's filled with rats."

"*What?*"

"They gotta live somewhere, Lisa."

"Of course they do, and better in that tree than anywhere near me. So, what's the point?"

"I guess the point is, that's my neighborhood now. And I really love it. I like the full-world view that it provides. Remember that trip we took to New York? Remember how we observed the way the City just lets everyone—all cultures, all languages—coexist in a way that inches slowly toward a sense of equality?"

"Yeah, I kinda do remember that trip," Lisa says, her tone softening even more. "We were still living in Chicago."

"Right," Martin says, he, too, becoming a bit quieter. "Anyway, I've always loved New York, and I really love this part of L.A."

"Green parrots and rats, huh?"

"Co-existing."

"You sound good, Martin," Lisa says then.

"Thanks. You sound happy, too.

"Hey!" he adds. "Congratulations on the upcoming nuptials in Vegas! You're going this weekend, you say?"

"Yup. Just as soon as we get off of work, we're hopping in the car, and heading for what Glen calls the arithmetically progressive freeways."

"Arithmetically progressive?" Martin asks.

"We take the Five to the Ten to the Fifteen," Lisa explains.

"Wow," Martin responds. "What would happen if you then got on the Twenty?"

"We'd probably end up in Utah, and I'd be sharing Glen with about six other wives."

"You don't want to do that."

"No," she agrees. "I don't."

"Well, I wish you the best, Lisa. Really."

"You, too, Martin. Thanks for being so kind."

"Goodnight," he says.

Martin smiles at his phone after pushing the *Off* button. That was probably the most cordial conversation he has had with Lisa in three or four years. He's glad she's happy. And he's glad his own life allows him to feel that way.

He puts the phone down on the table beside his computer stand and looks at the clock on the monitor. It's almost six-thirty. Strange. He was predicting something closer to midnight.

He closes the message from Lisa, a virtual reply no longer necessary, and he moves to the remaining bold subject in his in-box: **Hey, Boss** from Alice. Written at two-thirty that afternoon. He opens it.

```
Hi, Martin.

I hope all is well with you. I forget when you
start your new job. Two weeks? Regardless,
enjoy the time between as much as possible.

I'm taking a "mental health day" today, at my
husband's urging. Which is to say, I called
in sick. I might go ahead and be sick again
tomorrow. I had lunch with Barry over the
weekend, and I wanted to give you a heads up.
There's a good possibility that the firm has
been involved in some shady deals. You're
lucky to be out of there, but that doesn't
mean you won't be brought into any discus-
sions. Barry has already heard from the big
boys in New York. He's been told to get a
lawyer. So that's the news I have.

Feel free to call me at home anytime.

- Alice
```

Martin is glad he opened the emails in the order received. He's glad he was able to have that conversation with Lisa before reading this rather ominous narrative. He also is glad that one of his new best friends is a former partner of one of Los Angeles' most prominent law firms.

Martin did nothing wrong. He will remind himself of that fact several times tonight before he finally falls asleep.

CHAPTER FORTY

I

Between Zac's jetlag and Martin's joblag, it isn't surprising that they are both awake and "moving about the cabin" at seven o'clock on Tuesday morning. They first run into each other when Zac emerges from the bathroom.

"Morning, Uncle Marty."

"Morning. You know, I was gonna make some coffee, but there's also a really good restaurant we could go to. Good place. Good breakfast."

"I'm up for whatever," Zac replies, walking like a zombie back into the living room.

II

Because there's not a breakfast rush on Tuesday mornings, Martin and Zac are able to spread out quite comfortably in one of the semi-circular booths that grace the southern boundary of Home's quaint multi-leveled courtyard.

"I love this," Zac offers, stretching his arms out and embracing the booth's upholstery. "This neighborhood rocks."

"So," Zac says then, "I crashed out early last night. What'd you do?"

Before Martin has a chance to respond, their breakfasts are delivered. They had both ordered the Pomodoro Omelet with the requisite home fries and an English muffin.

"This looks great," Zac says, apparently incapable of inflecting—even a little bit—before noon or so.

"I agree," Martin says.

He then looks at the waiter. "More coffee, please?"

III

As they work their way through their omelets, Martin ends up telling Zac everything about Haley-Mitchell-Phelps. He tells Zac about how bored he had become over the years, but how he managed to still deliver the goods in an above-average way. He tells Zac about the sudden departure of Barry, which was preceded by his wife's shocking suicide. He tells Zac about the promotion, and how it seemed to come with perks and not-so-perks: the ninth floor accommodations; the trips to Chicago and New York; the constant hovering of Vivian. He tells Zac about the weird relationship between Vivian and Phil. He tries to describe Phil's enigmatic aura.

Having scarfed down his food quite efficiently during Martin's monologue, Zac places his fork on a plate that has barely enough remnants for a cat's scraping tongue. "Damn, Uncle Marty. Sounds like they were planning to set you up."

"Interesting comment," Martin says, as the busboy approaches and they both point to their coffee cups. "How do you mean?"

Zac sits back, holding the mug that is on its last dregs and will soon benefit from a refill. "It sounds to me," Martin's nephew says, "that they had you pegged as a high-performing company drone. I'm guessing Vivian—who seems to be running the show in L.A.—figured you'd just do whatever. So, if they had a shady deal in the works, it made sense to promote you, 'cause you'd just follow company policy. And they could fix the books to stick that shady deal on you."

The busboy arrives with a fresh pot of coffee. He fills both their mugs—mugs that don't match, because this is Home.

"How did you get to be so smart?" Martin asks, smiling at the twenty-year-old whose listening skills are consistently thoughtful.

"I've taken a few Psych classes," Zac replies. "Actually, I've taken three, which is a pretty remarkable number for someone who isn't majoring in Psych. It's such a trip, though. Psych is a trip."

Martin takes a sip of the fresh coffee and shakes his head. He smiles at his nephew.

"Yeah," Zac says, now on some sort of caffeine roll, "and you know, the reason I probably wouldn't major in Psych is that I just would be fighting with the professors all the time. They're so zoned into their detailed theories. Me? I think there are two kinds of people in the world. Mean people and nice people. And I think if psychologists would accept my theory, they might zero in on things a lot faster.

"Take your office, for instance," Zac continues. "Vivian? Mean. You? Nice. Phil? Mean. Debora? Nice. Cody? Nice. Maybe a little too nice. And by the way, Uncle Marty, given how things are coming down, I kinda agree with Debora. I think you two might want to consider an intervention with Cody. That guy is not equipped to deal with the shit that is about to hit the fan."

Martin sits back and appears to be deep in thought.

"Provocative, huh?" Zac comments, observing his uncle's pensiveness.

"I agree with you about Cody. I'm supposed to have lunch with Debora on Thursday. I'll see if she can persuade him to join us... Your theory, though."

"What do you think of it?" Zac asks.

"It just makes me wonder about when otherwise nice people do mean things, and when otherwise mean people do nice things. I was thinking about Lisa, specifically."

"She got mean, right?"

"Right, and I spoke to her on the phone last night. The first conversation we've had since we split, and she was nice. She was remarkably nice," Martin says, nodding as he thinks about their dialogue.

"I think when nice people are mean, they're just in the wrong place," Zac suggests. "The marriage wasn't working for her anymore, and she had to process that for a while. Being mean was a coping mechanism until she figured out what to do."

"Interesting," Martin says. "And I was a bit mean at times myself."

"What about the opposite?" Martin asks then.

"A mean person being nice, you mean?"

Martin nods.

"It's a tool," Zac explains. "It's a tool for them to get what they want. Mean people only care about themselves and the mean people who relate to them. I bet Vivian had some moments when she would 'play nice'."

"Yeah," says Martin, "but it was pretty transparent."

"That's probably because you were done with the place."

Zac removes the leaf that has just dropped into his coffee cup. "Yeah," he says then, studying the leaf's now-wet veins, "and I bet there were moments when you were meaner to Vivian than you would generally be to another person."

"Yup."

"That's just your psyche's way of telling you it's time to move on," Zac asserts, once again stretching his arms across the back of the booth and looking charmingly self-assured.

"So what are you going to major in?" Martin asks.

"Something nice," Zac says, nodding.

IV

Martin has a lot to think about as he and his nephew walk back from their breakfast on Hillhurst. And as they take that walk, in silence, Martin is once again happy to have a blood relative who doesn't have to fill every moment with chatter. Zac was quite effusive while they were at Home. It's not altogether surprising to Martin that now, as they're heading back to his place on Vermont, Zac has become quiet.

"Oh, God," Martin says, in an amused tone, as they wait at the crosswalk near the newsstand. "That's my crazy neighbor Myra across the street."

Zac follows Martin's glance and sees two women. One, in a plumed cap, a blue and white striped tee shirt, mauve leggings, and rhinestone flip-flops. The other, in jeans, an oversized man's shirt, and what appear to be Keds. She is skinny and weathered. Her taupe-colored hair is long and thin.

"Which one?" Zac asks, as they begin to cross the street.

"The one in the hat. I don't know who the other lady is. Looks like someone asking for a hand-out.

"Myra!" Martin calls, as they near the sidewalk on the west side of the avenue.

"Martin!" Myra responds. "Have you met Jean?"

Martin's facial reaction indicates that not only has he not met Jean, he didn't know there was a Jean.

"Our dear Brittany's mother," Myra explains, as Martin and Zac approach the two women.

"Oh, hello!" Martin says kindly, smiling as he extends his hand.

"Hi, Martin," Jean replies, in a meek, rather high-pitched voice. "I think Britty told me about you. Are you the one with the cat who fell out of the window?"

"That's me! And, this is my nephew, Zac."

Zac exchanges handshakes and greetings with both Myra and Jean.

"I was just going up to 7-11 for some cigarettes," Jean says then. "I really appreciate Britty letting me smoke in her apartment."

"Your daughter's an angel, Jean," Myra says. "We all love her so much."

Jean lowers her head then, and when she doesn't raise it back up after several seconds, Myra places a hand on her shoulder and looks at Martin with concern.

"Are you and Brittany having a good time?" Martin asks, his light tone an attempt to bring Jean back to a more easy-going dialogue.

As she looks up to respond, she wipes a few tears off her cheeks. "I guess we are. It's hard. It's been so long. And I feel so sad when I think about what she lived with back in Nebraska. Was it your friend who made the phone calls?"

"Yes," Martin replies. "My friend Susan."

"I hope I get to meet her," Jean says. "I would like to thank her in person."

"I'm sure we can make that happen."

"Well," Jean says then, shrugging as she puts her hands in her denim pockets. "I should probably get going on my errand. I don't want Britty to worry that I got lost."

Jean then slowly heads up the street, looking down on the sidewalk, probably crying again.

Martin, Myra, and Zac don't say anything for a few moments. They just watch the frail back of Brittany's mother.

"So are you coming or going?" Martin asks Myra.

"Going," Myra replies. "I have a craving for a piece of Lemon Meringue Pie, and the almightly house on the corner is calling."

"Sounds like a good breakfast," Martin comments.

"Why not! Good to meet you, Zac," Myra says. "I hope I'll get to see you again."

"I hope so, too. Enjoy your pie!"

Martin and Zac watch as Myra saunters away, her confidence a contrast to Jean's issues. Martin then turns to Zac, an inquisitive look on his face.

"Both nice, I'd say," Zac comments.

"I tend to agree. And poor Jean, she had one helluva a mean husband."

"Brittany's dad?"

"Yeah," Martin says. "He's in prison now."

"That's also nice."

CHAPTER FORTY-ONE

I

Martin's cellphone rings just as he emerges from his car in the Mo's parking lot.

"Debora!" he says, after seeing her name on the screen.

"Hi, Martin," Debora responds, her tone sounding tired and a bit frustrated. "Cody and I are just getting down to the garage. Where are you?"

"I just got to Mo's."

"Sorry about the delay," Debora says. "We had another one of those impromptu two-hour meetings this morning. Anyway—"

Martin can hear Debora's car alarm chirp.

"We should get there in about ten or fifteen."

"No problem," Martin replies. "I'm not punching anyone's timeclock these days."

"Don't gloat," Debora says, before turning the call off.

II

"So what was the meeting about?" Martin asks, after the waiter has delivered their iced teas and walked away.

"Bullshit," Debora replies. "Pure, unadulterated bullshit."

"Would you agree?" Martin asks Cody.

Cody shrugs and smiles.

"Cody, come on!" Debora protests, in a light-hearted tone. She is facing her colleague, who is sitting at her left in the booth. "You can't be thinking all these meetings are necessary."

301

"I don't know," Cody responds. "I'm not sure what's going on. I just try to keep up, you know?"

Cody then looks directly at Martin. "I got about four more of your old accounts."

"On top of what you already had?" Martin asks.

"Yeah," says Cody. "I'm hoping it means I've got a healthy raise coming. My review is in a few weeks."

Martin smiles at Cody, whose naïveté is palpable. As Zac said, he is maybe a little *too* nice.

"So you're happy at H-M-P?" Martin asks Cody.

"Sure," Cody replies, again shrugging. "I mean, it's good money, and the work isn't that difficult, so..."

Debora catches Martin's eye. She's not sure where they can go with this, but she knows it's her turn to speak up.

"Tell me, though, Cody," she says, leaning into him. "Don't you think it's a little wrong that Vivian named Phil the Interim Senior VP?"

While Cody doesn't answer immediately (and even seems hesitant), Martin decides to jump in by pretending he hadn't heard of Phil's promotion.

"You're kidding!" he says to his former colleagues. "Phil is a Senior VP now!? That's crazy. He's only been there eight months, whereas you two have, what, about seven or eight years between you?"

Cody remains posture imperfect as he dips a fry into ketchup. "Yeah, but I think he has more experience generally. Also, didn't he and Vivian work together at another firm back in New York?"

Martin and Debora exchange a quick look. This is news to both of them.

"Well then," Martin says, casually. "Maybe that's the reason for the appointment. The history thing. She's comfortable with him."

"She certainly seems to be," Cody offers.

Debora rolls her eyes and is hard-pressed to squelch a disgusted sigh as she stabs at her Chicken Caesar Salad.

"So, Debora," Martin says then, slicing into his chicken, "I guess you also got some new accounts?"

"No," she replies, finding an available hand to twirl some available hair. "I haven't."

"Are you kidding?" Cody asks, incredulously.

And Martin believes that Cody's disbelief is genuine. Martin believes this because Cody was just about to take a bite out of his cheeseburger. But now, he's put that bite on the back burner. He's returned his cheeseburger to his plate.

"Seriously?" Cody says to Debora. "You've gotten no new accounts?"

"No new accounts," she replies, her dimples deepening so much they might split open.

"This really sucks," Cody says then, causing Martin and Debora to raise four eyebrows between them, in hopes of their young boy beginning to see the light.

"This really sucks," Cody says again. "I mean, it's blatant sexism, right?"

Martin and Deborah both put down their forks. And without knowing it, they also are both considering the type of guy who would appeal to a kindergarten teacher from Iowa.

"I don't know if it's sexism," Martin offers. "I mean, Vivian's a woman, so—"

Cody, who's just stuck a fry in his mouth, begins to laugh.

He takes a few moments to chew and continue to laugh. And when he is done, he waves his hands. "Sorry, you two. I just keep forgetting that Vivian's a woman."

III

"I think we should forget about it," Debora suggests, exasperation in her tone.

"Yeah," Martin agrees, keeping an eye on the route to and from the men's room. "He's either genuinely and completely clueless or he doesn't *want* to know. It's not worth trying to figure out.

"So, no word from Children's Hospital?" Martin asks then.

"I don't know," Debora responds, extracting her cell phone from her purse. "Once we got out of that meeting, I wanted to get over here, so I wasn't able to check my messages."

She pushes a few buttons on her cellphone and raises her eyebrows. "Maybe, maybe," she says, putting the phone to her ear.

Debora is listening to a message when Cody returns to the booth and takes his seat. "Did we get the check?" he asks.

"Yeah," Martin replies. "This one's on me."

"You didn't have to do that!"

"Don't worry about it," Martin says. Then, he looks at Debora, who is returning her cell phone to her purse. "Good news?"

"Potentially very good news," Debora replies.

Cody looks at her inquisitively.

"About the place where my husband works," Debora explains.

IV

"As your friend and as a lawyer," Susan says, opening the fridge to retrieve the lasagna, "I think you need to stop thinking or talking about it at this point. It's potentially dangerous, and people who are intent on behaving illicitly have very smooth ways of putting innocent bystanders in incriminating positions.

"If and when the time comes that you or Debora or even Cody need counsel," she continues, "I will make sure you get the best. But until then," she says, opening the oven and sliding the lasagna onto the upper shelf, "seriously: disengage."

"But what about—" Martin begins, prevented from completing his question when Susan plants a very firm kiss on his lips.

"I will not be your enabler," she says, smiling.

"You mean, any time I mention the firm, you're going to kiss me? That's not a very discouraging response."

"Then I'll come up with another one. Truly, though. I won't listen to it because I think your talking about it is a very bad idea."

Just then, they hear some uproarious laughter coming from the living room, where Brittany, her mom, Myra, Zac, and Jason are gathered around the coffee table, and where—if the conversation has not changed much in the last five minutes—Myra is telling stories from her wild days in the 'Sixties.

Susan smiles as she removes salad fixings from the chiller drawer in her fridge and as Martin reaches for the cutting board and finds a knife. "It seems like things are going well with Brittany and her mom," Susan says, quietly.

"It looks that way," Martin agrees. "What can I do?"

Susan places the tomato, the cucumber, and the onion on the counter beside the cutting board. "Slice," she says, as she reaches into a cupboard below and retrieves a large salad bowl.

"That was so sweet of Jean," she comments then, "bringing me that Lamb of God prayer candle."

"So, you gonna put it on your altar?" Martin teases, as Susan empties two bags of Baby Spinach into the salad bowl.

"Be nice," she responds, crossing the room to retrieve her wineglass.

"I'm sorry," he offers, as he continues his painstaking approach to slicing cucumber, "Anyway, Brittany said her mother *loved* Wacko. She said that between there, Ozzie Dots, and Uncle Jer's, they killed all of yesterday afternoon."

"Have you taken Zac to Wacko yet?"

"He went today, while I was in the Valley. Came back with a few books and an ashtray for one of his friends back in Philly."

"So, I'm assuming the ashtray says something amusing," Susan states, enjoying the opportunity to sip on her wine and let Martin continue prepping the salad.

"It's really kinda funny," Martin admits, as he tosses the cucumber slices into the salad. "It says 'Jesus hates it when you smoke.' And the best part is that Zac's smoking friend, Adam, shares an apartment with a guy named Jésus, who gets a little intolerant if Adam and his fellow smoking friends spend too long a night in the living room."

"Oh, God, has Zac seen the tee shirts at Fred 62?" Susan asks.

"We did see a few funny ones when we had lunch there on Monday. Why?" Martin asks, as he cuts up the red onion. "You thinking of one in particular?"

"Yeah. It says, 'Jesus is our dishwasher.'"

"Oh," Martin laughs. "That is *bad*."

"So bad it's good," Susan suggests.

"You seem to be having a nice time with your nephew," she comments then.

"I am," Martin states, contorting his face as he resists the onion's desire to make him cry. "A lot, in fact. His mind kind of blows me away."

"Smart?"

"More than that," Martin says, scraping the pungent onion pieces into the bowl. "He's wise. He's just unbelievably wise."

Susan stretches to give Martin a quick peck on the cheek. "I'm glad you're having a good time with him," she says.

V

When Martin and Susan re-enter the living room a few minutes later, the cast of characters is down by two. "Where are Jason and Jean?" Martin asks.

"They're outside having a smoke," Brittany responds.

"Oh, they don't have to smoke outside!" Susan says, crossing to the sliding glass door that leads to the back yard. "Come on in, you guys. You can smoke inside. I'll get you an ashtray."

"Are you sure?" Jean asks in her meek voice, entering the room just ahead of Jason.

"Absolutely," says Susan, as she opens a drawer in one of the end tables and extracts an ashtray. "My husband used to smoke cigars. One almost every night."

"Is that why you left him?" Myra asks.

"I didn't leave him," Susan responds. "He got killed."

While Jean twitches through an extremely nervous, uncomfortable smile, Myra does nothing to cover her shame. "Good God!" she blurts out, "if I stick my foot in my mouth one more time this week, I'm going to get a case of athlete's jaw!"

"It's okay," Susan says, smiling as she places her hand on Myra's shoulder. "Really. It's been twelve years. I'm well onto the other side of the grieving process. And your assumption was perfectly reasonable."

"How did he die?" Jean asks quietly.

"He was a cop. Killed on duty. He was—"

Susan then cuts herself off. "I'm sorry," she says, "I just remembered the bread, and if I don't deal with that now, the memory will be gone and may never return."

As she heads to the kitchen, Martin appreciates his friend's quick thinking. He knows, because Susan told him, that her husband was killed when he was called on a domestic violence incident. This is not something Jean needs to hear.

But, as he glances at Brittany's mother, who is hunched over and looking at the floor, Martin realizes that she probably feels that she has asked a bad question.

"It's okay, Jean," Martin says. "I think it was an armed robbery situation."

"That's too bad," she says, quietly. "He was probably a nice man."

Martin looks at Brittany then, and he can tell, by the gentle way she is smiling at her mother, that Brittany is benefiting from this visit. Whatever issues, anger, or sadness she might have carried with her from Nebraska to the streets of Hollywood seem to be fading away. And they are gradually being replaced by love and empathy for her mother.

CHAPTER FORTY-TWO

I

"This is good coffee, Uncle Marty," Zac says, returning to the living room.

"Thanks," says Martin, smiling at the nephew who will probably start espousing snippets of wisdom by the time he's halfway into the current mug of caffeine.

"So what time are we leaving tomorrow morning?" Zac asks.

"I think we should get a fairly early start. There's a great breakfast place in Summerland, and then there's a place—and I can't remember the name for some reason, but it's really well-known—anyway, it's about thirty minutes or so south of the Monterey Peninsula. We can stop there for a late afternoon light meal. It's incredible. Tables on a bluff overlooking the ocean."

"Cool. So, what's the plan for today?"

"I'm gonna drive up to the Valley at around noon," Martin says. "I'm having lunch with my former assistant, Brenda. You're welcome to come along if you feel like cruising Ventura Boulevard for an hour or two."

"What's there?"

"I don't know. More retail basically."

"I like the retail here," Zac says. "Maybe I'll see if Brittany and her mom want to go for a walk."

"Her mom left yesterday," Martin reminds his nephew. "And Brittany is back at work today."

"Oh, that's right."

II

Martin is in the bathroom when the phone rings at around eleven. "Zac! Can you pick that up! It might be Brenda."

A few seconds later, Zac is standing in the short hallway, just outside the bathroom. "It's Debora," he says, "and it's urgent."

Martin rolls his eyes as he flushes the toilet. He does not want to engage in any work talk. It's going to be hard enough avoiding that goal when he has lunch with Brenda.

Martin emerges from the bathroom and takes the phone from Zac.

"Hi, Debora, what's up?"

"It happened."

"What happened?"

"Some S.E.C. investigators just escorted Vivian out of the building, and someone said Phil is currently behind closed doors with some other suits."

"Fuck."

"My sentiments exactly," Debora says. "I had that interview this morning, so I arrived late. Just in time, in fact, to see Mizz Viv taking the walk of shame out of the main floor elevators."

"Fuck," Martin says again.

III

Arriving at the pita place about five minutes after their agreed rendezvous time, Brenda looks like a deer in headlights.

"Martin," she says, breathlessly, "oh my God."

"I heard. At least, I heard from Debora about an hour and a half ago."

"So you know about Vivian and Phil."

"Phil got hauled out too?"

"Unbelievable!" Brenda says. "But, boy, those two. I mean, Phil has been a bastard to Vicky since day one. You have no idea. He's cruel."

"I'm sorry to hear that," Martin says. "Good riddance, right?"

"Alice thinks there's going to be a lot of fallout. Like, we're going to be dealing with this for a while. Interrogations and stuff."

"How is Alice?"

"She seems okay. She said to say 'hi,' by the way."

Off Martin's inquisitive look, Brenda adds: "Yeah, I just saw her as I was leaving the building. She was heading out to lunch with Cody. He looked pretty shook up."

"Well, I'm glad he's talking to Alice, then."

Martin doesn't want to dwell on the developments, and he hopes he'll be able to change the subject. They should be talking about futures, not pasts or what others have done to the present. He reaches for two menus from behind the condiment tray and hands one to Brenda.

"God, I don't even know if I can eat," she says, staring at the list on the laminated sheet. "My stomach is all in knots."

"Well," Martin says, smiling and reaching for a lighter tone. "Let's just order. If you need a doggie bag, we'll get you one."

IV

Susan arrives at nine-thirty, just a half hour after her shift ended. Earlier in the evening, Martin had asked Zac if it would be okay for Susan to come and spend the night. "Sure," Zac had said, smiling. "But you guys aren't going to make a lot of racket in there, are you?"

Martin laughed at his nephew's question. He also wondered if this dialogue would settle with Reggie. Probably not.

"I brought some Two-Buck Chuck," she says, as she enters the apartment. "Figured you might want a glass of wine after the day's developments."

"Thanks," says Martin, leading the way into the kitchen.

He finds the corkscrew fairly quickly and begins the task of corkage.

"And I was able to reach Nathan during my lunch break," Susan says.

Martin's facial response tells her to explain.

"One of my former colleagues. He's phenomenal. One of the best litigators I've ever worked with. Anyway, he said he had already gotten wind of the case. He also said he'll be happy to represent you if the need arises."

"Did he think it would?" Martin asks, remarkably uncorking the bottle with a few smooth manipulations.

"No way of knowing," Susan responds, reaching into the cabinet for some glasses, "but don't worry about it. The guilty parties have been identified and removed, it seems. And *you* are going to Big Sur tomorrow. Are you excited?"

"I am, actually," Martin says, pouring an inch of wine into the two glasses and then calling into the other room. "Zac? You want some wine?"

"I'm cool," Zac calls back.

"Have you been up there before?" Susan asks.

"Oh yeah. Lisa and I used to go for Thanksgiving, if we didn't have plans to see either of our families. We probably went about six or seven times."

"Good," says Susan. "So you know the places to go."

"Yeah. And, I was telling Zac about it earlier, but I can't remember the name of that restaurant on the edge of—"

"Nepenthe?"

"That's it," Martin says. "Nepenthe."

Susan spontaneously places her glass on the counter and puts her arms around Martin. She hugs him tightly, then pulls away and plants a strong kiss on his lips.

"What's that about?" he asks. "You don't want me to say Nepenthe?"

She smiles. "No. I just am really glad I met you."

CHAPTER FORTY-THREE

I

Martin is spreading a little more apple butter on his English muffin. This will be his breakfast's dessert.

Zac has been quiet while eating his pancakes. In fact, he's been fairly quiet since they left Los Feliz nearly two hours ago. He probably needs more coffee.

"Thanks," Zac says to the Summerland Beach Café waitress who seemed to read Martin's mind just then. As soon as he thought the word "coffee," she arrived at their table carrying a fresh pot and ready to pour.

"I'll take some, too," Martin says.

"And you can take this," he adds, referring to his plate.

"You ate fast, Uncle Marty."

"Or you're eating slow," Martin says, tossing a teasing glance at his nephew.

"I seem to be doing everything slow this morning."

"Did you sleep well last night?" Martin asks.

"Yeah," Zac responds. "And you kids were pretty quiet. I appreciate that."

Martin smiles and feels a bit of redness cover his face.

"I think you've found a pretty cool woman, there, Uncle Marty."

"I do, too."

"So, tell me," Zac says then, "I never got to know Lisa very well. How are they different?"

"Hmm... I'm not sure that's an answerable question. I'm also not sure it matters."

"Maybe that's because you're different. I mean, different from the man who married Lisa."

"I'm older," Martin replies. "And there's a lot to be said for that."

"So," Zac says, "you been thinking about all that scandal stuff?"

"No. Susan is my *pro bono* counsel on that score, and I've taken her advice."

"What was that?" Zac asks.

"She said that anytime a firm-related thought enters my head, I need to banish it. Even if that means saying 'delete, delete, delete' out loud."

"I haven't heard you say that today."

"I've been saying it to myself," Martin explains.

"How often?" Zac asks.

"Oh, I don't know, every ten minutes or so."

"I think you should start saying it out loud," Zac suggests. "It might be helpful if I monitor you."

II

After they'd left the Summerland restaurant, Zac offered to drive. Martin hadn't considered sharing those duties, but it made sense to do so. Zac could at least get them as far as San Luis Obispo. Then, Martin could take the wheel. Once they got on the Pacific Coast Highway, Zac would want to give his full attention to the surrounding landscape and the grace of the almighty ocean.

Martin likes sitting in the passenger seat. It is something he rarely gets to do anymore. Riding shotgun on this arm of this particular itinerary, though, is familiar. When he and Lisa used to take their Thanksgiving excursions, they always divided the driving so that Lisa was in charge of the Ventura Freeway and Martin was in charge of Highway 1. Toward the end of their marriage, and specifically on that last trip they took to Monterey—just seven months ago—Martin was resentful of their division of labor. He remembers feeling pissed at her during the first four hours of the drive. Looking at the same landscape that is passing him now, he was filled with contempt. He remembers thinking that she always had a way of *getting* her way. Whether that meant enjoying the best views as a passenger (that is, the views that appeared the minute Martin took the wheel in San Luis Obispo) or ensuring that they would always spend Christmas with her family, Lisa just always seemed to be "the decider."

Martin smiles as he entertains these recollections. He smiles because he understands the whole marriage differently now. Lisa "got her way" because she could. Lisa got her way because Martin never *had* a way. And so Martin's resentment was really misplaced. He realizes now that it wasn't fair for him to blame her. She was just being. She was just being herself.

Martin remembers a phone conversation he had with Rachel, probably early last December. He and Lisa had had such a lousy time in Monterey that last Thanksgiving that it was becoming increasingly obvious: their marriage was either over or in desperate of some sort of long-term therapeutic counseling. They had reached a stage where they could barely stand looking at each other. They were two nice people who were acting mean far too frequently.

During that early December phone conversation, Rachel had shared with Martin an experience from her late twenties. At the time, she was in counseling to address some relationship and work issues. And, one day, apparently, the therapist started talking about marriage.

"What's weird," Rachel had told Martin, "is that I wasn't even talking about marriage myself. But I think Charles—that was my therapist—was having some issues with his wife. I think *he* needed to talk about it. Anyway, he said he viewed marriage as a crapshoot, a total gamble. Because you *can't* know, you just can't know, when you pledge all that 'til death do us part stuff. You can't know if you and your spouse will grow at the same pace or even at complementary paces."

And maybe, Martin thinks now, marriage can even stunt growth.

"It's just a total risk," Rachel had said. "And if you think about it, it's kinda crazy. I don't know, maybe that's why people have kids—to make sure they'll always have something in common."

Martin laughs quietly.

"I don't hear any 'delete, delete, delete'," Zac says from behind the wheel. "You must be thinking about something else."

"I was just thinking about a phone conversation I had with Rachel several months ago. You know, she's a funny girl."

"She is," Zac says, nodding. "She's quirky with a capital K."

"So what made you think of Rachel?" Zac asks then.

"Lisa did."

"God, Uncle Marty, does she still have that much power over you?"

Martin turns to Zac and looks at him in a faux-scolding way. "Delete it, dude."

III

Once they began the climb just north of Morro Bay, Zac became transfixed.

"This is amazing," he said at one point. "I get it now."

"What's that?" Martin asked from behind the wheel.

"I get it that the Earth quakes. It's huge and powerful. It's amazing."

"Yeah," Martin had said in response. "There's something about California that keeps reminding us that we're not completely in charge."

Now, they are at the midpoint, and Martin pulls into the little parking lot of the Gorda market.

"Is this the restaurant you were talking about?"

"No, that's about thirty or so miles ahead," Martin replies. "This is just a good place to get out and stretch."

They both cross the two lane highway and stand near the bluff. They take in the Pacific below and beyond. The Pacific forever.

"Big Sur," Zac says then. "This was a good idea, Uncle Marty."

IV

Zac is beyond mesmerized when Martin makes the turn into the Nepenthe parking lot.

They find a spot easily, and after getting out of the car, they walk together in peaceful silence up the steps that lead to the restaurant.

"Cool phoenix," Zac says, when he sees the wood sculpture that is a focal point of the eatery's outdoor terrace.

"You know about the phoenix, Uncle Marty?" Zac asks, as they take a prime table with a bird's eye view of the coastline to the south and the Pacific everywhere else.

"I just know something about rising from the ashes," Martin replies.

"It's from Egyptian and Greek mythology," Zac states. "The phoenix lives for between five hundred and a thousand years, and when its time comes to die, it gathers twigs of myrrh to create a nest. The nest catches on fire and so does the phoenix, but after it's all reduced to ashes, another phoenix egg appears, and the new bird lives as long as the old one."

Martin smiles at his nephew. The knowledge just keeps spewing forth somehow.

"Some of the mythologies say, too," Zac continues, "that the phoenix could regenerate after it was wounded or hurt. It's about resilience, really."

"Are you ready to order?" asks the waitress, who has appeared out of nowhere.

"We haven't looked yet," Martin says, passing a menu over to Zac and keeping one for himself.

"How about drinks?" the waitress inquires.

"What beers do you have?" Zac asks.

"Anchor Steam is our top seller."

"Sounds good," Zac says.

"ID?"

"Sure," Zac responds, reaching into his back pocket.

The waitress studies his Pennsylvania driver's license. "Sorry, sweetie," she says, "you have to be twenty-one in California."

"That's cool. Iced tea, then," Zac says, returning his wallet to his back pocket.

"Then I'll take that Anchor Steam," Martin says.

"Good," says the waitress, as she quickly moves on.

"We can do a switcheroo when she's not looking," Martin suggests.

"Cool," says Zac, smiling.

Zac then looks at the menu's title line. "Nepenthe," he says. "Nepenthe."

"Sounds like a mantra," Martin comments. "I wonder what it means."

"Greek mythology," Zac states.

"And how many of those courses have you taken?"

"Just one. Fall semester this past year."

"So tell me," Martin says, smiling at his nephew. "Tell me about Nepenthe."

"The reference showed up first in Homer's *Odyssey*," Zac explains. "Nepenthe is an opiate. The 'Milk of Amnesia.' In the *Odyssey*, an Egyptian queen gives nepenthe to Helen of Troy. It's meant to chase away her sorrows. And that comes from the literal translation. The 'ne' means 'not;' and 'penthe' comes from 'penthos,' which means 'sorrow' or 'grief.' Nepenthe."

"No sorrow," Martin states.

"That's right," Zac agrees.

"Here you go, guys," the waitress says, placing the iced tea in front of Zac and the beer in front of Martin. "Do you know what you want to eat?"

"We haven't really looked yet, but... you know what—?" Martin says. "Why not just bring us one of those fruit and cheese plates."

Zac nods in approval, and the waitress walks away.

They switch beverages while the coast is clear.

As Zac takes a swig from the bottle of Anchor Steam, Martin looks out at the landscape and the ocean that meets it. For some reason, he suddenly thinks about Lonzo and that flyer that was placed in the old elevator on Vermont. *Missing Man.* Martin wonders if Lonzo will ever show up to anyone who might be concerned about him. Or if he just disappeared in Vegas one night, last seen at a roulette table.

Martin wonders how many people go missing in the course of a day, a week, or a year. And then he considers how many more might be on the list if you opened the definition of "missing." There's the physical kind—like Lonzo—when someone is no longer where they were last seen. But there's another kind that might be equally tragic. It's when a man is missing to himself. He goes about his business, does his job, pays his bills, but it is as if his spirit has left his body. Who puts up the flyers when that happens?

Martin doesn't know when the disappearance began for him. It was gradual, and so it was sneaky. But, he knows it happened because now, taking in the view from the cliffside restaurant, he realizes that for the past few months, he has been in the process of returning. Now, he is fully back inside himself.

He's returned from the ashes.

He no longer feels any sorrow or grief.

Nepenthe.

ABOUT THE AUTHOR

Katie Gates is a resident of Los Angeles by way of rural Virginia and New York City. Her first novel, *The Somebody Who,* was nominated for a 2009 Library of Virginia Literary Award. *Martin Lost and Found* is her second novel.